Dear Target Reader,

Thanks for picking up this exclusive edition of *Why Not Tonight*, book three in my Happily Inc series. If you haven't read any of my other books, don't worry, you won't be lost. This story works as a stand-alone.

My longtime readers will be thrilled to know that in this book, you'll visit our beloved Fool's Gold one more time. No spoilers, just a teaser—Ronan Mitchell will return to his hometown to resolve some issues that have impacted him for years, so he can finally and truly open his heart to the love that awaits him on the other side.

What first attracted you to this cover? Was it the romantic kiss in the soft rain under the colorful umbrellas? Was it the Happily Inc logo, which promises a lighthearted love story? Or maybe, just maybe, you were drawn to this book because of Natalie's trademark red glasses. I cheered when I saw them for the first time on the cover because heroines with glasses are underrepresented on romance covers—but we deserve love, too!

When I begin a new book, the first thing I do is write a scene from each main character's point of view. (By this point, I will have been thinking about the characters for a couple of months, but I won't have written a word.) I write until I hear his or her voice in my head. That's when I feel I know who they are. Then I stop writing and plot the story, scene by scene.

As I was writing Ronan's first scene, he surprised me, big-time. I had thought he was going to be much more moody and dark. He's still reeling from discovering a shocking family secret that has changed how he views himself, his parents and his brothers. But underneath all that, I discovered he's the same lovable heartbreaker he once was. Quirky, funny, determinedly upbeat. Natalie is just the woman to remind him that life can be very, very good.

I fell in love with Natalie and Ronan while writing this book, and I hope you will, too. Don't miss the bonus content at the end—wedding stories for a few of your favorite Happily Inc couples, in print for the first time, exclusively for Target shoppers.

All my love,

Susan Mallery

Also by Susan Mallery

When We Found Home
Secrets of the Tulip Sisters
Daughters of the Bride

Happily Inc

Not Quite Over You
Why Not Tonight
Second Chance Girl
You Say It First

Mischief Bay

Sisters Like Us
A Million Little Things
The Friends We Keep
The Girls of Mischief Bay

Fool's Gold

Best of My Love
Marry Me at Christmas
Thrill Me
Kiss Me
Hold Me
Until We Touch
Before We Kiss
When We Met
Christmas on 4th Street
Three Little Words
Two of a Kind
Just One Kiss
A Fool's Gold Christmas
All Summer Long
Summer Nights
Summer Days
Only His
Only Yours
Only Mine
Finding Perfect
Almost Perfect
Chasing Perfect

For a complete list of titles available from Susan Mallery, please visit www.SusanMallery.com.

SUSAN MALLERY

why not tonight

ISBN-13: 978-1-335-00595-3

Why Not Tonight

This edition published by arrangement with Harlequin Books S.A.

For questions and comments about the quality of this book, please contact us at CustomerService@Harlequin.com.

www.HQNBooks.com

Printed in U.S.A.

When I was nine years old, my parents took me to the eye doctor, where he told me I had to wear glasses. I was devastated and crushed and sobbed with the broken heart of a little girl who believed she would never again be told she was pretty. When I was fifteen, I convinced my father to get me contact lenses. (And I'm not ashamed to admit I might have used a little guilt from my parents' recent divorce to get what I wanted.) Order was restored to the universe, although, let me tell you, contacts are a pain.

One LASIK surgery later, I needed neither contacts nor glasses. But alas, my correction slowly faded until now I need glasses to drive and see a crowd. Enough time has passed that I no longer mind wearing them, but I did always wonder why there weren't more romance novel heroines who wore glasses. And wore them on the cover of a book. Well, now there's at least one. So this story is for those of you who wear glasses, too. May you always know how beautiful you are.

why not tonight

CHAPTER ONE

NATALIE KALETA DROVE up the mountain, prepared to beard the dragon in his lair. She was brave, she was fearless, she was on a mission. Only was "beard a dragon in his lair" right? Did dragons have beards? And if they did, was it just boy dragons or did the girls have to deal with a beard, as well, which seemed desperately unfair.

Okay, so the dragon-beard issue was questionable, but she was totally sure about the lairs. Dragons had lairs. Cool-looking caves with secret rooms and hidden treasures and maybe a chandelier because a chandelier would look great in a lair and the light would bounce off the dragon scales in a really beautiful way.

Although electricity was an issue. It wasn't as if the dragon could call the local utility company and get a line brought in. How would they use a phone with their little claw-hands and how would they pay for a phone, for that matter?

Candles could work. Dragons were tall enough to

be able to light the candles and replace them when needed… Still, if a dragon couldn't buy a phone, how would she buy candles? Unless she made them. It wasn't that hard. Natalie had taken a class once, when she'd been wanting to experiment with wax in her art.

Okay, so a candle chandelier with a beardless girl dragon and no cell phone.

Her mental image reestablished, she turned off the main highway when her phone told her to and headed up the mountain. In the rain. Although *rain* in no way described how much water was falling. *Monsoon* was more like it. It was late August and still the season for crazy rain in the desert.

Natalie's tired, battered twenty-five-year-old Volvo wheezed as the road got steeper. She downshifted, offered silent words of encouragement and wished for a dragon to give her car a little push…or her a ride.

"You can do it," she told her car, hoping she wasn't lying because she did not want to get stuck on the side of a mountain, in the rain or, frankly, any other time. Seriously, when was it convenient to get stuck by the side of the road?

Natalie turned right when instructed. The road narrowed and the rain came down in even bigger buckets.

This was no fun, she thought, driving more slowly, less by choice than by the limitations of her taxed car engine. She shouldn't have volunteered to go check on Ronan, only someone had to. No one had heard from him in almost a week and he wasn't answering her texts.

Ronan Mitchell disappearing into his work at his house for days at a time wasn't uncommon, but no matter what, he always answered her texts. As the part-time office manager for the Willow Gallery, Natalie was responsible for all the local artists. All three of them. Nick and Mathias were never any trouble, but Ronan was a giant, somewhat good-looking pain in her butt.

Oh, sure, his work was amazing. What he could do with glass—turning something that should be static and not that interesting into movement and beauty—was astonishing. She could spend hours watching him create. But he wasn't very friendly and, more significant to her, when he disappeared like this he stopped communicating to the point that she had to text with a very pointed, Are you home sulking or are you dead? Which always got a response. Only not for the past five days.

As far as anyone knew, he hadn't taken a trip. Ronan wasn't big on travel, and when he did, it was for work, so the gallery would know. His brothers had no knowledge of anything other than his normal reclusiveness, or as she liked to call it, brooding artist pouting.

She'd tried to talk her boss into checking on him, but Atsuko had only laughed and told Natalie to keep track of the miles so she could be reimbursed. Which was why Natalie was still driving up, up, up in a horrendous downpour and wishing there were indeed dragons. Or bigger guardrails should her tires lose their grip.

"Just a little farther," she whispered.

She'd only been to Ronan's a couple of times. Once to deliver some packages—yes, being the office manager of a gallery came with mind-boggling responsibility—and once to take a piece of his art back to the gallery. Both tasks had been accomplished without him having to let her inside his gorgeous house. If she arrived in one piece, she was going to insist on a tour…and maybe a snack. Honestly, it was the least the man could do after not admitting he wasn't dead.

Unless he was.

Natalie didn't want to think about that but why else would he not answer her? Maybe he was hurt, she thought, although was that better? If he was so injured he couldn't text her back, then there might be blood, and while she had many excellent qualities, the ability to deal with blood was not one of them.

"I'm fine," she told herself, trying to ignore the bile rising in her throat. "There's no blood. Just rain. Look!"

She gripped the steering wheel with both hands as she continued up and up, the water racing down the road in the opposite direction, lightning flashing in the sky. She slowed even more, her car complaining loudly. An unfortunate knocking began from somewhere in the engine area. An ominous red light flashed on her dashboard.

She was pretty sure she was close to his house. Nothing looked the same in the driving rain but she was confident that just around the bend in front of her was—

She screamed as her car hit a river of mud and started to slide off the road. She'd barely begun to panic when she slammed into something hard and unmoving. Her body jerked, the car engine died and there was only the sound of the rain.

"This can't be good," she murmured, taking the key out of the ignition and unfastening her seat belt. She peered through the curtain of rain and thought she saw Ronan's house up ahead. She must have made it onto his driveway, only to be swept into—

"Well, crap!"

She'd been pushed into a tree. A big tree that had probably put a sizable dent in her already-on-its-last-legs car. While her boss was willing to pay her mileage, she doubted Atsuko would cough up repair money. Plus her favorite mechanic had told her there was nothing that could be done anymore. That her car deserved a decent burial.

Which she was working on. Ah, getting a new car, not the burial. She had savings, but she wasn't ready yet. Regardless, she had to make her way from here to the house without getting swept away.

Natalie glanced at the umbrella she'd brought and knew it would be less than useless. She zipped up her lightweight coat, grabbed her handbag and opened the car door.

Rain immediately pelted her, but that was nothing when compared to the six inches of cold, wet mud swirling around her ankles. She shrieked and bolted for the house, only to realize there wasn't going to be any bolting. There was too much mud everywhere. She had to physically drag each foot out of the muck before planting it down again. The mud seeped into her ankle boots and splattered her legs. In the middle of the storm the temperature had dropped enough that she actually shivered.

In a matter of a minute, she was totally soaked. Her hair clung to her head, water dripped off her glasses and, about five steps in, she lost one of her boots.

"Damn you, Ronan Mitchell," she yelled into the storm. "You'd better be dead or I'm going to kill you!"

The house, a huge stone fortress that normally looked as though it had grown up out of the mountain-side, was barely visible in the deluge. She kept moving because to stand still was to be swept backward. She fought her way to the front door and rang the bell, then began to bang on the door.

It opened without warning and she nearly fell inside. Ronan Mitchell stared at her, his eyes wide, his expression confused.

"There's a storm, Natalie. What are you doing here?"

"A storm? Really? I hadn't noticed, what with sliding off the road and almost drowning on my way up the walk. Wow. A storm! Who knew."

He grabbed her arm and pulled her into the house. "Now I know you're upset. You're almost never sarcastic. What happened?"

"What happened?" she asked as she dripped on his tile floor. "That's not the question." She tried to wipe the moisture off her face only to realize her wet hair was the ongoing source. "The question is, why aren't you dead?"

Ronan stared at her for a second. "Did you hit your head?"

"No. I didn't. I slammed into a tree, which was not my fault, by the way. It was the mud." She felt herself starting to shake, no doubt from shock and his air-conditioning. "You didn't answer your phone. I texted, then I called like eleven times. Everyone was worried, and since they're all more important than me, I was tasked with coming up to check on you."

"I left my phone in my locker at the studio in town." One shoulder rose and lowered. "Probably why you couldn't hear it when you called."

"At work?" Her voice grew louder. "You left your phone at work and because of that I had to come all the way out here?"

The same shoulder rose and lowered again. "Sorry." He looked her up and down. "You're soaked and freezing. Come on. Let's get you dry." He turned away and started down a long hallway.

Natalie tried to go after him only to realize she still had just one shoe. She toed it off, then followed him barefoot, dripping and shivering. Not exactly her finest hour.

"This is your fault," she said as she caught up with him. "You could have—"

"I don't have a landline."

"Sent an email," she said triumphantly. "When you realized your phone was missing, you should have emailed one of us."

"I didn't think it would matter. It was only a couple of days."

"Five. It's been five days since anyone saw you."

He glanced at her, his eyebrows raised.

"Oh, please. I only know because it's my job to know. Don't flatter yourself."

Not that she didn't find Ronan attractive. How could she not? He was tall and muscled, with light brown hair and green eyes all put together in a dreamy package. A woman would have to be totally, well, she wasn't sure what not to notice his good looks, but still. There was no way he had to know that.

"Do you think I like babysitting you and your brothers?" she asked, trying to sound haughty and put-out, which was tough considering how hard she and her voice were shaking. "If you'd all just show up and do your jobs, but nooo. You have to live out here in the mountains, like some troll."

She followed him into a huge bedroom dominated by a big bed and a stone fireplace. She was about to continue complaining about how all this was his fault, but then she caught sight of a massive piece of glass by a turret-shaped window. Stunned, amazed and overwhelmed, she thought she might never speak again. How could she in the presence of something so incredible?

The statue had to be at least eight feet tall and was done in every shade of blue known to God and man. Part sprite, part fairy, all female, the glorious creature seemed to twirl right there before her. The wings appeared to keep her aloft and her feet would dance any second. She was curvy and naked, both sexual and otherworldly.

Natalie squished across the hardwood floor to the piece and put her hand as close as she could without touching her. Her face was beautiful—all angles and lines, as if to emphasize she wasn't quite human. Her hair was short and spiky, her lips parted in such a way that Natalie half expected to hear song or at least words.

"No wonder you don't have a girlfriend," she said before she could stop herself. "Who could possibly measure up?"

"We've never actually had sex." His tone was dry, almost amused.

"You should have made her anatomically correct." She circled her, studying the beautiful lines of the piece and wishing she were a quarter as talented as Ronan. "Although the positioning would be tough. Still, she would be worth it."

"Is there anything you won't say?"

She thought for a second. "Probably not. I try not to be mean or hurtful, but otherwise I'm not much into self-editing. It takes a lot of work."

"Come on. You need to get warm."

It was only when they entered the huge bathroom complete with steam shower, a tub for four and matching vanities that she realized they'd been in his bedroom and now were in his bathroom.

Yes, she thought Ronan was very handsome, and okay, sure, she'd had the odd naughty daydream about him, but shouldn't there at least be a bit of conversation first?

"Wh-what are you doing?" she asked as he punched several buttons on a complicated keypad outside the shower.

"Getting you warmed up. Wait here."

He disappeared into what she guessed was the

closet, then reappeared with a T-shirt, socks, a sweatshirt and sweatpants.

"They're going to be way too big, but you have to wear something while your clothes are drying. We'll wash them when you're done."

"Will we?"

He walked back to the panel and pushed another button. After a couple of seconds, water came on and the shower began to fill up with steam.

"I'm going to leave now," he told her. "Take a shower. A long one. When you're warm and dry, come find me. I'll be in the kitchen."

Not waiting for her in bed? The thought occurred without warning and caused Natalie to wonder if maybe she *had* hit her head. At best, Ronan saw her as a cross between a useful piece of office equipment and a baby sister. At worst, he found her annoying. Men did not, as a rule, find annoying women attractive. Plus there was the sprite. Who could compete with her?

"How do I turn off the shower?" she asked.

He pointed to a red button with the word *Off* printed on it.

"Oh. Good. I can do that."

"I have every confidence. Now get in the shower."

"There's no need to be bossy. I was doing a good thing when I drove up here to find out if you were dead. And I have no idea what I would have done if there'd been a body. So technically, this is your fault. You could have emailed."

"You mentioned that already." He pointed to the shower. "Get in."

She pointed to the door. "Get out."

One corner of his mouth turned up. "Yes, ma'am." He turned and left.

"Annoying man," she muttered as she tugged her wet, muddy, clammy dress over her head and dropped it on the floor, then put her glasses on the counter. But the words were said without much energy, and as she stepped into the shower, she found she was smiling.

RONAN CLOSED THE bathroom door behind him before walking out of the bedroom. He stopped in the doorway, turned and looked back at the glass piece by the window. Even in the dim light of the storm, she seemed almost alive.

He'd created her—had designed the various segments that made up the whole, had played with color until he found the right combination and had, with help from his brothers, brought her to life from inert glass. She was one of his best. Something he could be proud of. He should hang on to that because he was unlikely to do better. In the past few months, he'd discovered he was unlikely to do much of anything at all. Whatever talent he'd had, whatever creative ability, was gone and he had no idea how to get it back.

He turned away from the window and headed for the kitchen. Once there, he boiled water for tea, then walked into the fully stocked pantry to see what the part-time housekeeper had left for him that Natalie might like. He settled on a can of chicken soup and put it in a bowl to heat in the microwave.

Living on the side of a mountain had its advantages—peace and quiet for one, and not many drop-in visitors. The downside was there was no takeout nearby and when the weather turned bad—something that happened maybe once or twice a year—he was trapped either up or down the mountain.

He collected his laptop and quickly logged on to the Happily Inc county website, then shook his head as he viewed the map of the area. There were several mudslides and blocked roads already. He had a feeling Natalie was going to be his guest for a while.

He emailed his brother Nick to let him know what had happened and that Natalie was safe, then glanced out the window at the torrential rain and blowing wind. He had no idea how she'd made it up the mountain in that damned car of hers. It was old and barely running. He couldn't believe anyone would have sent her out in this weather driving that car. When he got back to town he was going to have stern words with his brothers and Atsuko, the owner of the gallery and Natalie's boss. They should take better care of Natalie.

"You're looking fierce." Natalie walked into the kitchen. "Have I created a disturbance in the force by my very presence? Is it because I'm a woman? Am I messing with your male energy?"

Despite himself, he smiled. "I'm more than capable of deflecting your energy," he told her.

"Nuh-uh. Women have been messing with men's energy for centuries. It's part of our mystique."

"Did you just say 'nuh-uh' as part of your argument?"

"I did and it was effective."

"Is that what we're calling it?"

He watched her prowl the kitchen. Despite her curves, the borrowed clothes were ridiculously large on her. He was six-two and she was barely five-three. She had to hold up the sweatpants with one hand and the sweatshirt hung well past midthigh.

Her shower had washed off any makeup, leaving her looking young and vulnerable. Her normally wavy hair was damp and curlier than he would have imagined. Tight ringlets grazed her shoulders.

"It's a miracle you got here in one piece," he told her. "I can't believe my brothers and Atsuko sent you out in the storm. That pile of trash on wheels you drive isn't safe."

Her expression immediately turned guilty. "Yes, well, I was supposed to take Nick's truck, which has four-wheel drive, only it's so big and I'm not comfortable driving it, so I didn't. Don't be mad at them. They didn't know." She paused. "They probably do now."

At least that was something—now he wasn't going to have to beat up his brothers. At one time he would have been more than happy to take on one or all of them, but lately he'd found himself disconnecting instead—walking away rather than acting. A philosophy that summed up much of where he was these days.

She pushed up her red-framed glasses as she sniffed. "Is that soup? Did you cook for me?"

"I opened a can and everything."

"What a guy." She sat on a stool at the island and grinned. "You can serve me now."

"Can I? Will you let me?"

The teasing earned him a smile.

Natalie was one of those naturally sunny people. She was always in a good mood, always excited about whatever life had to offer that day. He supposed he should find her annoying, but he didn't. Being around her made him feel better about everything. He liked knowing she hadn't been troubled by tragedy. She was bright, funny and talented, although he had a feeling she would disagree with the latter. According to her, she only played with paper, nothing more.

He knew differently. Natalie was a gifted artist who used paper and found objects to create unique works. She would say she was still a lowly starving artist but he was confident her time would come.

He set the bowl of soup in front of her, along with a package of Goldfish crackers. After pouring boiling water into a mug, he offered her a box of different tea bags. She picked one and plopped it in the steaming water. He leaned against the counter.

"You have quite the setup," she said after she'd tasted the soup. "Crackers, tea, soup. I know you don't do the grocery shopping."

"My housekeeping service keeps the pantry and freezer stocked. They also do the laundry."

The wind howled outside. Natalie glanced up at the lights. "Not even a flicker. Generator?"

He nodded. "I have city water and power, but when the weather gets bad, the lines can go down for days at a time."

"And they say no man is an island."

She ate more soup, then opened the crackers. After

shaking a few goldfish into her bowl, she offered him the package. He took it and ate a couple.

"Where did you leave your clothes?" he asked.

"In the bathroom."

"When you're done eating, we'll start a load of laundry. It shouldn't take long. Not that you're going anywhere."

He glanced toward the window. It was late afternoon and the rain showed no signs of stopping. According to the weather report, the storm should pass by morning. Depending on whether or not there were mudslides, the roads could be impassable for a couple of days. Even if they weren't blocked, there was no way he would let Natalie drive her POS car down the mountain until he knew the route was safe.

She followed his gaze. "You're thinking I'm stuck, but I don't think so. It's all downhill. That's my car's best speed."

"You're not going anywhere until the rain has stopped and I've had a chance to check out the roads."

For a second, he thought she was going to stick out her tongue at him. Instead she wrinkled her nose and said, "You have always been the bossiest of your brothers. Not that I know Aidan and Del that well, but still. Of you, Nick and Mathias, you are Mr. Bossy Pants. You think you're all broody, but you're not. You pout and you're bossy."

"Mr. Bossy—"

"Pants. Yes, that's what I call you in my mind. Now you know."

He wasn't sure what to do with that information. "You're still not driving home in the storm."

"Stuck in the dragon's lair."

Before he could ask what she meant, she brightened. "At least there's a chandelier in the entryway. It's really beautiful. I thought maybe candles, but the electric lights are nice, too."

"I have no idea what you're talking about."

She smiled. "You usually don't. That's okay. I move quick."

"Implying I don't?"

"You can be fast, probably faster than me, but quick is different."

He had no idea what to make of her. Two years ago Natalie had started working at Willow Gallery as the office manager and herder of the three Mitchell brothers. She monitored inventory, tracked sales and paid them when their pieces sold.

He had always found her appealing. She was pretty and sexy and it had been a long time since he'd had a woman in his life. But the more he got to know her, the more he valued her happy spirit. He was not a happy-spirit kind of guy and he didn't want to take the chance of changing her, of making her like him. So he tried to avoid her at the studio and kept to himself any interest he might have expressed.

Having her in his house now wasn't going to be a problem, he told himself. It was temporary. He would enjoy the Natalie-size interruption, be grateful for the distraction and, when the weather cleared, send her on her way.

A gust of wind rattled the windows.

"I'll huff and I'll puff and I'll blow your house down," she said with a laugh. "I'm glad this is the stone house and not the one made of straw."

"Me, too."

Lightning cut through the late afternoon, making the kitchen as bright as the sun. It was immediately followed by a boom of thunder that shook the house. They both jumped, then turned at a massive *crack*.

Natalie sprang to her feet. "What was that?"

Before he could say he had no idea, there was a colossal ripping sound, then a rumble, as if part of the mountain were being torn away.

Ronan started for the front of the house, Natalie at his heels. He jerked open the front door in time to see a hundred-foot tree falling, falling, falling as the ground beneath it slid away. It started a cascade of trees around it swaying, then drifting toward the ravine in slow motion, pulled along by the mudslide.

The noise was deafening and the whole earth trembled. The last of the trees trembled and hovered, as if it hadn't decided which way it was going to tumble. Ronan saw the trajectory, took a step toward it, then stopped. There was nothing he could do—nothing anyone could do. The last tree hovered for a second before crashing to the ground. The only thing in its path was a very wet, very battered twenty-five-year-old Volvo. The tree hit Natalie's car, crushing it flat. Then the tree and the car slipped away down the side of the mountain.

"Holy crap," she breathed, then started to laugh. "Did you see that? It was incredible."

Worry nibbled at the back of his mind. He'd always thought she was funny. Had he mistaken mental instability for humor?

She did a little dance, then bounced back in the house and grinned at him as he closed the door.

"You know you just lost your car down the side of the mountain, right?"

She shimmied on the tile and spun in a circle. "It's gone, it's gone, it's gone." She faced him and clapped her hands. "I'm so happy."

"Which is not a normal response to what just happened."

She stopped dancing and drew in a breath. "My insurance agent told me to drop collision or replacement or whatever it's called on my car because it's so old and wasn't worth it. Only I didn't want to because it seemed, you know, kind of mean. Like I'd given up on it."

He was no less worried by her response. "You didn't want to hurt your car's feelings?"

"Exactly." The smile returned. "They're going to have to pay me the value of my now-totaled car. I've been saving for a new one—well, new to me, anyway—but I don't have enough yet. I wanted to pay outright and not take out a loan. But with the insurance money, I can finally get my new car. Woo-hoo! I hope I can find a red one."

She began to dance again. Ronan looked out the windows at the raging storm, the mud on the driveway, and doubted the roads were the least bit passable. They were stuck until the county road crew got up the mountain and cleaned things up. It was going to be, he realized, a very, very long couple of days.

CHAPTER TWO

RONAN SEEMED UNABLE to grasp the glory of the moment, so Natalie stopped trying to explain it. Losing her car was fantastic, but if he couldn't see it that way, then she would be happy on her own.

"I emailed the county while you were in the bathroom," he told her. "I should hear back on the status of the roads in the next hour or so, but if those trees fell, I'm sure others did, too."

"So I'm stuck," she said, turning the idea over in her mind. "Is that going to freak you out?"

One corner of his mouth turned up. "I'm not easily freaked."

"Then I guess we're good." She wasn't worried about staying with Ronan. He was basically a good guy, and they had food and a generator, so she would be fine.

He showed her the laundry room, which was so much nicer than the one in her apartment building.

"I can figure it out," she told him, eyeing the sheets

in the dirty clothes hamper by the shiny, front-loading machine. "I'll use those to make a load. I'll be fine, if you want to go, um, work."

He studied her for a second, then nodded. "I'll be in my studio for a couple of hours," he told her. "Then we can figure out what to have for dinner."

She'd just had soup and crackers, so wouldn't be hungry for a while. Not that she wasn't always up for a meal, but still. "Sounds great."

She watched him leave, put her sopping clothes into the washer, added the sheets and detergent, then started the cycle. Only then did she wonder if he really was going to work. Lately he hadn't been producing. She didn't know if she was the only one to notice, or if his brothers had, as well. She wondered if the lack of work was the reason Ronan had been so withdrawn over the past few months. To be as gifted and incredible as he was and then to not be able to work would be... Honestly, she couldn't imagine. Maybe the saddest thing ever. To have that creative gift taken away was the definition of cruelty.

The front-loading washer door locked into place. She watched it for a second, realized there was a timer that told her she had forty-seven minutes until the cycle was over and knew there was no way she could stay here watching laundry wash.

The right thing to do would be to quietly sit somewhere, minding her own business, maybe playing a game on her phone, but the burning need to explore the huge, intriguing house was so much more appealing. She wouldn't go anywhere *too* personal, she promised herself. A quick tour of mostly public spaces should be okay.

She retraced her steps through the kitchen and into the entryway, wanting to start at the beginning. The double front doors were huge. They looked as if they'd been reclaimed from some castle teardown, not that they had many of those in the southwestern part of the country. She ran her hands over the wood and briefly imagined barbarians using a battering ram to break down the door.

The foyer itself was large and circular. A massive chandelier hung from the ceiling two stories up. It seemed to be from the same design era as the front doors—wrought iron and glass twisted into a medieval feel. To her right was a staircase hugging the curved wall. Beyond that was a hallway. To her left was a shorter hallway leading to the kitchen-slash-family room, and there was a half-open door straight across from her. Inside was a very prosaic but necessary powder room.

She headed down the hallway to the right. It led to a beautiful formal dining room with a big table and eight chairs. Ronan wasn't the type to host a dinner party and she couldn't imagine him buying the furniture. Had the house been furnished when he'd bought it?

She went back into the kitchen. It was just plain big. Starkly modern with stainless-steel appliances all in fancy brands like Sub-Zero and Wolf and gorgeous quartz countertops. The backsplash was done in swirling glass tiles that morphed from gray to blue to green to yellow and back to gray. The shapes fit together like a puzzle, and depending on where she stood, the colors seemed to blend and merge or stand out on their own. What on earth?

"Duh," she murmured to herself as she pressed her hands against the cool-to-the-touch backsplash. Ronan was a gifted glass artist. He would have made the tiles himself.

The glass door to the pantry had an inset that matched. She saw a built-in wine cellar that was filled, and plenty of cupboard space. After glancing over her shoulder to make sure she was still alone, she opened one of the cupboards and saw a stack of dishes. Nothing noteworthy. Everyone had dishes. Only these were special.

She picked up one of the plates and studied it. The pattern—one that was similar to the backsplash—was unfamiliar, but she recognized the work. Mathias, Ronan's brother, had made them. Mathias sold all kinds of dishes, serving pieces, light pendants and blown-glass sinks. As the part-time office manager, she cataloged his work, but she'd never seen these before. Had he made them specially for his brother, and if so, when had that happened? While they weren't estranged exactly, she couldn't imagine Ronan asking for something like this.

She put back the dish and turned to the family room. It was definitely a man's room—the large black sectional faced a movie-theater-size television. There were a few pictures on the wall but what really got her attention was the wooden carved bear in the corner. It was life-size and incredibly realistic. The only thing that kept it from being terrifying was the cup of coffee it held in one paw. She moved closer and saw a plaque at the bottom that read Vern.

Natalie laughed, then touched the wood. She knew the artist of the carved bear as well as she knew the maker of the dishes. Nick was a third Mitchell brother.

She had to admit she was confused. She would swear that Ronan was almost entirely disconnected from his brothers. He barely spoke to them when he was in the gallery workshop and he was spending more and more time up here, on his own. Yet he had their work in his house.

She walked back to the foyer and debated the stairs or the longer hallway. The curved staircase was too intriguing to be ignored, so she went upstairs and found herself in what she assumed was a guest room. There was a queen-size bed, a dresser with a TV on top, a small desk and an adjoining bathroom stocked with basic supplies.

She tried not to shriek when she saw herself in the mirror. Her hair had curled as it dried and was now a bouncing riot of brown ringlets. Oh, to have her blow-dryer and some decent styling product.

She went downstairs and headed down the long hall. She came to a study with a big desk and lots of books. No doubt where Ronan liked to sit and count his money, she thought with a grin. She walked out and glanced to her left. There was only one more doorway and she knew it led to the master bedroom. Temptation whispered, but she ignored the voice. She was exploring, not prying. Besides, she'd already caught a glimpse on her way to the bathroom. She knew what it looked like, even though she very much wanted to spend some quality time admiring his roommate, the sprite. Determined to be a courteous guest, she returned to the foyer, grabbed her tote bag and went into the kitchen.

She sat at the table and pulled a flat plastic box from her bag. She opened it, then flipped through the various pieces of square paper until she found a deep green sheet. She studied it for a second, then began to fold the paper.

Less than two minutes later, she'd finished the origami dragon. From the laundry room, the washer beeped that it had completed its cycle. She got up and put her clothes and the sheets in the dryer, then left the small dragon on Ronan's desk in the study.

Back in the kitchen, she noticed two doors. One led to the garage and the other led to yet another hallway. No, that wasn't right. It was a covered walkway, but instead of traditional walls, these were made of glass, allowing her to see out into the storm on both sides. The flooring was stone. She sucked in a breath before taking her first step.

As she followed the path, she realized the glass was curved. There was a door at the other end. A door with a lock. She tried the handle and it turned easily, opening to a much smaller foyer. More doors. One stood open; the other was closed. She moved to the open door and stared into sacred space.

Ronan's workshop was enormous—probably at least a couple thousand square feet. The ceilings soared. There were two ovens, equipment everywhere. Benches, bins, raw material for making glass and, on the wall opposite, a to-scale-size drawing of his current commission.

On the left was a beautiful swan, on the right an equally stunning dragon. The ten feet in between showed one creature transforming into the other. It was magical enough on paper, but the finished product would be done entirely in glass.

There was a similar rendering back in the gallery workshop. She knew parts of it were finished, but not enough, mostly because these days Ronan wasn't working. Even now, both ovens were cold and dark.

It occurred to her a second too late that coming into the studio uninvited was much more of an intrusion than going into Ronan's bedroom. He was an artist and this was—

"Natalie?"

She jumped and turned as Ronan approached. He stepped out of the shadows, all handsome and broody.

"Everything all right?" he asked.

He didn't look mad or concerned about her being in his studio, which was a relief. She managed a smile.

"Yes, I'm doing laundry. It's going great." Ack! That was an incredibly inane thing to say, but he'd startled her.

"I talked to the head of the county road crew. The way down the mountain is blocked. They're going to try to get it cleared as soon as possible, but the storm has to pass first and the main roads will have priority."

He paused as if waiting for her to react. She replayed his words and realized the significance. She wasn't going anywhere anytime soon.

"So I'm stuck. Sorry. You must hate that."

His expression turned from concerned to quizzical. "You just lost your car and now you can't go home. You're the one who gets to be upset."

"I'm totally fine. The house is great and we have power and food. It's not a problem. Really."

"I would have expected more demands."

She laughed. "From me? Seriously?"

"No, not from you. You always seem to take things in stride. There's a guest room at the top of the stairs. Make yourself at home." He hesitated. "I'm sorry I left my phone at the office. I didn't mean to make you come all this way and then lose your car and get trapped."

"Let the car go." She grinned at her own pun. "You know what I mean. It's really a happy thing. Now I can get a new one. It's going to be red, that's for sure. Bright red, if they have one. Anyway, I'll go get settled."

"Dinner at seven?" he asked before she left.

"Sure." For a second she nearly added, "Thank you for asking," only to stop herself in time. He wasn't asking her out on a date—he was feeding an uninvited guest. She wasn't a stranger—they knew each other from work, but she doubted he was superexcited about her presence. The one thing she knew about Ronan for sure was he loved, loved, loved to be alone.

She gave a little wave as she left. She'd had plenty of alone time since she'd lost her mom nearly seven years ago. Alone was something she didn't like at all. People should be together, preferably surrounded by those they loved. She didn't have family, but she was doing her best to build one of her own making. Ronan had his brothers so close and yet he rarely spent time with them. Talk about stupid and wasteful.

Not her rock, she told herself. She was a temporary guest, nothing more. He wasn't interested in her opinion and she wasn't going to give it. Really.

RONAN FOUND HIMSELF in the uneasy position of feeling out of place in his own house. He couldn't believe one petite, unassuming woman could have that much of an impact on him, but although he couldn't see Natalie or even hear her, knowing she was around was unsettling. He was torn between avoiding her and wanting to find her and…and…

Best not to go there, he told himself. She was his guest. He knew better, which was something because he didn't seem to know much else.

When had it happened? When had he left the world of normal people and become some kind of misfit recluse? It hadn't been his plan. When he'd first bought the house, he'd assumed he would have his brothers over all the time to hang out. He'd figured they would come up here to work as a change of pace from Atsuko's studio. Only none of that had happened. Instead he'd used his house as a retreat, at least at first. Now it was little more than a self-imposed prison.

Which was way too dramatic, he thought as he set out a casserole left by his housekeeping service. It would serve two and looked like something Natalie might like.

He read the label with a list of ingredients and the heating instructions. There was chicken. She ate meat, didn't she? He was pretty sure he'd seen her devour a hamburger more than once and she'd had no problem with the soup earlier. She'd been at the gallery at least a couple of years. He should know more about her aside from the fact that he thought she was attractive and maybe a little sexy. And he sure as hell shouldn't be worried about talking to her. Dear God, what was wrong with him? He'd always been the smooth twin when it came to women. He'd been the one to approach the girls in high school, the popular one as he and Mathias had gotten older. But it, like so many things, had been lost. He wasn't sure when that had happened—he hadn't been paying attention—but that confidence was gone now.

He turned on one of the two ovens, then returned to the refrigerator and pulled out fixings for salad. Not that he ever ate salad, but the service left the vegetables every week. Women liked salads, didn't they? Women…

His brain flipped over as he realized Natalie had lost her car, was stuck in his house and he'd basically left her to do laundry on her own. He hadn't asked if she was okay or sat with her or anything. He'd walked out like some brooding gothic figure.

He swore. What was wrong with him? He wasn't dealing with an alien species. He wasn't some thirty-something virgin alone with his first woman. He had to get a grip, or at least fake it better.

Natalie breezed into the kitchen. She had changed back into her dress.

"Doing okay?" he asked, wondering if she'd bothered to look around when she'd been alone in the house. It wouldn't matter if she had—it wasn't as if he had secrets. At least, not the kind he kept in drawers. There wasn't even a dirty magazine for her to find.

"Much better. Not that I don't appreciate you lending me clothes." She wrinkled her nose. "Which I'm going to need to continue to borrow while I'm here. I was going to say I should keep a packed bag in my trunk, but that wouldn't have helped, either." She held up a hand. "Please don't apologize about my car again. It's really a lucky break."

Something he didn't understand, but was going to have to believe, based on how many times she'd said it. He supposed the real problem was that he'd been so successful for so long he'd forgotten what it was like to have to save up for something like a car.

He wondered if it would be okay for him to offer to replace hers, then realized that was not a topic they should get into while she was stranded in his house. He might not know how to talk to a woman anymore, but he knew better than to say something that might be considered upsetting. And "Hey, let me buy you a car" fell firmly into the scary, weird-guy category.

"I like your hair," he said instead, thinking everyone enjoyed a compliment.

She groaned. "The curls? Really? I hate them. Hate." She squeezed several in her hand. "They were torturous when I was growing up. What is it about boys in elementary school and a girl with curls? I was teased constantly."

"You were different and they thought you were pretty."

"Oh, please." She sat at the stool by the counter. "I was not pretty when I was little."

"Why would you say that? You're pretty now. There's no reason to think that's changed." He raised his brows. "Trust me. When a boy in elementary school teases you like that, it's because you've flustered him."

"I honestly don't know what to say," she admitted.

"There's a first."

Natalie laughed. "Are you saying I talk a lot?"

"Yes, but it's nice background noise."

She looked around. "Hmm, nothing safe to throw. Someone as annoying as you should keep decorative pillows around. Background noise? You didn't actually say that."

"It seems I did, and what I meant was when I'm working and you're talking to Mathias or Nick, your conversation makes it easier to work."

"Oh. Well, that's different. I like that I make it easier for you to work. I didn't know what you thought of me." She looked at him quizzically. "Is this the softer side of Ronan Mitchell? The secret man at home?"

He realized he wasn't as uncomfortable as he had been, which was a relief. He would hate to think he'd totally lost who he'd once been. To be honest, he was enjoying the teasing.

"I have depths."

"I'll bet." She slid off the stool. "What's for dinner?"

"A chicken casserole left by the service. I have ingredients for salad."

"No, thanks. I'm not really a big fan of lettuce. Dressing I love, but I try to avoid it except on special occasions." She walked over to the refrigerator, pulled open the door and peered inside. "Yay, look!" She held up a tube. "Fresh baked biscuits. Okay, not exactly homemade, but close enough and very delicious." She glanced at the stove. "You even have two ovens, so I can bake these at the same time. It's a sign."

"Obviously."

He got out a cookie sheet for her, then went to the far side of the island to watch her work. Not counting the housekeeping service, she was the first woman he'd had in this house. More proof that he was pathetic, but still true.

He'd thought when he moved to Happily Inc that he would be able to put his past behind him and start being himself again. He hadn't realized he'd simply dragged it with him and had been dealing with it—or not dealing with it—ever since. He hadn't been in anything close to a relationship for nearly four years. He was cut off from everyone he cared about and he couldn't work.

Despite everything, he laughed out loud.

Natalie pushed up her red glasses and glanced at him. "I wasn't talking, so I know I didn't make a joke. Are you hearing voices and are they funny? Although humorous voices would be better than ones telling you to start killing people." She paused. "Oh, can you see dead people?"

"Only on alternate Wednesdays."

"I'm not keen on the whole seeing-dead-people

thing, although I would like to communicate with my mom. I lost her when I was twenty."

"I'm sorry." He hadn't known, but then, he knew very little about Natalie. She was a part-time artist, part-time office manager, and after that, he had nothing.

"Me, too." She checked the timer for the casserole, then slid the biscuits into the second oven. "This is going to be delicious." She paused. "Oh, did *you* want salad? I can make you some."

"I'm good." He shifted and reached for the door to the built-in wine cellar, then held up a bottle. "Interested?"

Her mouth curved into a smile. "Yes, please. It looks fancy. I love fancy wine."

"Because..."

"Because I can't afford it and it's fun to have." She held up her hand. "I know what you're going to say. That I should prioritize. Not that wine would be a priority, but still." Her expression turned earnest. "My art is really important to me. I work as much as I need to so I can pay the bills, but all my free time goes into creating. Maybe one day I'll be able to support myself with what I create, but so far, not so much." The smile returned. "I'm lucky—I work with paper. It's a pretty cheap medium. It would be hard if I had to have the equipment you need to sculpt with glass or bronze." She raised her arm and felt her bicep. "Of course, working with bronze would be a really fun workout."

He couldn't begin to know where to start with that info dump. Guilt was overwhelming most of his other emotions. Guilt that he'd been blessed with a selfish bully of a father who had nonetheless gifted him with incredible talent and, more important, had provided a name that had opened doors from the time Ronan had been a teenager. He didn't have to worry about money or finding people who enjoyed what he created. He was Ronan Mitchell—the world came to him. At least when he let it.

He found himself wanting to buy her a year's worth of art supplies, or maybe a house so she wouldn't have to work at the gallery and could devote herself to whatever she wanted, which landed him back firmly in the scary, weird-guy column.

He swore silently. When the roads were clear and he could get to town, he was going to show up to stuff more often. Maybe start meeting women online and take up a hobby. Anything, because in the last couple of hours, he'd been forced to admit he was not good at being human anymore.

CHAPTER THREE

WHILE RONAN OPENED a bottle of merlot, Natalie set the table. She waved one of the plates.

"Your brother made these."

"I know."

She gave him a slight eye roll. "I *meant* I'm surprised you have your brother's dishes in your house."

She was cute when she was sassy, he thought. Attitude in the face of car loss and being trapped by a storm—he could respect that.

"Why? I like his work and I need dishes."

"Does he know?"

"I think so." Did Mathias know Ronan had his dishes? Had he ever said anything? Years ago, they'd been twins and had known everything about each other. Now he was less sure about any of that.

"I'll mention it when I get back to the office," she told him. "He'll want to know."

Ronan doubted that, but if it made her happy. He crossed to the built-in sound system and turned it on.

Soft music filled the room. Natalie listened for a second, then smiled.

"Jazz. I like it."

"Good." He poured them wine before they both went into the kitchen to collect dinner.

There were a few minutes of setting out food. Then they sat across from each other at the big dining room table. As he was trying to remember how to make small talk with a woman he found attractive, Natalie looked at him.

"You didn't have the house built, did you? I mean, parts of it are really you and the style suits you but I'm not sure it's really, you know, *you*, if that makes sense."

"You went exploring?" he asked, his voice teasing.

"Well, yeah. You left me alone for hours. What was I supposed to do?"

"Read?"

"The only books are in your study and I'd never invade your personal space that way."

He didn't bother pointing out that to know about his study, she had to go *in* his study. "I don't mind you looking around."

"What if I find something I shouldn't?"

"You won't. I have no secrets."

"Everyone has secrets."

"What are yours?"

The question seemed to surprise her. "I guess I don't have any that I can think of. There's stuff about me you don't know, but it's no big deal."

"Such as?"

She raised her glass. "I really like fancy wine."

He grinned.

"So the house," she prompted. "How'd you get it?"

"I bought it. The place was partially finished when I first saw it. The owners had an odd construction style, almost completing it room by room rather than all at once."

"I knew it." She pointed her fork at him. "You didn't furnish this room at all, did you? Because while it's really nice, this is not your style. I see you more modern—more clean lines, with glass and metal. This furniture is too heavy for you."

"I never much thought about it."

"That's because you're a guy."

He looked around the dining room and realized he didn't much care for the big pieces, especially the hutch.

"The chairs aren't comfortable," he admitted.

"First time you've sat in them?"

He nodded. "I decorated the family room."

She raised her eyebrows. "Really? You?"

He chuckled. "I hired someone to decorate the family room, and the master bedroom. I designed the studio myself."

"That I believe. You would know best what goes where. Work space is intimate. It has to feel right." She looked at him. "Not that you don't know any of that."

"Do you like the studio at the gallery?"

She had a small area in the corner. He and his brothers had taken over most of the rest of it.

"I do. There's good energy. I like it best when the three of you are working. There's a lot of creativity and the way you talk to each other is fun." She grinned. "And you like it when I talk to Mathias and Nick. What did you call it? Background noise?"

"I meant that in the nicest way possible."

"Uh-huh." She opened her biscuit and spread butter on each half. "These are my favorite. Along with, you know, the fancy wine. The casserole is good, too."

"There are cookies in the freezer. We can defrost them after dinner if you'd like."

She winced. "I put on weight pretty easily. I should probably pass on the cookies."

He started to say she looked good to him but stopped himself. Under their present circumstances, that might be best left unsaid, even though it was true.

Natalie was petite, with plenty of curves. She had the energy of a person four times her size, with an easy smile. He meant what he said—he always liked it when she was in the studio. She was a balancing force for his demons.

"You might be stuck for a couple of days," he said instead. "We can save the cookies for another time."

"Tempting me with bakery goods. I never would have guessed."

Her eyes were big and brown, half-hidden behind her glasses, but still expressive. He realized he didn't know anything about her, other than the fact that she'd started working at the gallery two years before.

"Where did you move from?" he asked.

"When I came here? Sacramento."

"What made you move?"

Her expression was quizzical. "You don't know?"

He shook his head.

"I thought everyone had heard my sad little story." She smiled. "I was practically stood up at the altar."

What? He hadn't expected that. "You don't seem upset."

"It was a while ago and probably for the best. My mom warned me I came from a long line of women who were not lucky in love. I didn't want to believe her, but I guess it's true." She sipped her wine. "Back in Sacramento, I was trying to make it as an artist and failing, so I took an office job and through that I met this guy—Quentin Jones."

She paused dramatically and sighed. "He was very handsome and smooth. Just supercharming."

Ronan felt a twinge of something he couldn't name but he sure didn't like how it felt. "And?"

"And we started going out. His family owned a couple of car dealerships. One in Sacramento and one in San Diego. I met his parents and they were so nice." She looked at him. "I liked being a part of a family after losing my mom. When he proposed, I knew it was going to be wonderful. We had a plan. He was going to take over the San Diego dealership and I would run the front office. We'd get a little place of our own."

Her voice sounded regretful.

"What about your art?" he asked. There was no way Natalie belonged in an office—not full-time. She was meant to be wild and creative, not cooped up.

"I thought being in love was more important, I guess. I'm not sure. When I was with Quentin, my art didn't seem that important." She frowned. "He wasn't exactly encouraging about it, which I didn't realize until later. Anyway, we planned our wedding here, in Happily Inc. A destination wedding with a princess theme." She laughed. "I don't know what I was thinking."

"You'd make a very beautiful princess."

"Thank you. I like to think so but one never knows. I sold pretty much everything I owned, packed up my clothes and drove to town to get ready for the wedding. Three days before the big event, Quentin called and broke up with me. He said he wasn't sure anymore and his parents had never liked me and it wasn't going to work."

Ronan hadn't expected a happy ending to her story—he knew Natalie wasn't married—but he hadn't expected that.

"He dumped you over the phone? What a jerk. Did he help cancel the wedding?" He held up a hand. "Never mind. I know the answer."

Her mouth twisted. "Yeah, not so much with the cleanup. I was stuck doing everything and paying for most of it. It took me a full day to grasp what had happened. Then I had to scramble. What I hadn't expected was how nice everyone was. Pallas only charged me her expenses to date at Weddings Out of the Box. In fact, everyone did that. I had to pay maybe thirty percent of what I owed, but it was still a lot. It wiped out my savings and left me with some credit card debt." She sipped more wine. "A lot of credit card debt. But I was so surprised by how supportive everyone had been that I decided to just stay put until I figured out what

I wanted to do next. Then I found the job with Atsuko at the gallery and a little apartment and here we are."

He felt an odd flush of pride that his adopted town had come through for her, along with a very understandable need to find the ex-fiancé and smash in his face. Maybe he would take one of his brothers along so they could do a good job of teaching the asshole a lesson.

Natalie leaned toward him. "I'm fine and you're sweet to be protective."

"I didn't say anything."

"You didn't have to. You looked all mean and scrunchy. Thank you."

Scrunchy?

"I know," she told him. "Not an expected compliment, but I mean it that way, all the same. Once I settled in Happily Inc, I realized that I had found here what I'd been looking for with Quentin." She lowered her voice. "Family. If you don't have one, you make one. At least, that's what I learned. I have friends and my art and there are giraffes at the animal preserve just outside of town, which you know because your sister-in-law is the curator." She shook her head. "Is that the right word?"

"I'm not sure someone can curate giraffes. At least not legally."

She giggled. "Oh, wow, the wine is so going to my head."

It had been a quarter of a glass. "I'm glad you're not driving."

"That would take a car." She did a little dance in her seat. "I'm getting a red car. I can't wait."

"You have other criteria, don't you? Other than the color?"

"No." She sighed. "Okay, fine, yes, safety, but red. Red, red, red."

"I'm going with you," he muttered. "You aren't allowed to go on a car lot alone."

"Mr. Bossy Pants. Just like I said. Do you have any kids?"

He'd been swallowing and nearly choked on a piece of chicken. "No. Why do you ask?"

She drank more wine. "Kids are great. The unlucky-in-love thing is a serious drag, but just because I can't have romantic love doesn't mean I can't have children, right?"

He cleared his throat against an imaginary tight collar. Somehow the conversation had gone in a direction he hadn't expected. "Ah, sure."

"Your family is pretty healthy. There aren't any big diseases in every generation, are there?"

The question touched a sore spot, but Ronan kept his face emotionless. "Not as far as I know."

How could he know?

"You're athletic—I've seen that. Did you do well in school?"

"I guess. Math was easy. I didn't love history. Why are you asking all these questions?"

"Practice." She reached for her wineglass, then put it down. "Can you keep a secret?"

He could but he had a bad feeling that, in this case,

he didn't want to. But instead of saying no, like a man with a working brain, he found himself nodding.

"I have a new app."

Not the secret he would have expected. "Congratulations."

She giggled again. "No. That's not the secret. It's what the app is for. It's called Baby Daddy." She frowned. "Or maybe Daddy Baby. I can't remember. It's for finding a sperm donor. You know, so I can have a baby."

He was on his feet before he realized he was moving. "Are you—"

"Asking you?" She wiggled her eyebrows. "No. You can sit down. The app comes with a list of questions and I was trying out a few. Don't panic. I'm sure you have great sperm but you can keep it to yourself. Or not. I mean, I don't need it. Or them. I don't need a donation."

He lowered himself back onto his chair. "No more wine for you."

"MBP," she whispered.

It took him a second to realize she meant Mr. Bossy Pants. Well, hell.

BY MIDNIGHT NATALIE was sober, slightly chagrined and wide-awake. It made sense that half a glass of wine would metabolize quickly and she'd always been a night owl. Working a job with traditional hours had been a challenge. Given the choice, she would be up all night. She loved to create when the rest of the world was asleep. The quiet, the darkness, seemed to fuel her creativity. As for chagrined, well, she had no one but herself to blame.

In retrospect, she had to admit that maybe it hadn't been a good idea to test her find-a-sperm-donor app on Ronan, only she'd just downloaded it the day before and she was curious about how it worked. There were tons of questions—she'd barely started with Ronan and now she doubted he would be willing to answer any more.

Not that she wanted him to donate sperm. Sure, he was good-looking and smart and gifted and funny—in fact, nearly everything she would want in the father of her child. But he was someone she worked with and kind of knew. Having his baby would be awkward, to say the least. No, if she went the baby daddy sperm donor app route, she was hooking up with a stranger.

She paused on the landing outside her bedroom. Not hooking up, she corrected. Making medical arrangements with. She had no interest in sex with a stranger.

The house was dark and quiet. She could hear rain and wind outside, but with the thick stone walls, the weather seemed to be at a safe distance. She was itching to work—her fingers practically trembled with the need to do *something*, only she didn't have any supplies with her. Just her usual stash of origami paper and she'd already left little animals, flowers and shapes all over the house. She wasn't in the mood for TV, so maybe she should try reading. There was a whole library of books in Ronan's office. She would creep downstairs, collect one and return to her bedroom to wait for elusive sleep.

She grabbed the waistband of the baggy sweatpants—she'd hung up her dress for the night—and tiptoed down the staircase. When she reached the foyer, she paused to get her bearings in the dark, turned toward what she assumed was the hallway and ran smack into something big, solid and warm.

She screamed and the big, solid, warm thing grabbed her arms.

"It's me," Ronan said in the dark. He released her and clicked on a light. "You okay?"

She blinked in the sudden brightness. Ronan had changed his clothes, or pulled on new ones. He wore jeans and a sweatshirt. They were both barefoot, which felt oddly intimate or weird, depending on one's perspective.

"Did I wake you?" she asked. "I was trying to be quiet. I wanted to get a book."

"Can't sleep?"

"I'm a night owl."

"Me, too."

He gave her a slow smile. It was one she hadn't seen before, or if she had, she hadn't been paying attention. Or maybe it was different because of the time of night. Regardless, the curve of his mouth was unbelievably sexy and totally caught her off guard. She suddenly felt breathless and young and intensely aware of the fact that she wasn't wearing a bra.

He pointed down the hall. "Go find a book. I'll make us hot chocolate and maybe that will help you sleep."

"I, ah, thank you. Hot chocolate would be nice." She wanted to say something to make that smile return, but honestly, her mind was totally blank, so she headed down the hall, only to stumble when she stepped onto the rug, which was just so typical.

Ten minutes later, book in hand, she walked into the kitchen. Ronan had a small pot on the stove and two mugs on the island. There was a blue oval tin, trimmed in gold, sitting on the counter.

"What did you pick?" he asked as she settled on one of the stools.

She waved a hardcover thriller. "Nazis, missing gold treasure and genetically modified twins. I'm not sure it can get better than that."

He chuckled. "You have unexpected reading tastes."

"Given my choice, I would much rather sink into a steamy romance novel, but you don't seem to have any of those on your bookshelves."

"My apologies. I'll order several first thing in the morning."

"I doubt that, but thank you for offering." She pointed to the tin. "First, let me say how impressed I am that you have hot chocolate in your house."

"I don't have it often, but every now and then you gotta indulge." He measured out several tablespoons of the dark powder, then handed her the container. "It's my favorite. It's German, from a little shop in what was East Berlin."

She studied the label and tried not to laugh. "And they ship it to you?"

"Not just me. They'll ship to anyone."

"Uh-huh. You can't just get the stuff from the grocery store like everybody else?"

"It's an indulgence. Why not have what I really want?"

A philosophy she planned to emulate just as soon as she had an extra nickel or so, she promised herself. For now, her indulgences were things like meat and paying her light bill.

He stirred the powder into the milk for nearly a minute, then filled each of the mugs. He pulled one of those whipped cream spray cans from the refrigerator and added a generous dollop to the mugs before handing her one. She inhaled the scent of sweet chocolate and nearly moaned.

"You do know how to treat a girl," she said before taking a sip.

Not moaning became even harder. The drink was smooth and sweet, without being too sweet. The chocolate flavor indulged her senses, especially her taste buds.

"This is so good it's dangerous."

Ronan settled next to her and grinned. "Women and chocolate."

"It's a thing. We can't help it." She took another drink and sighed. "Oh, man, I could get used to this and I bet it has like a billion calories. Does it?" She held up a hand. "Never mind. I don't want to know."

"I'll send you home with the can."

"Thanks, but don't you dare. I'm short and curvy. I told you, weight finds me much more easily than it does my leggy friends. I try not to be bitter, but sometimes I can't help myself. And don't say you understand. You're a guy and you have a job that's physical. You can eat the entire grocery store and not gain a pound, which annoys me and I don't want to talk about it."

He studied her for a second, then smiled again. "I see the late hour doesn't make you any less feisty."

Feisty? He thought she was feisty? That was very close to sexy. She told herself not to think about her braless state. She was wearing an incredibly baggy sweatshirt. He would never notice. Still, it was nice to pretend, even for a second. Although after the conversation they'd had at dinner, he would probably be terrified if she made the slightest move. Speaking of which…

"I'm sorry about the app."

One brow rose. "Putting it on your phone or discussing it?"

"Talking about it. I really was just checking out the questions. There are a lot of them and some are really interesting. I didn't mean to scare you."

"*Scare* is strong."

She rolled her eyes. "You were terrified."

He chuckled. "Your words, not mine." He lifted his mug. "What do you normally do when you can't sleep?"

"Work. It's relaxing and eventually I get tired enough to sleep. I would have done that tonight, but I don't have anything with me except a few sheets of origami paper."

"Do you ever paint?"

"Sometimes. I'm not very good at it. I used to paint all the time. One day I finished a watercolor and realized it was awful. I got so frustrated I tore it up. When the pieces settled on my desk, they'd created something really beautiful and that was the beginning."

"From failure, success."

She smiled. "Exactly. I enjoy the unexpected and I've been working with mixed media ever since."

"Which explains the trash."

Ronan and his brothers often teased her about her found objects that she worked into her pieces. "It's not trash. Just because someone doesn't want something doesn't mean it's trash."

He held up his free hand. "Don't get riled. You're supposed to be getting sleepy."

"Trash," she grumbled. "Your inability to see the potential in things is surprising, given what you do for a living."

"Like I said, feisty."

There was a tone to his voice. Or maybe she just wanted to hear something. Regardless, she liked the slightly affectionate, slightly teasing sound. Maybe it was the late hour or the storm raging outside, but she liked this Ronan. He was much more approachable and charming than the one she knew at work.

He'd always been appealing, and not just based on his features. There was something…wounded about him. She knew the danger of the brooding, damaged guy and had always avoided the type, but there was something about him that drew her in.

"Would you like to work?" he asked, drawing her attention back to their conversation.

"Sure."

"Then come with me."

She thought he would lead her to his studio behind the house. Instead he went upstairs, toward the guest room.

For a second, she wondered what he was going to do. If he pulled her close and kissed her, well, she had no idea how she would react. The thought of Ronan touching her was kind of intriguing. She felt a slight shiver low in her belly.

But instead of heading to her bedroom and making her question his definition of "work," he stopped on the landing in front of the curved wall decorated with molding. He pressed in and the wall popped open to reveal a hidden door.

Natalie jumped back and nearly spilled the rest of her cocoa. "I had no idea that was there."

"I think that's the point. I'm not sure why the builder put in the secret room. I didn't know what to do with it, so I made it into an art studio." He walked inside and turned on the lights.

She was about to say he already had the custom studio he'd built when she followed him inside and saw this space was totally different. There weren't any ovens, no raw materials for making glass. Instead there was a long counter at desk height, a drafting table and several easels. Cabinets filled the walls on either side of the door.

The room itself was in the turret, she realized as she looked around. There were huge windows that would let in light during the day. Tonight the storm raged just beyond the panes. She could practically feel the fury as the wind howled.

Ronan began to open the cabinet doors, revealing stacks of paper in all different sizes, canvases, bags of clay and boxes of brushes. Another cabinet held paints—oil and acrylic—along with colored pens and pencils, markers, glue and a glue gun. There was yarn, string, crochet hooks, scissors, rubber stamps, ink, X-Acto knives and ribbon.

She turned in a slow circle, then stared at Ronan. "But you work with glass."

"Most of the time. Every now and then, I need to be inspired."

"It's a magical place."

"I'm glad you think so. While you're here, consider it yours."

"What? No. I couldn't."

"Sure you could. I rarely come up here. Indulge your inner artist. Keep your own hours."

It was a gift beyond measure, she thought, slightly light-headed at the thought of all the possibilities. "You're sure you don't mind?"

He gave her that smile again. "I don't mind. Have fun, Natalie. I'll see you tomorrow."

She nodded and moved toward the cupboards. She wasn't sure what she wanted to do first. A collage, or maybe paint. She was a horrible painter, but sometimes the wretchedness of her work inspired a mixed-media piece. She would have to—

The sound of a door closing caught her attention. She turned and saw Ronan had left. The door to the landing was easily visible from this side of the room.

How amazing, she thought, setting her cocoa down

on the long table. Energy flowed through her. Paint first, mixed media second, she decided, reaching for a canvas. And in a few hours, she would get to watch the sunrise through the storm. Honestly, it didn't get better than that!

CHAPTER FOUR

RONAN HAD NO idea what time Natalie finally went to bed. When he got up after a handful of hours sleeping, the house was quiet. Despite the storm still milling around, he checked with the county road crew and was not surprised when they said there was no way they could begin to clear roads for at least another twenty-four hours.

He went into his office to send an email to his brother Mathias, telling him what was going on. As his laptop booted, he noticed a tiny green origami dragon sitting next to his computer. He picked it up and held it on the palm of his hand.

The workmanship was precise, the lines perfect. There was something compelling about the tiny creature. He finished his email, then put the paper dragon on his bookshelf before heading to the kitchen to brew coffee.

As he waited for the machine to work its magic, he prowled the family room, spotting a tiny paper mouse on an end table. There was a turtle in the dining room and a classic crane in the foyer.

Once the coffee was done, he picked up the turtle and carried it with him to his studio. As he passed through the long hallway, he felt the force of the storm outside. According to the weather reports, it would blow itself out by the end of the day and then the cleanup would begin.

He put the turtle on his desk and began to sketch. He wasn't sure it was possible for glass to capture the sharp edges of origami. He couldn't use a sheet of glass and fold it—that would be too thick. So he would have to create the illusion of folds and lines.

Hours later he stared at the molten mess he'd made. It was a green blob that was more failed science experiment than turtle, but he'd learned from his mistakes and was eager to try again. His stomach rumbled, reminding him he hadn't eaten since dinner, so he went back into the house.

He found Natalie sitting at the island, a mug in front of her. She was back in her dress, with her hair all curly and her eyes slightly sleepy. She looked soft and rumpled and sexy as hell.

For a second, he allowed himself to simply look. To take in the perfect line of her cheek and the way her glasses added an impish air.

Something stirred inside of him. Not the need to recreate her in glass—no, the sensation was more base. Desire, he thought with some surprise. He wanted to know if her skin was as soft as it looked, and how her scent would surround him when he got close to her.

He wanted to kiss her and taste coffee on her lips. He wanted to know what she was like in bed. Was she as feisty as she was in the rest of her life, or did she yield with a sigh designed to drive a man to madness?

She looked up and smiled. “Morning.”

He mentally turned his back on his imaginings and glanced at the clock. “Barely,” he said, his voice teasing.

“I know, I know. I indulged my inner night owl and worked until sunrise. It was glorious.”

“The work or the sunrise?”

“Both. The storm was going hot and heavy, but I could still see the light on the horizon. Nature is miraculous. What have you been doing in your studio?”

“Playing, mostly. You?”

“I painted.” She wrinkled her nose. “It’s total crap, but that’s okay. From crap comes inspiration. I seem to often start with a horrible painting. I guess it’s because my mom was a painter, only she was brilliant.”

“Have you eaten?”

She shook her head. “I was trying to figure out what I wanted, although it would probably make more sense to see what you have and then decide on something.”

“Breakfast or lunch?”

“I’m open.”

“Let’s make it brunch. Omelets okay?”

“Sure.”

He headed to the refrigerator and started pulling out ingredients. He stacked eggs, cheese, a red pepper and mushrooms on the counter, then pulled a box from the freezer and handed it to her. Based on her reaction to the hot chocolate, he had a feeling she would be all in.

She read the label and groaned. "Cinnamon buns? What are you doing to me?"

"You don't want one?"

"I want all of them, but one will do."

He turned on the oven and got out a baking sheet, then washed his hands and began chopping up the pepper.

"How do you know how to do all this?" she asked. "You're very handy in the kitchen. I wouldn't have expected it."

"Mathias and I moved out when we were maybe twenty-two. Neither of us was crazy about takeout every night, so we took a couple of cooking classes. It was fun and we learned the basics."

"And it was yet another weapon in your attracting-women arsenal."

"Asking or telling?"

She grinned. "Oh, I'm telling."

He was surprised. While he used to be very successful with women, in the past few years he'd stopped trying. He preferred to be alone. So how would Natalie know whether he had an arsenal or not?

He finished prepping the vegetables about the time the oven chimed that it had reached the right temperature. He slid the cinnamon rolls into the oven and set the timer, then poured more coffee and joined Natalie at the island.

"Did you sleep at all?" he asked.

"About five hours. I'll take a nap later and then stay

up tonight." She pulled her cell phone out of her pocket. "You have great coverage up here."

"There's a tower on the edge of the property. It's close to the hiking trails. I think the state put it in for search and rescue teams."

"Makes sense." She pushed a couple of buttons. "Would you say you have a moral compass?"

The question surprised him. "Don't most people? Yes, and I try to follow it."

"Me, too. I hate to lie. I feel icky and then I can never remember. Better to just be honest." She paused. "Do you think people are basically good, but sometimes misguided, or do you believe there are actually evil people?"

He hesitated. Most people were basically good but there were others who seemed to be following a separate set of rules, like his father. Ceallach Mitchell wasn't evil, but he rarely showed compassion and thought kindness was for suckers. At the same time, he expected those around him to rotate in the orbit of his greatness and be grateful for the opportunity. No, his father wasn't evil, but he wasn't good, either. Ronan wasn't sure if—

He grabbed her phone and stared at the screen. The app logo made him shudder. "You said we weren't going to play this game anymore. I'm not going to be your sperm donor."

"Oh, I know. I just thought the questions were interesting." She smiled. "I hadn't realized you were so emotionally delicate."

"I'm a typical guy who doesn't want unexpected children wandering around."

Her smile turned impish. "That would be your moral compass at work."

"Good to know it's working." He glanced at the timer, then got up and began cracking eggs into a bowl. "Are you serious about having a baby on your own?"

"I don't know. Maybe. I'm playing with the idea. I'm not sure I'll ever be able to fall in love."

"You don't really believe you're unlucky in love, do you? You can't base all your decisions on the actions of a single jerk."

She hesitated just long enough for him to know there was more to the story. Something she wasn't telling him.

"He was a jerk who said he wanted to marry me and then changed his mind."

"That's on him, not you."

He got out a twelve-inch pan, figuring he'd make one big omelet, then cut it in half. He tossed the vegetables into the pan to begin to sauté.

"It was one guy, Natalie."

"My high school romance ended badly. He cheated."

"That was high school, and if you want to use those two men to plot a course for the rest of your romantic life, have you considered the problem might be your choices rather than a cosmically determined fate?"

She winced. "It's very early to be so judgmental." She sipped her coffee. "You're saying I have bad taste rather than bad luck?"

"I'm suggesting it might be something to consider before you jump into having a baby on your own."

"I'm not jumping."

"You're practicing for your interviews."

"I guess you're right. I have been looking at adoption, but it's not easy if you're single."

He kept the vegetables moving in the pan. When they were nearly done, he dumped them back onto the cutting board, then wiped out the pan. The oven chimed. He turned it off and set the cookie sheet onto a cooling rack, then added butter to the frying pan.

"What do you really want?" he asked, swirling the melting butter in the pan.

"What everyone does. To belong. To have family, to feel safe and loved and be the most important person in someone's life."

He glanced up in time to see her mouth twist. He had the most ridiculous need to go over and somehow make things better, although he had no idea how. Her desires required more than a friendly hug.

"You're talking about finding a partner, not having a child. Kids grow up and leave. Unless you're planning to keep him or her locked in the basement."

"I don't have a basement, and no, I'm not creepy. I just want..."

To be loved.

She didn't say the words, but then, she didn't have to. He heard them. He supposed nearly everyone wanted that. He had, at one time. Back before everything had changed, he'd assumed that one day he would fall in love, get married and have kids. All his brothers were married. He was, as they often put it, the last dog standing.

"You've given me a lot to think about," she admitted as he poured the whipped eggs into the hot pan. "I'm not sure that's a good thing."

He grinned. "You love it."

"That will depend on whether or not the cinnamon rolls are frosted." She raised her eyebrows questioningly.

"They wouldn't be cinnamon rolls without frosting."

She smiled. "You're the best host ever. I may never leave."

Words that should have scared the crap out of him but didn't. And what was up with that?

NATALIE WATCHED THE clock with a sense of anticipation. It was nearly midnight. She'd worked all evening, beginning the process of turning her flawed painting into mixed-media magic. She'd already done a quick sketch on thick paper that she'd mounted on canvas. Now came the painstaking work of layering in the various elements. Around eleven she'd started to feel restless, as if waiting for something important.

She knew what she was hoping—that once again she and Ronan would spend time together. It didn't seem to matter that they'd shared brunch and then dinner. She wanted to see him at midnight, as if the hour had some significance or mystical power.

Or maybe it was more the man. She'd never spent so much time with him before. He was pleasant enough at the gallery studio, but not chatty like Nick or Mathias. She'd always been aware of him when he was around, but that was more an energy thing than a personality thing.

Staying with him had changed everything. He was so…interesting with his brooding eyes and sexy smile. He could cook! He was more open than she would have thought, even as he kept his secrets. He was a good host and yet gave her plenty of personal space. She hadn't realized he had a sense of humor—it was subtle, but seemed to be coming out more and more. She had the feeling he was slow to trust people, cautious about opening up, and she liked to believe he was starting to let her into the inner circle.

She left her work space and went downstairs, hoping to run into him. She found him in his study, on his computer. In the second before he looked up, she spotted her origami pieces on a shelf. As if he'd collected them to put them somewhere safe.

"How's your work going?" he asked.

"Good. I'm making progress and I have an idea."

"Is this about the app?"

"No." She laughed. "The foyer ceiling is two stories with a nice updraft. We should fly paper airplanes."

"I haven't done that since I was a kid."

"Did you ever compete?"

He grinned. "You've met my brothers. Do you have to ask?"

"Did you ever win?"

"Sure."

"You won't tonight."

His gaze turned speculative. "Are you challenging me?"

"I am so going to kick your butt. Every single time. Even if you get lucky."

"You're on." He rose. "What's the wager?"

As he spoke, she would have sworn that his gaze dropped to her mouth. She felt heat and a sensation that was almost a kiss. Then he returned his attention to her eyes and she wasn't sure it had happened at all. Real or wishful thinking?

"You don't want to bet with me, Ronan," she said, hoping her voice sounded playful instead of needy.

"I'm not afraid."

"In the words of Yoda, *you will be*." She grinned. "How about this? We each do a practice flight, and then if you still want to bet, we will."

"Done."

He followed her upstairs to the turret. She'd put out paper, scissors and a couple of rulers to flatten the edges. They each sat at the long table and started to work. In a matter of minutes, he'd completed a traditional paper airplane. It took her a few seconds more to complete her gliding plane. The more snub-nosed design was reinforced with additional folds that would withstand the updraft from the furnace vents.

Ronan looked from her plane to his sleek design. "You think that's going to win?"

They walked to the landing. She smiled.

"In this confined space, winning is about staying aloft longer. Your plane is built for distance. It's going to soar out perfectly fine and then pretty much plummet. Mine is going to stay up in the clouds for hours."

Ronan's eyes brightened with humor. "You're a

ringer, aren't you? Instead of hustling for money at a pool table, you use paper airplanes. I've been had."

She tried not to look smug. "And you were so sure you'd win. Come on, Mr. Bossy Pants. Let's see what you've got under the hood."

Ronan turned and sent his plane soaring off the landing. As she'd predicted, it made its way across the foyer with great speed and grace. He threw it hard enough that it actually hit the opposite wall and then tumbled to the floor two stories below.

"Well, damn," he muttered. "You were right."

"I know. Isn't it great?"

She put out her arm and felt for the warm updraft from the air below, then aimed her stubby plane at the ceiling. It took off, looped once, then kept flying as it was slowly, slowly, oh so slowly, taken down by gravity.

"I want to learn how to do that," he said the second her plane touched the floor. "What other kinds of planes do you know how to make?"

They spent the next hour folding paper planes. She showed him a half dozen designs and they practiced with all of them. When the foyer was littered with their efforts, they went downstairs for hot cocoa. While Ronan heated the milk, Natalie pulled a bag of marshmallows out of the pantry.

"I found these earlier," she said, waving the bag. "I'm superexcited."

"About marshmallows?"

"Duh. Of course. Aren't you?"

He studied her for a second before he smiled. "I am. Now tell me how you learned to fly airplanes so well."

She settled on a stool at the island. "There weren't any girls on the street where I grew up. Just boys. It was fine when I was little, but by the time I was seven, they didn't want me tagging along. Whenever I convinced them to play with me, it was sports and they always beat me. I got tired of being humiliated. My mom was the one who came up with the idea of paper airplanes. I was already doing origami, so it was an easy transition."

She grinned at the memory. "They were woefully unprepared to be beaten by a girl and they didn't take it well. After about a dozen rematches, they stopped trying to beat me and I was still shut out."

"That must have hurt."

"It did, but then a couple of girls moved in, so I cared less. Plus anytime the boys tried to tease me, I reminded them they'd been beaten by a girl and they wilted."

"You're scrappy."

"I try."

He stirred the cocoa into the pan. The smell of chocolate filled the kitchen and her mouth began to water.

"I'm drinking up your supply," she said. "I should order you more." Although she had no idea how much it would cost to buy a tin of cocoa from the former East Berlin. There went her meat budget for the month.

"I already have." He poured the mixture into mugs, then handed her one. "It's nicer when it's shared."

"Thank you."

She looked up and saw he was watching her. For a second, their gazes tangled and refused to separate. She found herself leaning toward him, as if… As if…

He turned away and put down the pan, then passed her the bag of marshmallows. She took two and dropped them into her cocoa all the while telling herself not to be silly. Whatever she was feeling was obviously one-sided. Ronan wouldn't be interested in her *that way*. He was worldly and famous and rich. She was just a girl who couldn't find someone to love her and who tore up bits of paper and called it art. He was the real artist. Speaking of which…

"How did work go today?" she asked.

The energy in the room changed immediately. Ronan's face tightened. She had a feeling that if he hadn't already been sitting next to her at the island, he would have turned and walked out. She wondered if he still would.

For more than a minute, there was silence. Natalie told herself to keep quiet, to let him talk, but in the end, she couldn't help blurting, "Do you know *why* you're not working?"

He looked from his drink to her and back. "I take it you have a theory."

"I do. Several, in fact, but the one I like the best is that you can't work because you've closed your heart to your family. You're like Elsa in the movie *Frozen*. You have to believe in love again."

He turned toward her, his expression disbelieving. "Like Elsa?"

"In *Frozen*, yes. Have you seen it?"

"I know the song."

She smiled. "Isn't it great? And I love the movie. You should watch it sometime. You'll see what I mean. If you would just..."

She paused, not sure what he should just do. It occurred to her, perhaps a tad late, that there were things about his life she didn't know.

"Not that I'm an expert," she added quietly.

"What do you know about my past?" he asked. "About my family?"

He didn't seem to be challenging her. Rather he wanted to know how much she'd overheard, been told and figured out on her own.

"I know what your dad did. That he had an affair years ago and you're the result. I know you thought you and Mathias were fraternal twins and then you found out you weren't. I know he didn't tell anyone that you knew, so the two of you had to deal with it by yourself."

"That sums it up," he told her, cupping his mug in both hands and watching the marshmallows melt. "My father is a difficult man. He's gifted, cruel and selfish. Everything is about him. No one else matters. Not us, not his wife, Elaine—just him."

He glanced at her. "As you said, I'm the result. I was born a few weeks after Mathias. For reasons I can't explain or understand, when my birth mother gave me up, Elaine agreed to raise me as her own son. They told everyone Mathias and I were fraternal twins. That's how we were raised and what we believed. Elaine never hinted otherwise."

He kept saying *Elaine*. "You mean your mom."

His gaze hardened. "She's not my mother. She's the woman who raised me."

As far as Natalie was concerned, that was the same thing. "Okay," she said slowly. "So your dad dumped this on you and then you had to deal on your own." She hated to speak ill of someone she'd met for five seconds a year ago, but the man sounded like a butthead. Yes, he'd thought he was dying from a heart attack when he'd blurted out the truth, but what about after? Why hadn't he gone back to his sons and explained things better? It made her furious to think about.

"I'm sorry it happened, but I'm glad you and Mathias moved here," she said.

"*I* moved here. Mathias decided to come with me. I thought being somewhere else would help and it did for a while. Now, I don't know." He angled toward her.

"Everything is different. I'm not who I thought. I don't know where I come from. Ceallach is so much worse than you're imagining. I always thought I had Elaine to offset that. She's misguided in her devotion to my father, but otherwise a decent person. Now there's nothing in me but him."

"You've never met your birth mother?"

"No."

"Don't you want to?"

"No. She dumped me and ran. I don't need to meet her to know what she's like."

Natalie touched his arm. "Don't say that. She was young and scared. You need to find out who she is and why she did what she did. That could change everything."

"I know enough."

"You're stubborn. Just like Elsa."

One corner of his mouth twitched. "You're not going to let me wallow in this, are you?"

"I'm not going to stop you. I enjoy a good wallow as much as the next person. I'd just like to point out that, so far, it hasn't helped very much. You should talk to someone."

He drew back. "Like who?"

"You know, to a therapist. Someone who could give you perspective and help you brainstorm ways to handle this. You're too brilliant not to be working. I'm guessing you don't really need the money, but that's not what's important. Creating is who you are. Without that, I'm not sure you can be happy. I know I couldn't be and I'm nowhere near as talented. You need to learn to open your heart, Ronan. Or you're going to be trapped in your emotional ice kingdom forever."

He groaned. "That's another *Frozen* reference, isn't it?"

She smiled. "Admit it. You find me totally charming."

Figuring she'd pushed her luck about as far as she could, she lightly kissed his cheek, then rose and reached for her mug.

"Night, Ronan."

He watched her go without speaking. When she reached the doorway, she turned back and he was still looking at her. For a second she hoped he would come after her, take her in his arms and give her a hearty kissing. Or maybe more. Instead he didn't say anything and she was left with the uncomfortable sensation of wanting someone who probably didn't see her that way at all.

CHAPTER FIVE

DESPITE HIS CONVERSATION with Natalie, Ronan slept well. Maybe it was getting things off his chest. He never talked about his situation anymore. He used to discuss it with Mathias, but lately they only spoke about work.

He woke up early and, after making coffee, went into his studio, where he studied what he'd done on his commission. He couldn't work on it without help. Glass was a demanding mistress and creating the hundreds of pieces that would make up the final work required many hands.

He had interns and a few assistants scheduled, but with the weather, they couldn't get up the mountain and he couldn't get to town. A few days ago, he would have welcomed the excuse. Now he felt stirrings of energy about the project.

He walked around his studio, remembering how excited he'd been when the space was first completed. He'd had so many plans for what he and Mathias could do here. Because it had always been the two of them. Elaine had often talked about how they'd shared a crib until they were toddlers. At the time, he and his brother had assumed that story was about their unbreakable bond. After Ceallach had told them the truth, they'd realized they'd shared a crib because Elaine hadn't been prepared for a second infant and she'd had to make do.

Still, knowing the truth hadn't shaken the memories of all the times he and his brother had worked together as a single unit, and damn it all to hell, he missed that. He didn't want to, but he did. He missed having Mathias around. He missed knowing what he was thinking without having to ask. He missed their connection.

That bond had been severed with a few words. Ronan hadn't seen that at first. He'd been stunned by their father's revelation. He and his brother had left the hospital and walked around town for over an hour until they could finally speak. Only there hadn't been anything to say.

After a few weeks, Ronan had decided he had to leave Fool's Gold. He'd found Happily Inc and had made plans to relocate. When Mathias had found out, he'd said he was coming with him. And he had.

Ronan had thought being here, together, would make everything right. Only it hadn't. They were slipping farther and farther away from what they had once been. Sure, some of that was them growing up. Mathias was married now. But they weren't close anymore and Ronan knew he missed that.

The problem was he also didn't know how to get it back.

He put down his coffee and studied the disastrous faux origami piece he'd made the day before. He saw now what had gone wrong and decided to try again. He wanted to make it right so he could give it to Natalie. He had no idea why. She was—

He put on a thick apron and goggles and reached for a rod. It was one thing to lie to other people, but he should at least tell himself the truth. He wanted to impress her. Just like some sixteen-year-old dreaming of scoring the winning touchdown, he wanted to get the attention of the girl.

He smiled at the realization. It had been a long time since he'd been interested in a woman. He wouldn't have guessed she would be the one to light that spark, but she had and now the flame burned hot and bright.

Not that he would do anything about it. She was his guest and his responsibility. While she was trapped in his house, she needed to feel completely safe around him and not have to worry about him making a move. Still, a man could dream.

As he collected the material to begin his glass piece, he thought about what they'd talked about last night. How his father had once again produced drama. Yes, the situation was complicated and there was no good way to tell your son he wasn't who he thought, but as always, Ceallach had picked the worst possible way.

Ronan pushed thoughts of his family and his growing need for Natalie from his mind and began to work.

He'd come up with some ideas for making his piece look more like what she'd made—with the lines and angles.

Hours later, he had a series of small dragons. They were bigger than hers. The first three were crap but the last one was close. Damned close.

He held up the small glass dragon. Light flowed through the various thicknesses, creating the illusions of different shades of green. He hadn't done a good job with the scales, but he would do better next time.

He walked back in the house. As he passed through the long glass-lined hallway, he was surprised to see the shift in the light, now that the storm had passed. There was blue sky and, according to the thermometer hanging just outside the window, temperatures were climbing back to the normal summer sizzle. He'd been in the studio much longer than he'd thought.

He walked into the kitchen and found Natalie sitting in her usual seat at the island. She had piled her long, curly hair on top of her head and wore a different sweatshirt over the sweatpants. The second she saw him, she smiled.

"You've been working," she said happily.

He held the small dragon down by his thigh so she couldn't see it. "How do you know?"

"You look content and a little smug. It's your work face."

"I have a work face?"

"Who doesn't? Mine is a little more bemused, but then, I'm not the great Ronan Mitchell."

"I'm not him, either."

"One of us has to be and I'm pretty sure I couldn't convince anyone." She pointed to the window. "It's sunny. I spoke to the county road crew supervisor, who is a very nice man, by the way. He said the main roads will be cleared by the end of the day and that he'll make sure your road is passable first thing tomorrow. You'll be able to take me to town by midmorning and be rid of me."

He didn't expect the sense of being kicked in the gut. "You must be happy," he said. "Back to your own place."

She hesitated just a second before answering. "I am, of course. Just like you're thrilled to have your place all to yourself. Not that you haven't been the perfect host. I've enjoyed spending time with you."

"Thank you." He put the glass dragon on the island. "You've been an exemplary guest."

Her eyes widened as she picked up the tiny glass creature and set it on her palm. "Oh, Ronan, he's wonderful." She raised her gaze to his. "How did you get the folds in the glass?"

"It's not easy. I've been failing for two days. I still have to work on the scales, but he's getting there."

"I love him. Thank you." She smiled. "I finally have a Ronan Mitchell original."

Right—because she couldn't afford any of his regular pieces. He wasn't sure if she was teasing or not because if she really did want something he'd made—a real piece of art—she was welcome to any in his storage room. He started to say that, then realized the offer could easily come out wrong.

"I'm glad you're happy."

"I am. Very."

The polite response, he told himself. She was saying what you were supposed to say—nothing more. Yet he couldn't help wishing she was telling the truth about spending time with him.

NATALIE SEARCHED THROUGH the drawers in the turret art studio. There were so many supplies stored so haphazardly that she was never sure where she'd seen what she was looking for. Ronan kept his work space organized, so she wasn't sure why the turret was such controlled chaos. She wondered if he'd simply ordered every art supply he could think of, then had randomly stored them without giving them a second thought.

Not that she minded the search. As she opened cupboards and drawers, she found iridescent discs she could use, along with some black glitter. Her time with Ronan had a distinct dragon theme, one she was continuing with her piece.

She opened the small bag of clear, iridescent discs to make sure she had enough to be scales. She thought she might need another bag, which would mean another search. She would use the black glitter for the eyes and to tip the wings and the tail. She'd seen a box of small gold-colored paper clips in a drawer. Maybe if she used those with the discs she could add dimension to the scales and have enough material for the body. She also had some glass beads she wanted to incorporate and—

The hairs on the back of her neck stood up. She turned and saw Ronan walk into the studio. Her heartbeat instantly accelerated and her palms got sweaty. What on earth? Was she coming down with something?

"How's it going?" he asked.

"Good. I'm getting there."

"May I?"

She nodded and he approached to study her work-in-progress.

The finished piece would be large—maybe two feet by four feet. The canvas lay flat on the largest of the work spaces. She'd applied two coats of flat white paint to seal the material before drawing the outline of her dragon in pencil.

"I'm going to do a night scene," she said. "I haven't found the right material for the sky. I'm thinking I want something with texture like beads or maybe pebbles. The white showing through will be the stars."

She picked up a few of the torn pieces of paper she'd piled on the desk. "I'm not sure about these. Maybe bits of fabric would be better."

"They'd handle light differently," he said. "Do you want me to make you some black glass beads for the sky?"

"No! Are you insane? Ronan, no. You can't. You have a multimillion-dollar commission you need to be working on. I can buy glass beads."

"If you don't have a strong opinion," he said, his voice teasing.

"Make me glass beads," she grumbled. "As if."

He pulled up a chair and sat next to her. "Does the

inspiration always come from what you have around, or do you find your vision determines what you're going to use?"

"Both. I thought of dragons the second I drove up the mountain, so that's where the idea came from. Then I used what I could find in here." She grinned. "It's a pretty sweet setup. I have great light in my home studio, but it's just a boring bedroom. This is so much better." She glanced toward the window. "I would love to see what it's like up here when the sun has been shining for days. You have southern exposure. It makes me wish I was a better painter." She wrinkled her nose. "But we all know that's not going to happen."

"You like working in paper."

"I do. It's fun. Not just the origami, but other things. I've done a few paper mobiles for baby gifts. That's been interesting. Sometimes Pallas asks me to help with a wedding."

"Nick's Pallas?" He sounded surprised.

She nodded. "You do remember that she owns a destination wedding business, right? Couples come from all over to be married at Weddings Out of the Box."

"I've heard rumors, yes."

"Most of the weddings are variations on a theme, but every now and then one of them is totally custom. If there's something I can do to help, I will. It's fun for me and a nice bonus for the income stream. One of the Valentine's Day weddings was all things hearts. Not original considering, but still. I made origami hearts that held the place cards for the reception, and a lot of bigger folded hearts for decorations. Last year for an under-the-sea wedding, I made little turtles and starfish that were scattered on the tables." A lot of work, but she'd enjoyed the challenge.

"Nick helps Pallas with a lot of her decorations," Ronan said. "He enjoys the work."

"You made the glowy orbs for the alien wedding." She remembered how cool they'd looked with all the other decorations. "It's nice to be a part of things. Maybe I should learn to do caricatures."

"For weddings?"

"At the reception. As a memento. I'd have to be really fast, though, which probably takes a lot of practice."

"You're not going to settle on just one thing, are you?"

"Maybe if I could sell it for a lot of money," she said with a laugh. "I love being an artist, but I do enjoy paying my bills. For the right price, I could be bought."

Her record sale had been for nearly two thousand dollars, but that had been for an entire collection, and for a fundraiser. She hadn't seen a cent. She'd yet to sell a single piece for more than three hundred dollars, and she had to split her sad little payment with the gallery. Oh, to be in the four-figure range.

She glanced at Ronan. His pieces sold for several hundred thousand dollars. What must that be like, to never have to worry about money? She and her mom had always pinched pennies, but her mom had made it fun—like a game. Their frugal habits had served her well as an adult.

Having a baby would be a financial responsibility,

she thought as she remembered her baby daddy app. She would need savings and more regular income and better medical insurance.

Ronan frowned. “What are you thinking? You’re looking fierce about something.”

“Just that I might not be ready to have a baby by myself.”

“Rethinking the app?”

“I’m still going to play with it, but I’m not ready for a donor at this exact moment.” But if she started seriously planning, then maybe in the next year or so.

She knew she wanted a family—connection. She talked about having bad luck with men because it was an easy almost-truth. The real story was harder and more painful. First she’d lost her mother, her *only* family. Later, when Quentin had dumped her, she’d not only lost the man she’d loved, she’d lost the promise of belonging. Until he’d told her otherwise, she’d believed that his family cared about her and wanted her to be one of them. But she’d been wrong and once again she’d been left alone. A baby would mean being part of something again.

She would have to think on it and decide what was the most important to her. Was she willing to work full-time and put her art on the back burner for the chance to belong? Because that would mean she could get pregnant much sooner. Life, it seemed, was always about choices.

“Come on,” she said, standing and walking to the door. “I defrosted some cooked chicken and a loaf of bread overnight. I thought we could have chicken salad sandwiches for dinner." She paused by the door and wiggled her eyebrows at him. "I'll even cook."

"Impressive."

"I know, right? Oh, and maybe we could eat in the family room instead of the dining room."

He paused in midstride and stared at her. "Why?" he asked, his voice more than a little suspicious.

"I thought we could watch a movie."

"Uh-huh. Which one?"

"Which one do you think?"

"Not *Frozen*. I mean that, Natalie. We are not watching a kids' movie over dinner."

She walked onto the landing and started down the stairs. "It's so strange. I know you're talking but all I hear is a buzzing sound."

NATALIE WAITED UNTIL the credits finished rolling before turning to Ronan. "Admit it. You have to. You know I'm right. You loved every single minute of it."

Ronan leaned back in the big sofa and shook his head. "I'm not admitting anything." Then he glanced at her. One corner of his mouth turned up in the sexiest way possible. "It was okay."

She threw a pillow at him. "You are so lying. It was wonderful. You laughed, you got scared, you were totally engaged."

"I wasn't scared."

"The ice monster scared you. I could tell." She stood and stretched. "Olaf and Sven are the best. And Elsa and Anna. I wish I'd had a sister with magical powers. Or maybe just a regular sister. Didn't you love the animation? The Disney team is so talented. And the way they seamlessly blended in the songs. Wouldn't it be fun to do that?" She drew in a breath, then stopped herself. Singing was not her thing. Or at least not in front of other people. She was actually pretty decent in the shower.

Ronan rose and faced her. "You're a little like a pinball, heading in forty-seven directions at once."

"Am not." She considered his statement. "Okay, maybe a little. It's just everything is so interesting. We should make cookies. We'll want them later. You've got the premade ones you only have to bake. You know, for our midnight snack." She leaned close and put her hand on his chest. "Later, when 'Let It Go' is stuck in your head, you'll remember tonight."

She expected him to laugh, or groan or do something other than put his hands on her waist and pull her close right before he settled his mouth on hers.

His move was so unexpected she almost didn't react. Or rather she almost *did* react by pulling back and asking him what on earth he was thinking. Only she managed to stop herself in time, which was a really good thing because Ronan's kiss—even a casual, practically chaste kiss—was a not-to-be-missed experience.

His mouth was warm against hers. Purposeful without being too demanding. He kissed with intent and intensity, all the while not moving or taking or doing anything but holding his lips right there, on hers, until her whole body began to burn, and she knew, she just *knew*, nothing would ever be the same again.

He drew back. His gaze was determined, his expression unreadable. She had no idea what he was thinking, but if she had to guess, she would say he was making a decision. To do more? To stop? To—

"I'm sorry."

"Noooo." She drew back and put her hands on her hips. "Do not apologize. That ruins everything."

"You're my guest."

"So?"

"I want you to feel safe while you're here. I shouldn't have done that."

Because she was his guest? "Do you really think that I'll be afraid you'll break down my bedroom door to have your way with me?" She asked the question half-seriously and just a little bit hopeful about the answer.

"I wouldn't do that, but yes. You're stuck here in the house. I don't want you feeling unsafe."

There it was—the unexpected nice-guy moment. When it followed an amazing kiss, it was twice as deadly. "Does it occur to you that having that concern means you don't have to have that concern?"

When he only looked confused, she added, "Ronan, I'm not worried you're going to do anything untoward." She made air quotes around the last word. "I trust you and the kiss was very nice, so you can't take it back. That would hurt my feelings."

"All right. I won't take it back. I'm glad you liked it."

She smiled. "You liked it, too."

"I did. Now let's go make cookies. It will defuse the tension."

"Ooh, you think we have tension!"

He growled low in his throat. “Don’t start with me.”

“I have to start with you. There’s no one else here.”

He sighed. “Fine. Tell me about the baby app. You’re really considering that.”

She burst out laughing as she headed for the refrigerator. “Wow, you really *are* desperate to distract me. You’d rather talk about my baby app than the kiss? I’m going to remember how easy you are to rattle. Brace yourself. The next time you get on my nerves, I am so taking you down.”

“I never get on your nerves.”

“You have no idea.” She found the cookies and tossed the package onto the counter, then collected a couple of cookie sheets.

“How could I annoy you?”

He sounded genuinely confused, which was seriously cute, she thought as she washed her hands before ripping open the log-shaped package.

“You have it all and you don’t appreciate it.” She cut the dough into slices, then divided each slice into quarters. “You have a great career. Your work is literally sought after all around the world. You have family—brothers who care about you. Mathias followed you here. Do you get that? He totally uprooted his life, left everything he knew, so he could still be your twin. I have the feeling you don’t appreciate that enough.”

She thought about what he was dealing with—his family, his inability to work—and wished she had words of wisdom, but she’d been blessed with a sunny disposition rather than the ability to help people with their problems.

She glanced at him. He was watching her, but she had no idea what he was thinking.

"And Nick," she added, figuring she was on a roll and should just keep talking. "He moved here, too. To be with you and Mathias. That's a big deal. I know you think Ceallach isn't a good father—and from what I've heard, he isn't—but still, that's some powerful DNA."

"There's a price for that DNA."

"Your mom is a nice counterbalance."

She spoke without thinking, then could have slapped herself. Ronan didn't know who his mother was and he didn't accept the woman who had raised him as that person.

She finished with the cookies and walked to the sink to wash her hands. Silence built in the kitchen until it threatened to suck all the air out of the room. She dried her hands, crossed to him and stared into his green eyes.

"You know what I meant," she said softly.

"Elaine isn't my mother."

Elaine had raised him—she'd loved him, worried about him, done her best for him, so yeah, she was his mother, but Natalie wasn't going to die on that particular hill.

"You are such a pain in my ass," she murmured. "Honestly, if I thought it would do any good, I would so slap you upside the head."

Things could have gone a thousand different ways. She half expected him to stalk out of the kitchen, never to be heard from again. Or he could have gotten really mad and yelled at her. Or he could have been sarcastic and maybe hurt her feelings. Instead that very wily, very appealing corner of his mouth twitched slightly, as if he were trying not to smile.

"You're not as bad as people think," she whispered, allowing herself to get lost in his eyes.

"You're about ten times worse."

She raised her eyebrows. "You mean that in the nicest way possible."

"Yes, I do."

The tension returned, but it was a lot more interesting than it had been before. She couldn't help thinking about the brief, chaste kiss they'd shared. Imagine what he could do if he put his mind to it. Or his body.

Without having anything close to a plan, she stepped close, put her hands on his chest and said, "While sex is never the answer, it can sometimes be a nice distraction."

Emotions skittered through his eyes. She didn't bother trying to figure out what they were. Instead she waited for him to pull her close and—

"Natalie, no." He took a step back. "You're my guest. We had this conversation. I'm sorry, but we can't."

Before she could figure out if he meant what she thought he meant, he turned and walked out of the kitchen, leaving her and the cookies alone.

She stared after him, not able to believe he'd rejected her. Didn't he know that she'd never done anything like that before in her life? Just blatantly asked for sex? He was supposed to say yes, otherwise she never would have asked.

Humiliation burned hot, staining her cheeks and

making her run for the relative safety of her room. Once there she tried to slow her breathing, but she couldn't. Rejection more than stung—it made her feel small and less than. It made her want to disappear. Only she couldn't. Ronan had tried to warn her and she hadn't listened. She was well and truly trapped with nowhere to go.

CHAPTER SIX

RONAN DIDN'T KNOW what to do. He wanted to give Natalie space and distance himself from her, so he couldn't take her up on her amazing invitation. He retreated to his studio, locking the door behind him. The turn of the dead bolt was much more for him than for her. It was a tangible reminder that she was under his charge and therefore to be protected.

He knew better than to try to work. Sexual frustration and molten glass were not a good mix. Instead he paced for nearly an hour before settling down enough to plan out the next few steps in completing his massive installation. It was nearly eight o'clock when he finally allowed himself to go back into the house. The second he stepped inside, he knew she was gone. Knew it from the stillness in the air.

Panic and worry braided together to hang him, but before he could come up with a plan to go find her, he saw a note on the island, next to a batch of baked cookies.

The road crew called. Things went faster than they expected, so they cleared the way tonight. I caught a ride back to town with them. Thanks again for giving me a place to stay in the storm. N.

He carefully set the paper back on the island, knowing if he held it he would crush it. She was gone. Back to her place, back to where she belonged. His life was restored to what it had become. He should be thrilled. Delighted. Relieved. Only all he could think was how much he wanted her back, even as he knew that was never going to happen.

AFTER SHOWERING AND changing into fresh clothes, Natalie paced through her apartment. She rented the second floor of a converted house. The kitchen and bath had been updated, but what had drawn her to the rental were the big windows in the south-facing master bedroom.

The light was perfect. Nothing like it would have been in Ronan's turret, but still, plenty for her. She'd taken the smaller second bedroom to sleep in and used the master as her at-home art studio.

She fixed herself a sad little frozen dinner and made herbal tea, all the while thinking longingly of German hot chocolate and marshmallows and charming conversation and the man who had delighted her at every turn…right up until he'd resisted her advances.

"No means no," she whispered, stirring the slightly

gummy spaghetti and trying to find humor in her battered heart.

Not battered, she told herself. Embarrassed. There was a difference. Ronan had done what he thought was right to protect her and she needed to respect that. Her hurt feelings were her problem.

She ate her dinner, then carried her tea to her studio. She'd brought the dragon picture with her, but none of Ronan's supplies, which meant she would be changing direction partway through.

She touched the iridescent discs and the brass paper clips that covered part of one wing and a little of the body. Should she just surrender to failure and start something else? If she changed direction now she would have to…

She put the framed canvas on the long craft table, then went into the master closet. It was good-sized and she'd crammed it with bookshelves, plastic trays and drawers, all filled with odds and ends she'd found, bought or been given. There were those buttons her friend Violet had let her have for practically nothing. Weren't they iridescent? The shape and thickness were different, but that didn't matter.

She found the buttons along with some dark green feathers, brass-colored wire and half a yard of midnight blue velvet. She grabbed a bag of black volcanic glass and her trusty glue gun, then went back into her studio.

There were so many possibilities, she thought happily as she spread out all her supplies, then began to play with combinations. It was only midnight. If she concentrated, she might have the piece done by morning and then she would show it to…

She pressed her lips together. It had been three nights. Just over seventy-two hours. She would finish the piece for herself and decide if she wanted to take it to the gallery to see if Atsuko was interested in showing it. No one else's opinion mattered. She liked her life exactly as it was and now she had it back. She was happy about that. Really.

RONAN DROVE DOWN the mountain much earlier than he'd first planned. The long night had convinced him there was no way he could work in his private studio, so he'd emailed his interns and told them to meet him in town, where they would all get to work on his commission. He was ready, he was eager and most of all he was missing Natalie, but damn it all to hell, he couldn't admit that to anyone—not even himself.

He arrived at the studio behind Willow Gallery. The rear parking lot was empty. Ronan went inside and flipped on lights, then started the process of bringing the huge oven up to temperature. He studied the to-scale drawing on the wall—it was exactly the same as the one he had at home and detailed every part of the intricate design. The hundreds of individual pieces would be connected on-site.

By eight, both Nick and Mathias had arrived. His brothers looked alike with dark hair and eyes, both around six feet tall. Del and Aidan shared their physical description. Only Ronan was different, with lighter hair and green eyes. He'd always been teased about being different, his brothers joking that he wasn't really one of them. None of them had known they were telling the truth.

Mathias grinned when he saw Ronan. "You finally made it in. Pretty slick having your road wash out. I knew there was a reason you wanted to live up in the mountains."

"He was trying to get away from you," Nick joked. "I take it you survived the storm."

Ronan nodded.

Mathias glanced around, as if making sure they were alone, then asked, "With Natalie? How was that?"

"Fine. She stayed in the guest room up in the turret and used the studio there."

He was braced for more questions. Would they guess what had almost happened, what he'd *wanted* to happen?

"You made her cook for you, didn't you?" Nick asked, then chuckled. "So about her car. It's gone?"

Ronan grimaced at the memory. "Clean off the side of the mountain. Several trees came down. The last one fell on it and carried it down the ravine. I don't know if it can be recovered. Even if it is, it has to be totaled."

"That will make her happy," Nick said. "She's wanted a new car for a while. I told her it was silly to keep replacement value on that old piece of trash, but I was wrong."

Ronan didn't like that his brother knew that about Natalie. "She told you?"

"Five dozen times," Mathias said. "Bro, you need

to learn to listen when people talk. She wasn't hurt, was she?"

Ronan stiffened, only to realize his brother was talking about the car destruction, not anything else.

"She was in the house when it happened."

"Good thing. She wouldn't have survived that." Mathias slapped him on the shoulder. "Good to have you back."

"Thanks."

Mathias and Nick retreated to their areas of the studio. Nick reviewed his email before heading out back, where he was working on a huge wood piece. Once he'd done the rough cuts with a chain saw, the twelve-foot-high block would be moved into the studio for his detail work.

Mathias spent his days creating glass dishes, light pendants and bowls in various patterns. Every now and then he created something that would be considered "art" but mostly he preferred what he called his utilitarian collection.

For years Ronan worried that Mathias had given in to their father's judgment and was selling himself short by making everyday objects. Over the past few months Ronan had come to see that Mathias enjoyed what he did. For him, the act of creating was its own reward and having his pieces be on someone's table mattered to him.

Nothing their father would approve of, but maybe that was part of the joy of it.

Ronan's two interns arrived. They went to the local community college and worked for him a few hours a week. The morning went by quickly as they created piece after piece, building the parts of his installation.

A little before noon, the interns left and Ronan took a break. He drank some water, logged on to his email and checked on the new pieces, all in an effort to avoid what he really wanted to do. When he'd run out of distractions, he made his way across the parking lot to the gallery and in the back door, heading to Natalie's office.

She sat behind her desk, her slightly frowning gaze locked on her computer. Gone were the tight curls. Instead her straight hair had been pulled back into a braid. She wore a tailored jacket over a green blouse and she was wearing makeup.

This was work Natalie—he liked this side of her but preferred laughing, playful, relaxed-at-his-house Natalie better.

The need to go to her nearly overwhelmed him. He wanted to pull her to her feet, drop her glasses on the desk and kiss her senseless. Maybe unfasten her braid and a few other things. Need burned hot and bright, blinding him to the reality of where they were and the fact that they hadn't spoken since—

"Wocka!" Natalie jumped in her chair and pressed a hand to her chest. "You scared me. When did you get so stealthy?"

"Sorry. I wanted to make sure you were okay."

Color stained her cheeks. "I'm fine. The road crew guys were supernice and delivered me right to my door. I had my purse, which meant I had my keys. All is well." She gave him a cheerful smile. "It's really good

I don't have a cat. He would have been starving. Although I guess I would have called a neighbor or one of my friends to feed him, so he would have been fine. But I didn't." She cleared her throat. "What with not having a cat and all."

She was nervous—not a usual state for her. Was she concerned about what had happened before? He was sure he'd made it clear that while he appreciated her incredibly tempting invitation, he hadn't been able to act on it. Or was she having second thoughts and was concerned he was going to expect her to make good on her offer?

He swore silently. There had been a time when the whole man-woman thing had been ridiculously easy. Sadly that time was not now.

"I probably should have told you I was leaving," she told him.

"I know why you didn't."

"Do you?" She bit her lower lip. "I didn't mean to upset you."

"Me? Why would I be upset? I thought *you* were upset."

"No. Well, maybe. A little." She stared at her desk, then back at him. "I guess I'm not everyone's cup of tea."

"You are. I mean, I like tea. It was a timing thing. I meant that."

Dear God—what on earth were they talking about? He looked toward the open door, then back at Natalie. They were both at work and this was not the moment, but he wanted her to know that he hadn't been rejecting her.

She smiled at him. "I think I understand what you're saying. Did you get your phone?"

It took him a second to realize she meant his cell phone. "I have it with me and promise I will keep it close always. Did you call your insurance company?"

She laughed. "Yes, and at first they didn't believe me. But I got lucky. A tow truck driver found my car and is pretty sure he can drag it out of what I was afraid was its final resting place. Once he does, I can send pictures to my agent and get the paperwork started for them to total my car." She did a little shimmy in her seat. "Then it's new-car time for me! Well, new-to-me, but still!"

"Uh-huh. Are you still determined to buy a red car?"

"Duh. Yes. Red is my color."

"I'm going with you. You can't buy a car based solely on color. It needs to be reliable and safe, without too many miles and no accidents."

She waved her hand. "I'm not worried. I'm going to find a beautiful red car that is perfect. You'll see."

"Yes, I will because I will be right there. I want you to promise not to go car shopping without me."

"I'm perfectly capable of finding the right car."

"Not with color as your only criteria."

She mumbled something under her breath. He had a feeling it would sound very much like "Mr. Bossy Pants," but he didn't care. Natalie's desire for a red car was the same as wearing a T-shirt with the slogan Hey, Rip Me Off! He wasn't going to let that happen.

"Fine," she grumbled. "You can go with me. But I won't like it."

"That's my girl. Mature and open to the possibilities."

"I don't care what you say. I want a red car. And nothing is going to stop me from getting one. Not even you."

"There's an unexpected stubborn side to you, isn't there?"

"I am one with the feminine universe."

"And just a little bit crazy."

She flashed him a smile that nearly brought him to his knees.

"You have no idea, Ronan."

Maybe not, but he would very much like to find out.

NATALIE CAREFULLY CARRIED the plastic-wrapped tray of cupcakes. She'd been sucked in by a Facebook ad promising an easy way to make little flowers out of icing. When the tip had arrived, she'd had to try it out and had discovered that it worked really well. Lucky for her, the biweekly girlfriend lunch was the next day, so she'd packed up the cupcakes to bring with her. The alternative of eating them all herself was not a happy one. Not with the way her hips and thighs loved to pack on the pounds.

For the girlfriend lunches, hostess duties rotated. Whoever offered the location also provided the entrée. Everyone else brought another dish. Sometimes they ended up with three desserts and no salad, which was fine with Natalie—as long as the mix-up never went the other way, she was happy.

With the monsoon over, the California desert heat had returned. It was barely noon and already in the upper nineties. By four, it would be at least a hundred and five.

She crossed the street and made her way to her friend Silver's new place. The storefront with a loft-style apartment above was owned by Violet Lund, now the duchess of Somerbrooke. Silver had been looking for a new place about the time Violet had been falling madly in love and considering moving to England. A long-term lease between the friends had solved two problems.

Violet had used the street-level business space for her button shop. She'd also done alterations and some custom work on wedding gowns and bridesmaid dresses. Last fall she'd made an adorable dress for a sassy beagle name Sophie, who had been in Ronan's brother Del's wedding. Now Silver used the retail space for her own business.

Natalie opened the glass door and walked into the bright space. Silver had done away with Violet's displays of buttons and photographs of designer clothing featuring antique buttons. Her business—AlcoHaul—served local weddings. She owned a trailer that had been converted into a bar. As much of the town catered to theme weddings, Silver had decided to go all in. AlcoHaul could be transformed into a medieval tavern, a Wild West saloon or something from an alien landscape.

Her showroom displayed large pictures of the different themes. There were small vignettes set up, illustrating the idea with many kinds of glasses, bottles of liquor and custom drink menus. For today's lunch, Silver had pulled a couple of small tables together to form one longer one. The place settings were a mix of plastic plates, glasses and flatware from various weddings she'd worked on.

"It's me," Natalie called as she set her cupcakes alongside a huge covered casserole dish. She couldn't see what was under the foil, but even without visual clues, the smell was enough to make her mouth water.

Cheese, bacon and maybe a hint of jalapeño, she thought as her stomach rumbled.

"Hi." Silver walked in from the back room and smiled. "Tell me you didn't bring salad."

"I didn't bring salad."

"Good. I'm in a sugar, carb, fat kind of mood."

The two women hugged. Natalie had the brief thought that anyone looking through the front window would think of them as the most mismatched friends ever. Silver was tall and slim with just enough muscle definition to let the world know that, yes, she did work out. Her platinum-blond hair hung to the middle of her back. She wore tight-fitting black jeans and an equally snug black tank top. An open-work dark blue sweater slipped off one shoulder.

Silver was...exotic. Natalie shook her head. No, that wasn't right. Silver was the sexy bad girl you knew was the most fun ever. The closest Natalie ever got to out of the ordinary was to be called "bohemian." She was too short, too curvy and just too bubbly to ever be considered bad.

"How are things?" Silver asked, pouring a very purple drink into two ice-filled tumblers.

"Good. Busy. I'm working on a new art piece. I'm in a dragon mode right now and I'm not sure if that's good or bad."

"Does it have to be assigned a value? It's art—can't it just be?"

"Good point, *Mom*," Natalie teased. She took a sip of the drink. There was a fruit base and club soda for sure, along with something else she couldn't identify. "Is there liquor in this?"

"Would I do that at lunch? We all have to work later. I do make a version that would knock you on your butt in three minutes, but this is not that."

They walked over to the table and took a seat. Natalie glanced around at the displays. "You've made a few changes. The big pictures on the wall are great."

"Wynn did those for me."

Wynn owned the local graphics and print company. She'd started taking photography classes so she could take pictures for her clients. She always joked she was nowhere near wedding-ready, so wouldn't be putting any of their local photographers out of business, but sometimes a client needed corporate images or a head shot or, in Silver's case, a wedding setup. That was where Wynn came in.

Silver sipped her drink. "I need your advice. I've found a couple of trailers for sale."

Natalie leaned toward her. "Really? You're going to expand? You said you were thinking about it. Wow—that's exciting. Good for you."

"I haven't done it yet. I don't know. It's a lot. Not just the money, although that's a consideration. I have savings, but if I buy the trailers, I'll need to refurbish them so they work as bars and then I'll have to hire people to staff them." She looked at Natalie. "I can't buy them for cash *and* remodel *and* pay staff."

"I'm sure you can get a small-business loan."

"Probably. Maybe. But I've never done anything like that. It's scary to think about expanding. Right now it's all on me. I have a crew I work with, but I make all the decisions. With another trailer, I'm sending it out into the world without me. I'm trusting someone else to handle an event."

"Do you *want* to expand? What if you kept things exactly as they are?"

"I've thought about that, but it seems so cowardly."

Because Silver was always larger than life. "What about taking on a business partner?"

"No and no. I don't play well with others."

Silver's sweater slipped off her left shoulder, exposing the top of a tattoo on her upper arm. Natalie knew there was other ink on her friend's body, yet more proof she and her friend were wildly different.

"Change is uncomfortable," Natalie said. "Maybe if you look past that part to the end goal you want. You know, visualize your success."

"Because you don't see me failing?"

Natalie grinned. "Hardly. You're smart and determined. You will get wherever you want to go—I know that for sure."

"If you're not the nicest person I know, you're very close to it, and I don't mean that as a compliment."

Natalie was still laughing when their other friends arrived. Carol, Wynn and Pallas each carried a bowl or tray.

Carol, a pretty redhead, was married to Ronan's brother Mathias. She ran the local animal preserve next to the town dump. Carol was in charge of several gazelles, a few zebra, one water buffalo and a new giraffe herd. Wynn ran the graphics and printing company while Pallas owned Weddings Out of the Box. Bethany, the other member of their girlfriend crew, was visiting family in El Bahar.

Bethany had moved to Happily Inc the previous December. Actually, she'd come for a short visit and had ended up falling in love with Cade Saunders, which was in and of itself fairly notable, but not the real thrill of the story. Cade had purchased a stallion from the king of El Bahar's royal stable and Bethany had been the groom to accompany the horse while he got settled. Unbeknownst to anyone, Bethany was in fact the king's stepdaughter and a real, live princess. There had been quite the conversation when the truth had come out.

Natalie could sort of understand how life could be difficult if one were royal. Cade and Bethany had gotten engaged and Bethany had settled in Happily Inc. Natalie believed the two of them now both owned the ranch, but she wasn't sure.

There were greetings and plenty of hugs as the

friends got settled. Natalie was relieved to find out that there weren't three salads. Instead Carol and Wynn had brought different kinds of cookies, while Pallas had made a chopped salad.

Natalie studied it doubtfully. "Is that kale?"

"It's actually really good and it's healthy."

Silver handed them each drinks before leaning close to Natalie and whispering, "We can all see you're thinking 'but why' on the salad."

"I'm not," Natalie protested, even though it might be true. She understood the value of vegetables, if only they weren't so…vegetable-like.

In a matter of minutes, all the food was unwrapped and the five women were serving themselves before taking a place at the table. Natalie breathed in the scent of the BLT mac and cheese casserole (the *L* standing for *leeks*, which were technically a veggie but one Natalie actually liked) and made a mental note to get the recipe from Silver.

Natalie let the friendly conversation wash over her for a second as she enjoyed being with her friends. She would offer to take the next lunch. The gallery was closed on Mondays and Tuesdays. Atsuko, Natalie's boss, allowed her to use the space for her girlfriend lunches as long as Natalie cleaned up afterward.

"That was some storm," Carol said, passing the garlic bread around the table. "One of the days, most of the animals didn't even want to go outside in all that rain."

"That had to have been some barn cleanup." Wynn wrinkled her nose. "Hunter did a report on the zebras for his science class and couldn't get over how much they poop in a day." She waved her piece of garlic bread. "I can provide details if anyone is interested."

"No, thanks," Silver said, glancing at Pallas, who looked a little pale. "You okay?"

"I'm fine. It's the combination of lunch and poop that has me unsettled." Pallas turned to Natalie. "Tell us about your adventure, young lady. I've heard all kinds of rumors."

For a second Natalie had no idea what she was talking about. Then she remembered her trip up the mountain. She practically bounced in her seat.

"I'm getting a new car. New-to-me, anyway, and I'm superexcited."

"Good for you," Carol said. "Did you sell your old one or are you using it as a trade-in?"

"It's totaled. It fell off the mountain."

"What?"

"Are you okay?"

"What happened?"

Her friends all spoke at once. Then Pallas excused herself to use the restroom.

"I'm fine," Natalie told them. "I wasn't in it." She smiled. "Right at the beginning of the storm, Mathias and Nick realized Ronan hadn't been in for several days and he wasn't answering his cell phone. He doesn't have a landline, so someone had to go check on him."

Silver's eyes darkened. "They sent you up the mountain in your car in a storm? What is wrong with them?"

"Nick insisted I take his truck, but I was nervous about driving it. Anyway, I made it up to Ronan's with no problem, but I parked it too close to the edge. A bunch of trees fell and they took my car with them."

She sighed with happiness. "I'm going to be getting a check from my insurance company. That combined with what I've been able to save means I can afford a new car. I'm getting a red one."

Wynn reached for the salad. "That's practical."

"Now you sound like Ronan."

Pallas returned to her seat. "Speaking of Ronan, didn't you want to talk about your little getaway with him?"

Conversation ceased as everyone turned to look at her. Natalie felt herself blushing.

"What?" Carol and Silver said together while Wynn simply looked disbelieving.

"I so can't see you two together," Wynn admitted. "He's not your type."

"I agree." Carol looked concerned. "I'll admit he's really good-looking, in a brooding kind of way, but you're so light and fun and sweet. I'd be worried he'd suck the life out of you."

"Ronan would never do that. He's charming and has a great sense of humor. I beat him when we flew paper airplanes and he only laughed. A lot of guys would have gotten mad."

Silver picked up her drink. "Am I the only one wishing these had actual alcohol in them?"

"I hear you, sister," Wynn murmured. "Natalie, honey, maybe you should start at the beginning because the paper airplane reference is pretty confusing."

"Oh, right." Natalie thought about her adventure.

She would have to be careful so no one guessed about the kiss and his rejection.

"The trees that took my car over the mountain also made a mess of the roads. I had to stay with Ronan for a couple of days." And three delicious nights, but there was no reason to be that specific.

"You stayed with Ronan?" Carol's eyes widened. "In his house?"

"Uh-huh."

Silver's mouth turned up at the corners. "You are not at all what you seem, are you? So, pray tell, where did you sleep?"

"In the guest room. It's really amazing. It's upstairs by the turret. Oh, and the turret is this fantastic artist's studio. Ronan let me work up there. He has all kinds of supplies, and when there isn't a storm, the light's amazing."

"How disappointing," Silver murmured.

"We had a good time. I like him and you should, too. He's nice."

Carol and Pallas exchanged a look.

"Nice?" Pallas asked. "Are you sure that's the word? I know he's not mean or sullen, but he doesn't make an effort to hang out with Nick very much."

"He avoids Mathias," Carol added. "And they were twins."

"It's not his fault, okay? He's dealing with a lot. All Nick and Mathias found out is that he's only their half brother, but for Ronan, it was different. He has no idea who he is anymore. All he has is Ceallach, and would you want him to be your father?"

Natalie realized that she might have gone just a little too far with her defense of Ronan. All four of her friends were staring at her, their expression mirror images of concern and curiosity.

Uh-oh—that wasn't good. She honestly had no idea how she felt about Ronan, but she was in no way ready to have what she might or might not be thinking discussed on the friendship open market. She needed a distraction and fast.

She frantically searched for a distraction-worthy topic and realized she had one right in her own phone.

"Being at his house worked really well, timing-wise," she said quickly. "I got to play with my new app." She pulled out her phone and waved it. "I downloaded it last week, but haven't had a chance to explore the possibilities."

"Your new app?" Wynn sounded doubtful. "What does it do?"

"Help you find a sperm donor. You know, for women who want to have a child on their own."

Her distraction worked. Mouths dropped open, and Carol, who'd been drinking, began to choke.

"You want a sperm donor so you can have a kid on your own?" Silver asked, her voice incredulous. "Seriously?"

"Maybe. I'm not sure." Natalie tucked her phone back in her bag. "I love kids and always wanted them, but I come from a long line of women who are unlucky in love. Does that mean I don't get a family?"

"I get having your own baby," Pallas said. "Of

course you want to experience that, but, Natalie, what about falling in love first?"

"Besides, being a single parent isn't easy." Wynn picked up her fork. "It's great, don't get me wrong, but it's work. Hunter is the best thing to ever happen to me. If you're serious, we should talk."

"I don't know what I'm going to do," Natalie admitted. "I'd have to get my life together first. Financially and in other ways, but I do want to be a mother."

"What does the app do?" Carol asked.

"It helps in finding the right donor. There are all these questions as well as links to reputable sperm banks. It's kind of interesting."

"So you're looking for a donor, not a father," Silver clarified. "You want the guy to walk away."

"I guess." Natalie spoke slowly. "I really haven't gotten that far. Why?"

"Just asking in case I meet a qualified candidate."

Natalie rolled her eyes. "Whatever you're thinking, no. Did I say no? No."

Everyone laughed.

"While we're on the subject of breeding," Carol said. "It's official. We're bringing in a male giraffe."

The current herd was all female. Natalie pressed her hands together. "You're going to have baby giraffes. I can't begin to imagine that much cuteness! Is gestation long? Will they all get pregnant right away? Giraffe sex has to be kind of…"

"Awkward?" Wynn offered.

"Not to them," Carol said. "Giraffe gestation is about thirteen to fifteen months. We won't know for sure until she's fairly far along, although there are tests we can do. But we don't want to start breeding right away and we don't want the females getting pregnant at once, so I'll be putting them on birth control."

"Is it a patch?" Silver asked with a grin.

"I wish. It goes in their food and I have to make sure they eat it all or we'll have unexpected baby giraffes."

Which was probably not a good idea, but Natalie had to admit it was a sweet one. She loved the idea of little Millies in the animal park.

Pallas reached in her purse and pulled out a piece of paper. "Natalie, I nearly forgot to give this to you. They announced it at the last business council meeting. The news won't be going public for a couple of weeks."

Natalie took the paper and scanned it. The main bridge over the Rio de los Suenos had recently been refurbished. The city council wanted to invite local artists to decorate the bridge as a tourist attraction.

"I love this," Natalie said. "I'm so going to sign up for a section of the bridge."

Maybe she could get one section and have Ronan help her. Or even better, she could get *two* sections and give one to Mathias, while she and Ronan did the other one. That way the brothers could hang out and do a project together because they needed to be close again.

"You should use your totaled car," Silver told her. "Cut off the front or something."

Natalie's breath caught. "That is the best idea ever."

"I'm more than a pretty face."

"You are. We could use both the front and the back

and call it 'coming and going.'" She flipped over the paper and began to sketch out the concept.

"And we've lost her," Carol said with a laugh.

"Two minutes," Natalie muttered as she frantically drew exactly what she was seeing in her mind. "Three, tops."

Silver chuckled. "We'll give her three, then bring out the desserts. That will suck her back into our world."

Her friends knew her well, Natalie thought happily. Her ex might have broken her heart when he'd left her, but finding this wonderful town and the people in it had been worth it all. And she knew Ronan was going to be as excited as she was about their joint project. He just had to be, didn't he?

CHAPTER SEVEN

THE RESTLESSNESS THAT had dogged Ronan ever since Natalie went home refused to go away. It had been nearly a week and he was still not comfortable alone in his house, which was why he found himself back in town on Monday night.

In most towns, big or small, the time for going out and partying was the weekend, but not in Happily Inc. The income from all the destination weddings meant the town lived on a different schedule. Weekends were for weddings and therefore work. Monday was the big night out.

He didn't bother going to any of his brothers' houses. No one would be home. On Mondays they would be at The Boardroom—a pub-style establishment that celebrated all things board-game-related. Built-in bookshelves housed every board game ever invented. The tables were set up for easy play, and on Monday nights there were tournaments.

Ronan rarely bothered to go, but he'd been sucked

in a few times. Tonight his restlessness had caused him to walk in shortly before six, only to discover the place crowded with couples and groups of friends.

Posters on easels announced the night's game was Latice. There was also a plug for an upcoming outdoor charity challenge for teams of three to five participants.

Ronan looked around, trying to find someone he knew well enough to sit with. There was plenty of conversation and laughter—both designed to remind him how he was officially an outsider. He spotted Nick and Mathias sitting with their wives at a table for four and realized coming here had been a mistake. He didn't know anyone well enough to just join them and—

His brother Mathias spotted him. The other man's expression of surprise was nearly comical, until Ronan figured out he was trapped. Rather than retreating, he found himself responding to the wave and walking over.

"What are you doing here?" Mathias asked as Ronan stopped by their table. "You hate this kind of stuff."

Carol slapped his arm. Mathias looked at her. "What? He does. Crowds, conversation. Everything he avoids."

True now, Ronan thought, although it hadn't always been. Years ago, he'd been exactly like everyone else.

Before he could figure out what to say, he heard someone call his name. The second he recognized the voice, he relaxed and knew everything was going to be okay.

Natalie paused by his side. "You came! I wasn't sure if you would."

"Did you invite me?" If she had, he didn't remember.

She laughed. "No, but I thought about it, which is practically the same thing. Anyway, it doesn't matter because you're here and we're playing Latice."

"Is this like the paper airplanes?" he asked, knowing if it was, he would have to prepare to get his ass kicked.

She put her hands on his shoulders and leaned against him. "You can be on my team."

"We're not playing teams," Pallas said with a chuckle. "Good luck, Ronan. Natalie's a killer player. She always ends up with the wind tiles and totally knows how to score sunstones so she gets extra turns."

Natalie beamed at him. "She's right. I do have excellent Latice karma."

He knew he had to say something, but all he could think was how much he wanted to kiss her. More than kiss her. He wanted to pull her close and touch her all over. He wanted to take her somewhere quiet and private and prove that he hadn't been kidding before when he'd turned down her invitation because she'd been his guest.

He forced himself to remember where he was and sucked in a breath. "All right, Natalie. I'll take you on. But first I think I'll buy you a drink. You might be less deadly when you're tipsy."

"I don't think it works that way, but sure."

Natalie led him to a table that had two seats open. As they sat down, he thought he recognized the other couple. The woman ran some business in town and the guy was…

"Jasper Dembenski," the man said, holding out his hand. "You're one of the Mitchell brothers, right?"

"Ronan." He almost said "Mathias's twin" but caught himself in time. He wasn't, they weren't, and he still hadn't figured out how to accept the truth.

The man's name was familiar. Before Ronan could place it, the woman he was with spoke.

"I'm Wynn Beauchene."

She was beautiful with high cheekbones, black curly hair and brown eyes. For a second Ronan wished he sketched more, or painted. Wynn would make an excellent subject.

He sat down. Natalie took the last seat and grinned at Wynn.

"It's Latice night."

Jasper glanced at her. "What does that mean?"

"Wait and see," Wynn told him with a smug smile.

"I'm in trouble, aren't I?" He glanced at Ronan. "Wynn loves it when I get beaten by a woman."

"I confess, I do. Maybe it's wrong, but I'm willing to live with the flaw."

The games were passed out. Wynn and Natalie put the tiles face down and swirled them around until they were all mixed up.

"I believe I'm the youngest person at the table," Natalie said with a grin as she started taking tiles.

Wynn groaned. "I'd forgotten that part. Yes, Natalie, you get to start."

Natalie leaned close and lowered her voice. "Wynn gets crabby when she loses."

"You know I can hear you," Wynn said. "And that's not true."

"It's a little true," Jasper told her.

Wynn laughed. "All right. Maybe. I'll try to be on my best behavior."

One of the servers got on the loudspeakers and went over the rules. Ronan only half paid attention. He was more interested in how Natalie had shifted her chair a little closer to his.

Their server appeared with a beer for him and a glass of white wine for Natalie. A bell rang and play started.

The premise was deceptively simple—match tiles either by color or image. There was a strategic element Natalie had nailed. He knew that wind tiles allowed you to move a piece, and sunstones…well, he wasn't sure what they did, but within fifteen minutes, Natalie had an ongoing collection and seemed to play three turns for every one of his.

She won the first game. "We'll play two more rounds," she said, "with the winners advancing to the finals."

"Uh-huh. So I'll be going home early."

"We all will be," Wynn said with a grin. Then she touched Jasper's arm. "Come on. Let's get something at the bar. On our way, we'll discuss ways to end Natalie's reign of terror."

Natalie grinned as they left. When they were out of earshot, she leaned close to Ronan.

"So what do you think? Are they a couple? I mean,

I think they are, but Wynn never says anything and I don't want to ask."

"Since when? You ask me personal questions all the time."

"That's totally different. Wynn's one of my girlfriends. I have to respect her personal space."

"But not mine?"

"Not really."

She was tantalizingly close. He wanted to move that last inch and kiss her. But they were in public, and when he made his move, he wanted them to be alone.

"Who is Jasper? He seems familiar."

Her brows rose. "You don't know his face—it's his name. He's a writer. His books are thrillers and you've probably read them."

The information clicked into place. "I have. He's great."

"Are you going to go all fan-boy? I'm not sure how Jasper will react. Maybe it will be a sweet moment for both of you."

"Very funny."

"I am funny."

She was a lot of things, he thought as he stared into her eyes. Pretty and sweet and sexy. The kind of sexy that made a man ache all over.

"Am I interrupting?" Wynn asked as she returned to the table. "You two are looking intense."

Ronan straightened, not sure what to say. Natalie grinned at her friend.

"We were talking about you and Jasper, wondering if you were a couple."

So much for respecting a friend's personal space, Ronan thought with a chuckle.

"It's an interesting question," Wynn said serenely. "Now if only there were an answer."

NATALIE MADE IT to the final round only to have an unexpectedly bad couple of games. She wasn't sure how she'd become so distracted. It might have been the second glass of wine—something she rarely indulged in—or maybe the blame lay with not having Ronan sitting next to her.

She'd thought it was impossible to concentrate when the man was right there—breathing, talking, laughing. She'd been aware of everything. Of his broad shoulders, of how she could almost feel the heat from his body, of the way he had of looking at her as if she were the most interesting person in the room. It was a heady combination. Yet when she'd moved on to the final round and he hadn't, he'd left. Just like that, and she'd had, well, nothing.

The whole evening was confusing. While they'd been playing, she would have sworn he was interested in her. She'd tried to tell herself not to read too much into his attention. After all, he'd turned her down before. Yet she couldn't help thinking, *wishing*, that he were a little bit interested. But then he'd left and she'd realized she must have misread everything.

What was it about that man? Why him and why did he get to her the way he did?

She crossed the street and walked to her converted house. The front door opened onto a small foyer with three mailboxes, a table for packages, the doors to the two downstairs apartments and a staircase leading up to her larger apartment. She'd barely taken the first step up when she became aware that, despite the late hour, she was not alone. But before her breath could catch or she could start to panic, she recognized the man sitting halfway up the stairs. Recognized his light brown hair, green eyes and faint smile. When her heart rate picked up again, it had nothing to do with fear and everything to do with anticipation.

"Ronan?"

He stood. "I thought you'd be longer."

"I didn't make it past the final first round."

He waited until she reached his stair, then took her hand in his and led her to her front door. She unlocked it and they both stepped inside her apartment.

She had no idea what she was supposed to say or do. Offer him a beverage? Ask what was wrong? Throw herself at him and beg him to take her? The latter was the most intriguing but she couldn't help remembering the last time he'd turned her down. He'd been kind and gentle, but it had still been a no.

"So, ah, why are you here?" she asked.

He shoved his hands into his jeans front pockets. "I was waiting for you. I meant what I said before—at my place. I couldn't do anything while you were my guest. You're not anymore and I can't stop thinking about you, about what it was like having you in my house. Your invitation haunts me. I keep reliving our kiss and wanting to do it again. That and more. I want you, Natalie."

Oh. My. God! No one had ever said anything like

that to her before. No one had ever been so blunt, just putting it out there.

Deep inside, she felt a shiver, then another until she was trembling. She felt herself melting before he'd even touched her and wished she had something sophisticated or badass to say in return, but all she could muster was "Me, too."

Which, it turned out, was enough.

He reached for her, pulling her hard against him. Before she could catch her breath, his mouth claimed hers with a delicious power that left her gasping. His tongue teased hers even as his hands began to roam her body.

Everywhere he touched, she burned. Wanting exploded, shocking her with intensity and need. She'd always been a slow-build kind of girl. The sluttiest thing she'd ever done in her life had been to offer herself to Ronan a few nights ago and look how that had ended. Only now he was kissing her as if he couldn't possibly get enough.

He sucked on her lower lip before kissing her again even deeper than before. At the same time, he tugged on the hem of her shirt. Instinctively, she raised her arms so he could pull it off. Once it was gone, he ran his warm hands up and down her back before unfastening her bra and tugging it free of her body.

She barely had time to register her partial nakedness before his hands cupped her full breasts and began to massage them. Pleasure shot through her, making her whimper. It had been about a zillion years since she'd been with a man. Having that man be Ronan only intensified the experience.

He drew back enough to stare at her bare breasts. His eyes dilated and he swore softly, then dropped his head so he could take one of her hard nipples in his mouth. There was no elegant licking, nothing that tender. Instead he sucked hard, then used his teeth to lightly abrade her aroused flesh.

Her body's reaction was fast and to the point. Heat burned from her breast to her groin, leaving her barely able to stand. She groaned and cupped his head, encouraging him to do the same on her other breast.

"Just like that," she whispered, unable to stop herself from talking. "Like that, Ronan. Harder!"

He followed directions perfectly, going back and forth, sucking and nipping until she started to feel pressure build between her legs. Good pressure, the kind that told her she was alive and well and going to have an orgasm very shortly.

Without warning, he pulled back and dropped to his knees. He unfastened her jeans as she toed out of her loafers. Seconds later, her jeans and panties were on the floor and he was easing her back onto the entryway table.

The lamp wobbled. He set it on the floor, used his fingers to part the very center of her, then placed his tongue on her clit. For a second, that was it, just the pressure. Then he began to move. First back and forth, then in a circle that went around and over, again and again, until she was nothing but a quivering nerve begging to be satisfied.

The sensations were as intense as they were wonderful. She parted her legs as far as she could and hung on to the table to keep herself balanced in her half sitting, half standing position. Ronan didn't move any faster, but he pressed harder, pushing her closer and closer.

They were in her *foyer*, a voice whispered. She was *naked* and he had yet to take off a stitch. She should be ashamed of—

"I want this," she said aloud, silencing the voices.

Ronan chuckled. "Me, too," he said before pressing his tongue against her again. He moved just a little faster, pressed a little harder. It was too good, too much for her to resist. She tried to hold back, to keep it lasting just a little longer, but it was—

"Now," she breathed as the first wave hit. "Like that. Exactly like that. Oh, Ronan, I can't stop..." She sucked in a breath, then let it out, only instead of air, there was something very close to a scream as her body surrendered and she came and came and came.

Her orgasm went on for hours. Or maybe a minute, but it felt like hours in the best way possible. Ronan stayed with her, making sure she got to the end. When she finally stilled, he stood, pulled her to her feet and hustled her down the hall to her bedroom.

She was kind of in a daze and only vaguely aware of what he was doing, so it was a bit of a shock when she turned and saw he was already naked and reaching in his pocket for a condom.

While she knew she should be impressed that he'd, ah, come prepared, she was more interested in how he looked naked. He was muscled and masculine, broad-shouldered and fully aroused. At the sight of his erection, she felt a little *zing* of anticipation.

She stretched out on the bed and held open her arms. "You can just go for it, if you want."

His gaze locked with hers. She read his desperate hunger and knew she'd said exactly the right thing. She smiled.

"I mean that."

"Thank God."

He put on the condom, then joined her on the bed. After settling between her knees, he eased himself inside of her. She raised her hips to take all of him, then sighed as he began to move.

Yes, she thought happily. This was exactly right. Familiar pressure began. Slow and low, but there. She shifted a little to change the angle, hoping to get over the edge again.

"Natalie, touch your breasts."

Her eyes popped open and she found him watching her. What? Touch her…

"Please."

She'd always been kind of big on top and knew that some guys liked that, but she'd never thought that Ronan was a breast guy. She felt a little shy, but figured he'd made her scream, so she owed him.

She cupped her breasts in her hands and watched as his gaze settled on her chest. He continued to move in and out, going just a little faster. She moved her hands slightly, then squeezed her nipples. He groaned, which was fun, but she also felt a little jolt deep inside. What?

She did it again, harder this time. The jolt was bigger, deeper, and she suddenly got a whole lot closer. What had started as a show for him became a lot more interesting. She stroked her breasts, played with her nipples and found herself on the verge.

"You're killing me," he muttered.

She wrapped her legs around his hips. "I'm there, Ronan. Seriously, like two fast strokes and I—"

He groaned, seemed to gather himself, then shoved into her hard and fast, pushing her over the edge. She grabbed his hips, pulling him in as far as she could, then lost herself in her release. He continued to thrust in and out for a couple more seconds, then stilled as he came.

RONAN HADN'T DARED to imagine what it would be like to be with Natalie, which turned out to be a good thing. There was no way his imagination was up to the task. She was sexy and beautiful and curvy and about the hottest woman he'd ever seen, let alone made love with. She was uninhibited in a way he never would have guessed, and when she had her orgasm, it was the most incredible thing ever.

As they began to breathe normally and their heart rates slowed from hummingbird levels, his mind cleared just enough for him to think about how much he wanted her again. He wondered if it were possible to get enough.

She snuggled close and sighed. "Wow. Just wow."

"Yeah?"

"Oh, please. You know it was good. Do you need me to say the words? The screams weren't enough?"

"The screams were pretty good. And a bit of a surprise."

"For me, too."

He wrapped his arms around her. "Thank you."

"And wow?"

He kissed her nose and smiled. "Big wow."

She looked at him. "So, you're a breast man. I never would have guessed."

His gaze dropped to her chest. "I've never been into one specific body part before, but you have the most stunning breasts I've ever seen."

They were large and perfectly shaped. Or maybe it was her nipples or maybe it was just because they were hers. He had a vision of her on top, bouncing along as she rode him, and he went instantly hard. Fortunately they'd pulled up the sheet and she didn't notice. It was one thing to be enthused, but another to be desperate.

She glanced at the clock. "Okay, so here's the thing. I didn't get dinner and I'm starving. The Chinese place is open for another twenty minutes. Do you want me to call in an order for the two of us?"

Or do you want to go?

She didn't ask that part of the question, but he could read it in the faint worry in her eyes. In the two years he'd known Natalie, he'd never heard her talk about a guy. He had a feeling she didn't play the field and wasn't into one-night stands. Something he should have thought of before, because he didn't have a clue as to what he was doing—or wanted—except he knew he didn't want to go home. Not yet.

"Chinese sounds great."

She scrambled out of bed. "I have the number in my cell phone. Anything you don't like?"

She wasn't wearing anything and made no attempt to cover herself. He studied her curves, her full breasts and belly, her legs, and knew he had to have her again. She was lush and feminine and totally sexual.

"Ronan?"

"Get your favorites. I'm sure I'll like them, too."

"Okay."

She walked out of the room, giving him a view of her perfect ass. He swore softly, then began to dress. Once dinner was over, he promised himself, they were going to do it and she was for sure going to be on top.

CHAPTER EIGHT

Going out in the relatively cool night did little to tamp down Ronan's desire. Just having Natalie next to him in his truck was enough to get him going again. But he was determined to get through the meal without acting like some horny kid who couldn't keep it in his pants.

She tucked the big bag of takeout next to her feet and grinned at him. "I'm starving."

Her smile was infectious, her air of sexual satisfaction gratifying. He liked knowing he'd pleased her. More than pleased her, he thought smugly.

"Just to be clear, I know that wasn't baby sex," she said as he drove back to her place.

Shock nearly had him driving into a tree. "What?"

"From the app. It wasn't at all and I just wanted you to know."

That damned app. He'd totally forgotten about it. "Thanks for the share."

"Don't be grumpy. You would have thought of it eventually and totally freaked out."

"I don't freak out."

"Have you seen you? Because you do. But it's okay. I like you, anyway."

A baby. Damn. She knew how to break a mood. Not that he didn't still want her, but the need was about 20 percent less intense.

They arrived back at her place. He carried the food upstairs and waited while she unlocked the door. This time he got a good look at her apartment, only to grin when his gaze settled on the lamp sitting on the floor by the entry table. He carefully put it back in place, then glanced around.

The floor plan was surprisingly open. Living room, eating area and kitchen were basically one big room. She'd painted each of the walls a different color, which should have been chaotic, but was surprisingly pleasing to the eye. The door and window trim was uniformly pale lavender. Her living room sofa was oversize and done in a neutral medium brown, and the area rug pulled together all the colors.

Paintings and mixed-media pieces were everywhere. Some he recognized as her work; others were from artists he didn't know.

He carried the food to the kitchen and put it on the counter.

"There's wine in a rack in the entry closet," she said as she collected plates and flatware. "Don't worry. It's stuff you and your brothers have given me."

"I trust your taste in wine," he said as he opened the closet and saw all the bottles Natalie had been given over the past couple of years. Bottles that celebrated sales of her work or her birthday.

"You might trust my taste but you'd wince at my wine budget," she said with a laugh when they met up in the kitchen. She showed him where the corkscrew was and pointed to the location of the wineglasses.

After opening the bottle, he carried it and two glasses to the small dining table by the window. She'd already set out plates, which he recognized as his brother's design. But these were mismatched and obviously bought at Mathias's semiannual sale where his "mistakes" were offered at discount prices.

He poured wine while she opened cartons of Chinese food. The smell made his mouth water and reminded him he'd missed dinner.

"I already like what you chose," he told her.

She grinned. "There's plenty of garlic, but I have a spare toothbrush I'm willing to let you have."

He chuckled. "You're on."

They sat across from each other, with her facing the kitchen and him facing the living room. It was only then he noticed a blown-glass piece on a shelf in the corner.

It was a swirl of color—all blues and lavenders with a touch of gold. What was supposed to have been a vase had collapsed into a molten mess. He tried to remember when that had happened—maybe a year ago. Before the swan/dragon commission for sure.

He remembered being frustrated that something so simple had eluded him. He would have left the disaster to cool before tossing it. Natalie must have taken it instead.

"What are you—" Her expression turned rueful as she wrinkled her nose. "Yes, I have to confess to taking that. But you were going to throw it out and I thought it was beautiful the way it was. I didn't think you'd mind. Oh, I asked Atsuko first and she said it was fine."

"I don't mind, but why that one?" He had a storeroom full of pieces. She could have any of them.

She looked at him. "Seriously? That's your question. Hmm, let me think. Because I don't have three *hundred* thousand dollars to buy one of your quote real unquote pieces."

"I'd be happy to give you one. All you have to do is ask. You could pick whatever you'd like."

She didn't look the least bit impressed by his offer. "No. I appreciate it, but no. I'd be too tempted to sell it and finance myself for the next sixteen or seventeen years and it would be wrong to sell anything a friend gave me, so I would be torn and I don't need that kind of negative energy in my life."

She wasn't like anyone he'd ever known. He found himself wanting to offer her half his storeroom to sell and live off of, or keep—whatever she wanted. He had a ridiculous urge to create a grant and secretly fund her artwork.

He looked at her brightly colored apartment. Earlier, when he'd used the bathroom, he'd noticed that she'd made the master bedroom her art studio and that she slept in the smaller bedroom. She struggled financially every single day. Not that she was starving but he would bet there were months when it was tough to pay all the bills. And yes, she could work more hours and have a little extra cash in her wallet, but that would mean giving up her art, and with Natalie creating, the world was a much more wonderful place.

She passed him cartons. They both loaded their plates and began to eat. They talked about what was happening in town and who might have won the Latice tournament. When they were done, Ronan poured them more wine.

"I'd like to stay," he told her. "Tonight. If that's all right."

She studied him for a second. Emotions flashed through her eyes. He had no idea what she was thinking but the little curve at the corner of her mouth told him it probably wasn't bad.

Anticipation slammed into him as he again imagined her on top. Natalie was surprisingly uninhibited in bed—or maybe not. She did pretty much everything with total abandon—why not sex?

"We should probably talk about the elephant in the room, then," she said.

The… "What elephant?" One second too late, he thought of the baby app and nearly came out of his chair.

"You'll want ground rules. You don't want them in your art, but when it comes to your personal life, you like things tidy."

"How did you know that?" he asked, wondering if he sounded as relieved as he felt. As for the rules, he never much thought about it, but she was right.

"I see things." She picked up her wineglass. "I vote for fun without anything getting too serious. You can't lie to me and you can't cheat, and when it's done, just tell me."

"Yes, and the same from you."

She laughed. "I've never cheated."

"I haven't, either."

"But you've broken up with women before. I've never done that."

He grinned. "You've probably never dated a woman."

The laugh returned. "Good point. Oh, and it's okay with me if we don't tell anyone."

That surprised him. "You don't want anyone to know?"

"I'm fine with people knowing. You're the one who keeps your personal life private."

Before he could react to that particular truth, she stood, pulled off her T-shirt and her bra, walked over to his chair and straddled him, then put his hands on her breasts.

"We can keep talking," she said as she pressed her lips to his jaw. "Or not. You pick."

"I pick not."

"Oh, good."

NATALIE DROVE TO work because floating there would cause people to ask too many questions. But she could have floated, or danced, or simply willed herself there due to all the happiness bubbling up inside of her. She was happy, she was content, she was *quenched.*

Ronan had spent the night. They'd made love twice more and he'd left shortly after dawn. They'd laughed, they'd talked, they'd hung on to each other until their breathing settled and their bodies stopped shaking. Their time together had been magically amazing.

She had always enjoyed sex. She thought it was a natural and fun progression in a relationship. But she'd never experienced such a meeting of two bodies, where everything he did to her was more intense, more satisfying. She was glad he wanted them to continue to see each other—she wanted that, too. And if she had a thought or two that it would be nice if she could pretend it was going to last more than a few weeks, she knew she was only fooling herself.

She wanted family and belonging. Ronan had turned his back on all he had. She couldn't begin to understand how that was possible. To give up the *world.* They were too different in spirit for this to last, but for now…it was pure magic.

Once she was at work, she quickly cleared her gallery chores, then signed up for the refurbished-bridge art project. The sections were granted in five-foot segments, and artists were encouraged to work in teams. One side of the bridge would feature the artwork and the other would be a mesh material where people could put locks, like people did on Cologne's Love Lock bridge. The Happily Inc bridge had been reinforced to handle the heavy load of the locks and the artwork.

She filled out the paperwork and emailed it back and then sent an email to Mathias. Yes, she could have walked over to the studio and told him, but an email seemed more fun. Let him wonder what she was up to.

Around ten, she texted Ronan and asked if he could help her with something. As she waited for his response, she felt a little quiver in her tummy. Anticipation, she thought happily. Excitement. However temporary, she had a man in her life and she planned to enjoy every second of it.

A few minutes later, Ronan walked into her office. She gave herself a couple of heartbeats to enjoy his sexy smile, the slightly mussed hair, the clean-shaven jaw that had been delightfully bristly the previous night.

"You texted?"

His voice was low and teasing, and slightly secretive. She did her best not to sigh.

"Can I steal you away for about twenty minutes?" she asked. "I want to show you something."

His eyebrows rose and she giggled. "Not that. Something outside. In public."

"Damn."

They left the gallery and walked over to the bridge only a short half block away. The city had already put in the markings that would differentiate the various sections. Natalie counted out the spaces until she found the two she'd signed up for.

"The bridge has been reinforced and widened," she began.

"I can see that." He kept his gaze on her rather than the bridge.

"The city wants to make it into something beautiful that will attract tourists. We can't always depend on weddings. What if people stop getting married?"

"Unlikely but I see your point. Go on."

She pointed to the opposite side. "They're going to allow people to put up locks. They do it a lot in Europe. Everyone talks about the bridge in Paris but I like the one in Cologne better. Not that I've seen either, but still. Given your affection for East German hot chocolate, I thought you'd agree with me."

"I've already ordered more."

Her mouth watered. "That's nice."

"I'll let you know when it arrives."

"I appreciate that." Maybe they could drink it while naked. Or in bed. Or both. She cleared her throat. "On the other side, the city is asking for artists to create something fun or interesting or whatever, in five-foot sections." She touched the railing. "I signed us up for this one."

Before Ronan could react, she spotted Mathias walking toward them.

"Strange place for a meeting," he said as he approached. "What's up?"

Ronan looked between the two of them. He didn't look mad, which was great, but he didn't look happy, either.

"Let me guess," he said. "You want us to do one of these sections and Mathias to do the one next to it?"

"Something like that." She turned to Mathias. "You know about the bridge project, right?"

"Sure. Ten feet is a lot. I'm not sure what we'd do."

"I have some ideas," she said quickly. "I want to

use the glass you guys throw away. Work it in somehow. But I thought the centerpiece would be my car."

They both stared at her.

"How would we do that?" Ronan asked.

"In sections. We could cut it in half for starters. Maybe shorten the hood. The phrase 'coming and going' keeps popping into my head. It could just be sticking out a bit on our side, or it could be sticking out on both sides. I'm not sure how we'd secure it and the city wants to make sure it's supersecure so it won't fall. And we'd have to keep kids from crawling up on it and falling."

"Not just kids," Mathias muttered, peering over the side of the bridge. "That's a hell of a way down." He turned back to her. "When did you sign us up for this?"

"A little bit ago."

"When did you talk to the city engineers about what would be required to secure the car?"

She did her best to look wide-eyed and honest. Not that Mathias would get mad at her, but still.

"After I had lunch with my friends a couple of days ago. Silver was the one who suggested using the car. I don't want to take credit for her idea."

As she was talking, Ronan quietly eased between her and Mathias. At first she wasn't sure what he was doing, but then she saw he was acting as a physical barrier…protecting her.

So sweet, she thought, getting all mushy inside. She wasn't worried about Mathias. He was a really good-natured guy—he would never hurt her, but she liked how Ronan was taking care of her. She wondered if he knew what he was doing or if he was acting instinctively.

Mathias turned to Ronan. "It's not a *bad* idea."

"There are ways to make it work."

"You two deal with the details and let me know when you want to get together to start the work," she said as she walked away. "Oh, and talk to Nick about cutting up the car. He's good with power tools."

She kept moving toward the far side of the bridge and the safety of the gallery. She held her breath as she waited to see if they would come after her and insist she be a part of the planning, or worse, refuse to get involved. After a couple of seconds, she heard male voices. She was too far away to distinguish the words, but she knew the brothers were talking. Planning.

She released her breath and smiled. The bridge project would give the former twins a chance to hang out together without any pressure. With a little luck they would rediscover how much they enjoyed each other's company. From there it was a short trip back to being close again. Because Ronan had the gift of family and she was determined that he would appreciate that.

"DID YOU DO any research?" Ronan asked as he and Natalie drove to the used-car lot on the edge of Palm Desert, the closest semilarge town to Happily Inc.

"Some." She sat in the passenger seat of his truck, practically bouncing with excitement. He had a bad feeling her research had consisted of exploring the various shades of red available in cars in her price range.

"What are you looking for?" he asked, then added, "Aside from a red car?"

"Something, you know, safe and reliable. As late model as I can afford."

The words were what he wanted to hear, but he had a feeling she didn't mean any of them.

In the past couple of weeks, he'd gotten to know Natalie. She was bright, talented, funny and impulsive. When she got an idea in her head, it was impossible to budge. To her, the red car represented something important. All her talk about safety and model years was simply to humor him.

He knew better than to tell himself he wasn't going to get involved. That her car was her decision. The truth was he and Natalie were seeing each other and he cared about her—as much as he could, given his past. He wanted her to be safe and happy, which meant finding a car they could both agree on. And if they couldn't find a red one that was also reliable, he had the impossible task of convincing her that color shouldn't be a priority.

He thought about mentioning how she'd railroaded him into working on the bridge project with his brother… without checking with him first. That should get him something. Only he knew that Natalie wouldn't see it that way, and truth be told, he wasn't mad about working with Mathias. Maybe it would help them rediscover what it was like to be brothers. He missed his former twin and had wanted to get things back how they'd been. Maybe the bridge project was a start.

He drove onto the lot and parked. Before he could issue any last-minute instructions, Natalie was out of the truck and heading toward a red BMW convertible gleaming in the sun. Ronan caught up and held in a groan. Yes, the car was a head turner, but it was also more than double her budget.

"It's so beautiful," she said, holding her arms open as if she wanted to give the car a hug. "See the color? I'd look good in that."

"Yes, you would, but where would you put your various art projects? Some of them are big. The roof drops into the trunk, meaning you won't have any room when the top is down."

"Oh, you're right. That's okay. Plus I could never afford this one."

She spun in a circle and eyed the different cars. "What about that one?"

Ronan followed her gaze and saw a beat-up import. The paint job was decent but the car looked battered. There was something off on the hood, as if someone had done bodywork in a hurry.

"It's red," she said as she approached, her tone doubtful. "Is it just me, or does it look like it's been in an accident?"

Ronan studied the large As Is tag on the front windshield. "Not this one."

Natalie hesitated before nodding. "I think you're right."

They walked around on the lot. A salesman named Greg joined them. Greg seemed pleasant enough and wasn't pushy, nor did he balk when Ronan said he'd already made arrangements to have the car Natalie picked checked by a mechanic in town.

They found a great Corolla that met all of Ronan's requirements, except it was silver. Natalie agreed that it was in mint condition and had low miles. There were no accidents in its past and the interior was in excellent shape.

He watched her circle the car and saw disappointment in the set of her shoulders, then glanced at the red BMW convertible.

"Do you have any other red cars?" he asked, unable to believe he'd spoken those ridiculous words.

"Sure." Greg led them to a red Honda Fit. It was only a few years old with low miles and in perfect condition. It was also about four thousand above Natalie's budget.

"It's amazing," she breathed until she saw the price tag. "Oh, no. That is so not going to happen. I can't risk a payment."

Ronan glanced at Greg. "Give us a minute, please."

"No problem."

Ronan waited until Greg stepped a discreet distance away before touching Natalie's arm. "Let me pay the difference. It's the least I can do," he added before she could speak. "I'm the reason you lost your car in the first place."

"If I hadn't lost my car, I couldn't afford a new one now, so it's totally fine. You're not paying for part of my car."

He didn't know what to say or do. If only he'd thought to contact the lot ahead of time and arrange to pay down a good-condition red car. If only he could convince her that the extra money didn't mean anything to him.

"I owe you for the deductible on your insurance. You're going to let me pay that, aren't you?" Not that it would make up the difference.

She hesitated.

"I want to, Natalie. Please. I would feel a lot less guilty if I could at least do that."

She nodded. "Thank you. That's really generous. But nothing else." She looked at the Fit, then sighed. "I just can't swing it. If only the Corolla was a different color. I like how it looks and I know the car gets really good reviews."

A light bulb went on in Ronan's brain. "I'll get it painted," he told her. "It's only a few hundred dollars. Come on, Natalie. It's the perfect solution. You get a car I don't have to worry about and it's red." He leaned close and lowered his voice to a seductive pitch. "Candy-apple red."

Her eyes widened. "I could get the car painted?"

"No, I could. I'm pushing the sensible car. Come on. I'm an artist. Let me get it painted."

He hoped she wouldn't think to point out she was just as much an artist.

"You're sure it's not much?" She sounded doubtful.

"You've seen those commercials on TV, right? Painting a car is cheap."

He was lying through his teeth and he knew it. A decent paint job would be a few thousand, but he was willing to accept being a weasel about this if it meant she had a safe car that she loved.

"I want to double-check with Greg." She looked

at him. "I don't trust you not to try to give me something expensive."

"How would that be bad?"

She considered the question. "I'm not sure, but it would be." She waved Greg over. "If I took the Corolla, could I get it painted?"

"Of course. We have a paint shop right here in the service department. They do an excellent job and you'd get a discount."

"I'm going to pay for it," Ronan said easily, careful to stand behind Natalie so she couldn't see him. "It's only a few hundred dollars, right? Before the discount?"

Greg looked momentarily startled, then caught Ronan's slow nod and smiled. "Right. With the discount, it's practically free."

Natalie clapped her hands together. "Then it's the Corolla. Let's take her to the mechanic, and if she passes, then I'll buy her. I hope she's in good shape because I can already picture her bright, shiny red."

"There's some paperwork to fill out before she can go to the mechanic," Greg said. "Let's go into my office."

Natalie waved them toward the building. "You two go ahead. I need a minute more with the car."

"Take your time," Ronan told her. "You need to be sure she's the one."

He walked with Greg. When they were out of earshot, Greg said, "The paint job is a few thousand."

"I know. She's going to want candy-apple red. That's going to be more."

The other man stared at him. "You must really like her."

"Something like that." He passed over his credit card. "Just make sure she doesn't find out I did this."

"You got it."

Ronan watched Natalie to make sure she wasn't done bonding with her new-to-her car. When Greg handed him the receipt, he signed it without glancing at the final amount.

"If the car doesn't pass with the mechanic, I'll refund the money," Greg told him.

"Thanks."

Natalie started toward the offices. Ronan tucked the receipt in his back pocket and hoped his good deed wouldn't come back to bite him. If it did, he would have to deal.

CHAPTER NINE

"I DON'T KNOW what I was thinking," Atsuko murmured as she studied the brass statue. "Had there been wine at the meeting?"

Natalie carefully pressed her lips together, determined not to comment. Every quarter, Atsuko went over the gallery's inventory to determine what was and wasn't selling. The accounting software provided a list of everything waiting to be sold, but Atsuko preferred to look at the various pieces herself. She always said that while numbers were interesting, art came from the soul.

The first time Natalie had participated in the process, she'd been terrified. Not only had she been new at her job, she'd just had a small mixed-media canvas put on the wall. What if Atsuko decided it wasn't worthy? But her boss had simply walked by the small piece and two days later it had sold.

Atsuko had excellent taste and an understanding of what her clients wanted, but every now and then she made a mistake. The odd half man, half bull bronze casting might fall in that category.

Natalie waited, clipboard in hand, while Atsuko circled the eighteen-inch piece. Every now and then Natalie privately thought she wanted to be Atsuko when she grew up. The gallery owner was always perfectly put together, favoring tailored clothing with an Asian influence. She ran a successful business, sold incredible art for hundreds of thousands of dollars, all the while making everyone around her feel comfortable and happy.

Atsuko shook her head. "That one is going back. I'm sure it would sell eventually, but I don't love it."

Natalie made a note next to the small picture on her inventory sheet.

Every artist had his or her own sheet listing what was available for sale. The only exception was Mathias. His dishes, bowls, basins and lighting fixtures were managed differently—more as goods to be sold than individual pieces of art. As far as Natalie could tell, anything Mathias created sold almost immediately. Even his mistakes were offered at a discount and quickly snatched up.

Atsuko glanced out the window. Natalie followed her gaze and saw two cars driving around to the work studio parking lot.

"Ronan seems to be on track." Atsuko turned to Natalie. "Your doing, I presume."

"What?" Natalie felt herself flush. "Me? No. I just... He..." She sighed. "It's not what you think. Ronan is getting out more. Being around people helps him, plus working with his brothers. I think he needs the energy."

"Is that what we're calling it?"

Before Natalie could shriek, the gallery door opened and a man walked in. He was of average height, with light brown hair and glasses. He wore a blue button-down shirt tucked into khakis. For some reason he seemed vaguely familiar, but more in the way of someone she might have seen around town. He certainly didn't look like a typical gallery client. Plus it was Wednesday morning. No one shopped for art on Wednesday morning.

He glanced between Atsuko and herself. "Natalie Kaleta?"

Natalie took a half step toward him. "That's me. How can I help you?" She had no idea who the guy was or what he was doing here.

"Edgar Wooster." He offered his hand. After they shook, he handed her a manila folder. "I'm a scientist at the sleep research center north of town." He nodded at the folder. "That's my résumé, along with a health history. I've never wanted children of my own or a wife. Too much of a distraction. I'm all about my work."

Natalie glanced at Atsuko, who appeared equally baffled by Edgar's presence. "Okay," Natalie said slowly. "While that's interesting, I'm not sure why..."

Edgar frowned slightly. "I want to improve the gene pool. It's always been a goal of mine. To contribute to the species but without the messy emotional involvement."

Which sounded weird, but everyone had their own

ideas about things. What she couldn't figure out was why he was here and what he was telling her.

Edgar's expression became impatient. "I'm here to be a sperm donor. I heard you're looking for one." He dropped his gaze to her feet, then slowly raised his gaze until he met her eyes again, then smiled. "You're not unattractive. We could save the money and get you pregnant the old-fashioned way."

Atsuko gave a little burst of laughter, then excused herself, leaving Natalie to splutter alone.

"I… You…" What on earth had happened? Who was this man and how did he know about her baby app? And a sperm donor? No. No!

"Do you want to think about it?" Edgar asked.

"I don't need to," she said firmly. "While I appreciate the offer, I've decided to go in another direction."

"That's disappointing." He nodded at the folder. "If you change your mind, my contact information is right there."

With that, he turned and left. Natalie stood in the gallery, unable to believe what had just happened. In the distance, she could still hear Atsuko laughing.

Fire good, Ronan thought with a grin as he adjusted his face mask. Or in this case, a blowtorch was even better. He, Nick and Mathias were in the back of an auto repair shop where they'd had Natalie's totaled car towed. They'd let the local high school auto shop class pick over the vehicle for whatever parts they wanted and had been left with a stripped carcass. Now, wearing protective face masks, aprons and gloves, they prepared to cut her car in two.

Ronan and Mathias had agreed with the "coming and going" theme for the bridge and Mathias had already been in touch with the city's engineer to work out ways to secure the car and keep the bridge safe. Ronan had done some preliminary sketches and knew that he would have to reduce the length of the hood by at least two-thirds. Nick was along because it was cutting a car in half with a blowtorch.

Nick, who had won their round-robin rock-paper-scissors, got to go first. They'd marked where the major cuts would go—parts of the car would have to be separated with a saw and tin snips, but there were still large sections that could literally be blown apart.

"Everybody protected?" Nick asked, checking his own face mask. "I'm going in."

The sound of the blowtorch was very satisfying, Ronan thought as he watched the process of separating metal. The roof was thin enough that it cut quickly. As his brother worked, Ronan flashed to Natalie's mixed-media pieces and he briefly wondered if he could do something like that with metal and glass. He knew people did all-metal sculptures—some of them were huge and very detailed. But what about combining the two? He would have to play with some sketches and probably take a welding class. Last year Mathias and Nick had played around with welding and they'd nearly set themselves on fire.

Once the car was in two pieces, Mathias went to work on removing the back third, including a bit of the rear door and the trunk, while Nick and Ronan discussed the best place to cut the hood section.

"What's your outer limit?" Nick asked. "Don't forget you're going to have to put something over the headlights. You can't leave glass that thin out there. Maybe a mesh of some kind. Or replace them with a thicker glass that's safe."

"Good point." The last thing they wanted was glass that would splinter if broken.

He and Nick figured out the measurements, then had Mathias check their work. The three brothers worked together for most of the afternoon. They were hot, sweaty and tired when they were done, but everyone had a good time.

Ronan remembered when it had always been like this. The three of them in the studio, creating, experimenting, wanting desperately to be the best to show their father.

At first Mathias had been the most gifted. Nick had great talent, but he liked to try different things. Greatness meant perfection and perfection required discipline. Nick would rather experiment with a hundred different techniques than master five.

Mathias had been more than willing and the one Ceallach had watched the closest. Ronan had tried to outdo his brother. His work was consistent and always improving, but Mathias had a flare, a vision Ronan couldn't duplicate.

Ronan remembered their intense conversations about art and how great they were going to be. They were the twins—they'd always had each other. Everyone had known they were a team.

Maybe that was why Nick went his own way. Del and Aidan didn't have the gift—they were normal, so naturally hung out together. Ronan and Mathias were each other's best friend, leaving Nick odd man out. Whatever the reason, Ronan had known he could count on Mathias and his brother could do the same.

When Ceallach had destroyed an exceptional piece Mathias had created—no doubt because it challenged his own mastery—Mathias had switched to creating everyday objects. Ronan remembered their fights as he'd struggled to convince his brother not to let their father win. But Mathias had been adamant. He was what he was and he wasn't changing. A stubbornness Ronan happened to share.

Now he looked at his two brothers and wondered how things could have been different. If he'd found out the truth in some other way…or not at all. A part of him wanted to still be Mathias's twin—at least then he would know his place in the world. Now he was nothing but Ceallach's bastard and that was not a happy fate. Without a mother, there was no one to counteract the darkness that threatened.

Natalie would tell him he had his biological mother, but he wasn't sure she would be much help. The woman had slept with a married man, had his baby, then walked away from her kid. She wasn't a shining example of social correctness. For all he knew, she was as selfish and amoral as his father. Which left Ronan fighting demons with no chance of winning. Part of the reason he'd found it easy to stay away from his brothers.

Only now he was reconnected, and even though he knew he should go back to his solitary life, he couldn't seem to do it. He was drawn to town, drawn to their company and drawn to the safety and light of circling in Natalie's orbit. She had worked her magic and he was no match for her emotional power.

"Ready?" Nick asked, turning off the blowtorch before passing it over.

Ronan grinned, his introspective thoughts pushed away by the reality of tools that cut through metal. "Always."

BY THREE THE inventory was finished, Atsuko was no longer chuckling and Natalie had pretty much recovered from her unexpected encounter. On Monday she would be hosting lunch with her friends and she planned to get to the bottom of who might have mentioned her incredibly tentative thoughts on the baby front to total strangers. She was sure Edgar was a nice guy but jeez.

She supposed a case could be made that if she wasn't comfortable talking to Edgar about being a sperm donor, then she really wasn't ready or maybe even interested in the entire process. Not that her reluctance was exactly news. She was starting to suspect her thoughts about having a kid on her own were symptoms of a bigger problem. She wanted more in her life. She wanted a sense of belonging. She wanted to fall in love and get married and have a family.

She hadn't figured out an answer to her question when a very sweaty, very happy Ronan walked into the gallery.

"We did it," he told her. "We cut up your car. It was great. The kids from the auto shop class had picked over it like vultures. They'd taken everything that wasn't welded down. Mathias worked on the back half. He's got it sectioned to the trunk and just a bit of the back door. Nick and I worked on the front. I think I've got that where I need it. We'll have to check the final measurements. You're going to want to weigh in on color. Something that will look good with the sky. Also, we have to talk about how stylized you want this to be."

He grinned. "You know, we could put wings on this thing." His smile faded when she didn't respond. "What's wrong? What happened? Are you upset about the car?"

"No. Of course not. I'm glad it has a new purpose and you had a good time and that progress was made."

"I'm not convinced. What is it?"

She folded her arms across her chest. "A man stopped by. Edgar. He's a scientist at the sleep center. He brought me his résumé."

"For what?"

She drew in a breath. "I can't even believe I'm going to say this, but to be a sperm donor. I have no idea who told him about my baby app. You know and my friends know, and that's all. I did mention it the last time we had lunch, so it has to be one of them. Unless you told Edgar."

Ronan held up both hands. "I don't even know the guy. It wasn't me."

"I didn't think so." She doubted the man she was sleeping with would have offered her up for sperm donation.

"What happened?"

"You won't believe it. He just walked in here and started talking about how he wants to improve the species."

Ronan's lips began to twitch.

"It's not funny," she protested.

"It kind of is. Improve the species. Like he's all that."

Not exactly the response she was looking for. "You're not upset?"

"You're not going to take him up on his offer, so no."

He was far too calm, she thought, getting annoyed. An unusual state for her, but here it was and she was going to take advantage of it.

"Interesting." She studied Ronan. "He said I was attractive enough that he was more than happy to get me pregnant the old-fashioned way, if that makes a difference."

Ronan's green eyes darkened, his mouth straightened and his shoulders went back, as if in an unconscious attempt to make himself look bigger.

"What did you say?"

His voice was low and controlled and just a little annoyed.

"What?" she asked sweetly. "Are you concerned?"

"That some guy you never met wanted to have sex with you? Yes, I'm concerned."

"Good. Because it wasn't funny to me and you laughed."

He walked over and pulled her close. "You're right. I'm sorry. I should have reacted differently. Do you want me to go beat him up?"

"I'm not sure how that would help improve the species." She snuggled close. Now that he was holding her, she was feeling a whole lot better about things.

"Screw the species," he said right before he kissed her. "How can I make this up to you?"

She smiled at him. "Maybe you could show me the cut-up car."

"Happy to."

"And let me use the blowtorch."

"Not even for money."

She was still laughing when he kissed her again.

NATALIE LIKED WHEN the gallery was closed. Yes, it was a retail establishment where goods were bought and sold, but that was only when customers were around. On the days it was quiet and empty of anyone but her, she couldn't helping thinking the semilit space had a spiritual quality.

She loved to walk through the silence, pausing to admire various creations. She wondered what the artist had been thinking and how close they'd come to their vision. She got caught up in swirls and lines and color and depth. Looking at the art recharged and inspired her.

On this particular Monday she was a little more concerned with getting set up for her lunch than admiring the work around her, but she did pause to study a vase filled with elegant cut flowers. The piece was about three feet high and four feet wide and done entirely in glass. The true genius was how real the flowers looked, as if a leaf might fall off any second or a petal might droop.

Ronan had created a series of the flowers in vases—each one representing a different season. Mathias had played on that theme with seasonal dishes. Atsuko had created a display combining their work. The everyday and the untouchable, Natalie thought briefly before returning her attention to the table.

She had enough chairs, a place for their small buffet and the right amount of cutlery, plates and glasses. She'd bought a large superdeluxe chicken Cobb salad with extra avocado, tortilla strips and sesame seeds because there was so much yummy stuff on top there was barely any lettuce.

Right at noon Silver knocked on the front door. Natalie moved the Closed sign to let her in, then nearly groaned when she inhaled the scent of freshly baked bread. Her gaze dropped to the two long baguettes her friend held.

"You didn't," Natalie breathed.

Silver laughed before hugging her. "I did. I went to the bakery and they were just pulling these out of the oven. Brace yourself—it gets worse." She held up a small bag. "Irish butter."

"No. Not Irish butter."

At any given moment in time, Natalie was on the verge of gaining five or ten pounds, seemingly overnight. Her body just loved to be chubby, and while she liked to think she kept an ironclad schedule when it came to her exercise program, the truth was she didn't exercise much at all.

"I just finished eating like a rabbit for the past three days," she said with a sigh. "I took a walk this weekend." It had been more of a stroll, but still, there had been movement.

"Then you've earned French bread and Irish butter," Silver teased.

"Easy for you to say. You've always been skinny, and yet I still love you." Natalie pointed to the buffet table. "How are things?"

"Good. Busy. I had to turn down a couple of weddings. I can't be in two places at once and I was already booked." Silver pulled a cutting board and bread knife out of her tote, then set the loaves on the cutting board with the butter next to them.

"What about those two trailers you were thinking of buying? Have you decided?"

Silver made a face. "No. It's the money thing. I'm not comfortable taking out a loan."

"The bank would be happy to have you as a customer. You're a successful businesswoman."

"Maybe."

There was another knock on the door. Natalie let in Bethany Archer.

"I love it when lunch is here," the petite blonde said,

giving Natalie and Silver each hugs. "I feel so sophisticated surrounded by all the beautiful art."

"You're a princess," Silver said drily. "Shouldn't you feel sophisticated all the time?"

"You'd think, but no. So what's new?"

Natalie pointed to the buffet table. "Silver brought bread fresh from the bakery and Irish butter."

Bethany winced. "I'm on a diet. How am I supposed to be strong when you're tempting me like that?"

"If someone else buys it, the calories don't count," Silver told her.

"Great. Tell that to my thighs."

Wynn, Carol and Pallas arrived just then and greeted everyone. Pallas was still looking pale.

"Are you okay?" Natalie asked.

"I had a bug," Pallas said, her smile wan. "I'm getting over it."

"Whatever it was, I don't want it," Wynn said. "You've been sick for a while. Have you seen a doctor?"

"I have. She says I'll be fine."

There were more hugs all around. Then everyone wanted to take a quick tour of the gallery before getting to lunch.

Natalie did her best not to squirm as her friends walked around. Atsuko had taken the dragon piece she'd started at Ronan's and priced it at an astonishing thousand dollars. It was more than Natalie had ever gotten for an individual piece, and she had to admit she was nervous. What if no one bought it? What if everyone thought she was fooling herself, thinking she deserved that much for it? What if—

"You never said anything," Wynn called, pointing at the framed piece. "This is amazing. When did you do it?"

"Over the past few weeks."

Her friends gathered around to study the stylized dragon.

"Are those paper clips?" Carol asked. "They are! I never would have thought to use them. I love it. And hey, a thousand dollars! Good for you."

Natalie twisted her hands together. "I'm afraid it's too much," she admitted before she could stop herself.

"You have to value your work or no one else will," Wynn said sternly. "People try to get me to discount their projects all the time. At first I felt bad about saying no, but screw that. I have to pay for my equipment, my building and my employees. I do good work and that doesn't come free."

Silver linked arms with her. "You're so forceful and mature."

"I know. It's a burden."

Wynn grinned and everyone laughed.

"That sounds great," Carol said. "But it's not always easy to put a value on what we do. I work for a nonprofit, which makes asking for a raise difficult. Am I being realistic or taking away from the cause?"

"That would be a hard one," Natalie said. "But the animals love you and would want you to be happy."

"I don't know. I think the giraffes would rather have more of their leaf eater treats."

Everyone glanced at Bethany, who raised both hands in a sign of surrender. "Yeah, not a conversation I'm going to get involved with. I wrestle with having value all the time. Let's eat instead."

They headed for the buffet. Wynn and Carol had brought desserts, Bethany unwrapped a fresh veggie plate, while Pallas had provided an herbal sun tea and minestrone soup.

"Everything looks so good," Silver said as they served themselves.

"That bread," Carol whispered. "It's the devil."

"That's what I said," Natalie told her with a grin. "And the Irish butter? Why does she hate us?"

Once they were seated, Natalie carefully waited until her friends started eating. Then she picked up her fork and said as casually as she could, "So, who blabbed about me wanting to have a baby and maybe looking for a sperm donor?"

Bethany dropped her spoon. "What on earth are you talking about? I was gone all of two weeks, visiting my family back in El Bahar, and you're getting a sperm donor? What else did I miss?"

"Nothing," Silver assured her. "Don't worry. Natalie only *thinks* she wants a sperm donor."

"Still, details, please."

Natalie filled her in on the baby app, then returned her attention to her other friends. "Well? I'm waiting. One or all of you said something to the world at large and I want to know who."

Pallas looked only a little guilty as she murmured, "Why do you ask?"

"Gee, I don't know. Some guy showed up to give me his résumé. He was interested in improving the species and wanted me to consider him as a sperm donor." She set her fork by her plate. "Who is the guilty one?"

Her friends looked at each other, then back at her. Wynn cleared her throat.

"I'm so sorry. I did mention you were considering having a baby, but only in passing. I mean, I told a few people in passing."

Natalie wanted to whimper. "A few?"

"I might have said something, too," Silver told her.

"Might have?"

"Okay, I did mention it. But only, like Wynn said, in passing."

"I didn't say anything to anyone," Bethany said, sounding glum. "Because I didn't know and I'm so disappointed by that."

Natalie looked at Carol and Pallas. Pallas continued to look guilty while Carol seemed more smug.

"I told Millie," Carol said, naming her favorite giraffe. "I don't know who Millie told but I'm pretty sure they weren't human."

"Oh. My. God! I thought I could trust you." Natalie did her best to glare at everyone. "You just randomly told strangers I was thinking of getting a sperm donor to have a baby?"

"I wouldn't say randomly," Wynn said, not looking the least bit repentant. "Now that you're talking about it, I can see how it might have been a mistake to, you know, assume."

"You think?"

Silver leaned toward Wynn. "She's not as mad as she wants us to think."

"Yes, I am," Natalie said. "I'm furious."

Even Carol looked doubtful.

"Maybe not furious, but come on. I have no idea what I'm going to do." Plus she'd only told them about the sperm donor to distract everyone from the conversation about Ronan. "It's a secret."

"I'm sorry I mentioned anything," Pallas told her. "I mean that. I didn't know it was a secret."

"Probably because I didn't tell you." Her mistake, she thought. "So from now on, no sperm donors."

Silver grinned. "If I had a nickel for every time a friend said that to me."

They all laughed.

"So what else is going on?" Natalie asked, ready to change the subject. Because Edgar was not suitable lunch conversation.

"I have an interesting wedding come up," Pallas said. "It's based on a movie. *Batman & Robin.* The movie is an older version of our favorite dark and dangerous hero," she added. "It was out in 1997."

Natalie knew about the franchise but wasn't familiar with that particular film. "I don't think I've seen it."

"Oh, I have and it's fun." Silver grinned. "It's the one with George Clooney. Chris O'Donnell plays his sidekick and Arnold Schwarzenegger is the main villain, but I like the Uma Thurman one better."

Wynn sighed. "I adore Chris O'Donnell in *NCIS: Los Angeles*. He's such a cutie."

"Someone is picking a movie theme for their wedding?" Carol asked, sounding doubtful. "A movie based on a comic book?"

"A lot of people want to do comic-themed weddings," Pallas said. "You'd be amazed what's available to order through various vendors. People are so creative." She turned to Natalie. "The details aren't all worked out, but I've talked to the bride and we have some preliminary ideas, which is where you come in."

"Me?"

Pallas nodded. "Do you remember that paper bouquet you made for me a couple of months ago?"

"Of course."

The bride had wanted something special for her rehearsal, and when Pallas had asked about making flowers using origami, Natalie had been all in. She'd created a bridal bouquet entirely out of paper, matching the colors of the paper flowers to the actual bouquet. The bride had been thrilled to have a keepsake of her special day and Natalie had enjoyed the challenge.

"What about doing a small arrangement of flowers out of comic book pages?" Pallas asked. "They would be for centerpieces rather than for a bridal bouquet."

Natalie sat back in her chair. "I never thought of using comic book paper as a medium. I get the point of it—all the drawings and the words would add shading. I'd have to feel the texture of the paper. Maybe a comic print on different paper. I'm not sure. But it's really a fun idea."

"She already has the vases." Pallas hesitated. "We're talking fifteen tables and maybe three vases at each table, so a total of forty-five bouquets. And you'd only have about five weeks."

"I'd need to see the vases to figure out if it's possible, and if it is, I'd like to work up a bid," Natalie said. "The size of the vase will determine the size of the flowers and how many each vase will need."

"I'll drop off a couple later today."

"Then I'll let you know if I can do it and how much it will be by first thing tomorrow."

"Thanks. I hope it works out. I know my bride would love your work."

And Natalie would love the chance to try something new. Um, something artistic. Edgar would be new and she definitely didn't want to try him!

CHAPTER TEN

RONAN FINISHED PUTTING away his equipment. It was nearly six and Natalie was still at her small workstation, surrounded by open boxes. He picked up his backpack and walked over.

"You're working late."

She glanced up as he spoke. Her glasses had slipped down her nose and it took a second for her eyes to focus. She looked rumpled, harried and sexier than should be legal.

"What? Is it late?" She glanced at the big clock on the wall. "Six? How did that happen? Last time I checked, it was barely three."

He smiled before bending down to kiss her. "Occupational hazard, gorgeous. Want to get some dinner?"

Her full lips turned up. "Did you just call me gorgeous?"

"Yes."

"That's so nice. I'm starving, so dinner would be..."

She drew in a breath, then squared her shoulders. “Thank you, but no. Rain check, please.”

“Sure, but why not tonight?”

“I have to work.” Her expression turned impish. “I got the job. I have to make eight flowers for each of the vases the bride sent. That’s forty-five vases times eight flowers.” Her brows drew together. “That’s, ah…”

“Three hundred and sixty flowers.”

“Ack! How did you do that in your head? And so fast.”

“It’s a penis thing.”

She rolled her eyes. “It has nothing to do with your penis. You have a mind for math. Girls can do math just as well as boys and they’re more highly verbal in their early years. Don’t you start with me and math, bucko.”

He chuckled and held up both hands. “I’m sorry. I was joking. Women are as capable as men at math and science and computer programming. I believe that down to my soul. I won’t mess with you on that topic again. I promise.”

So Natalie was a bit of a feminist. Good for her. He liked her sass and her attitude. She was tough and stood up to him. Back when he still believed he was pretty much like everyone else, he’d wanted to have a wife and kids. If he was still that guy, Natalie would be tough to resist. He could imagine having kids with her. No, not kids. *Daughters.* He would want them to be exactly like their mom.

“You called me bucko,” he added.

“I know. I’m sorry.”

He sat on the corner of her desk and picked up a

mason jar. It had a black heart painted on it. The one next to it had a bat.

"So this wedding is based on a comic book character?" he asked.

"No, a movie. *Batman & Robin.* It was out in the nineties. I haven't seen it."

"I'll download it for us, if you'd like."

"I would. Tomorrow for sure." She picked up the bat mason jar. "I'm going to have to put together a schedule to get everything done on time. I don't want to be rushing at the end. So many flowers a day or maybe a week."

"What's the appeal with the project? I thought you enjoyed creating your mixed-media pieces. Are you going in another direction?"

She studied him for a second before standing and kissing him. "You're sweet and so naive." She touched a finished flower. "I'm getting paid to do this."

"You have a job at the gallery."

"I have a *part-time* job at the gallery. That's my choice and Atsuko always lets me figure out my hours. There's one week a month where I have to be in the office more because we're paying the artists and doing bills and inventory. The rest of the time, I work maybe twenty hours a week. That almost keeps me in mac and cheese."

He didn't like the thought of her struggling to get by, but sensed he wasn't supposed to say that.

"You use the rest of your time for your art," he offered instead.

"Yes." She lightly kissed him again, her gentle touch

arousing him a lot more than he would guess she suspected.

"I don't mind struggling for my art, so to speak," she continued. "I have it better than most. I'm selling fairly steadily at the gallery. My prices are going up, so yay. These flowers will go in my portfolio and they'll pay my rent for the next two months. That makes me happy."

He wrapped his arms around her and held her close. Unexplained feelings battled inside of him. He supposed if he had to pick just one, it would be shame.

He'd never once had to struggle. Not financially. He was a Mitchell—son of the great Ceallach. Doors had been opened to him before he'd been born. There was an assumption that what he created was brilliant. All he had to do was not screw up too badly.

But what about Natalie? He wanted to write her a check for a few hundred thousand dollars and change her life. He wanted to tell Atsuko to sell her work for twenty times the price. He wanted to fix the problem. Only he couldn't. It wasn't his right and she wouldn't want him to.

"I'm happy you're happy," he said, careful to keep his tone upbeat. He kissed her one last time, then released her. "Don't work too late."

"I won't." She smiled. "Tomorrow for sure."

"It's a date."

"Will there be sex?"

Blood froze in place before heading to his dick. "I'd like that."

"Me, too. Dinner, sex and a movie."

Did she have to keep talking about it? He was getting harder by the second. The next twenty-four hours were going to be hell.

"Count me in," he told her, and started for the door. "I'll see you tomorrow."

"You will."

By the time Ronan made it up the mountain to his house, he was marginally less aroused. As long as he didn't think about Natalie too much, he might make it through the night without too much pain. He let himself inside, but instead of heading to the kitchen or his study, he walked through to the hallway leading to his studio, then went into the storeroom he'd had built.

After flipping on the light, he looked at the shelves and tables, all filled with his finished work. There were dozens of pieces, maybe over a hundred. Some were small enough to fit on the palm of his hand while others stretched nearly to the ceiling. There were abstracts, animals, people, plants and creatures that had never existed outside of his imagination.

Some were promised to Atsuko. They had a plan to release various collections over time—a way of keeping his work in the public eye while he worked on larger commissions. But others were simple things he'd made because he'd seen something in his head and had needed to get it out. And here they sat.

He walked down one aisle and up the other, passing various creations. He'd never much thought about his personal inventory—why it existed or what he should do with it.

He paused by a display of flowers and thought of

how Natalie was spending her evening—working hard so she could pay the rent. He picked up one of the glass blossoms. He could easily get ten thousand dollars for a single flower—how fair was that? How ridiculous?

He hesitated, thinking he could also drop it, shattering it into a million pieces, and what would it matter to anyone?

Natalie wouldn't do that, he told himself. She would sell it or use it for something, but she would never destroy it. He could learn from that.

He turned slowly, taking in the collection of his work, and knew he couldn't just let it sit here gathering dust. He had to do something with it. Something Natalie would respect.

He walked up and down again, this time taking pictures with his phone. When he'd chosen a dozen pieces, he sent Atsuko an email, telling her he wanted to talk. A dozen pieces for a dozen charities, he thought. They could auction them off or whatever. Use the money to make a difference.

Before he left the storeroom he returned to the display of flowers and picked out a black one in honor of Natalie's wedding project. That one he would give to his girl.

NATALIE CAREFULLY FILED the receipts. She had to pay extra attention because she was a little tired from her date night with Ronan. As promised, there had been dinner, sex, the movie and then more sex. She hadn't gotten much sleep, but was hardly in any condition to complain. Not when Ronan did those delicious things to her body.

She picked up an invoice for one of his pieces and opened the file cabinet drawer devoted to him and his work. While Atsuko kept her records digitally, she liked to have a paper backup. Natalie checked the item sold, then searched for the correct file. She found it up front and pulled it out to add the invoice. It was only when a second folder fell to the ground that she realized she'd grabbed two by mistake. The second one contained his personal information, including his address, tax ID info and his birthday.

Natalie quickly closed the folder—she didn't want to pry—then opened it again and looked at his birth date. It couldn't be right—she must have read the date wrong. Only she hadn't. His birthday was next week! How could she not have known that?

She put the folder back in the file drawer and continued her work all the while trying to figure out how that information could have not been public knowledge. She knew when Nick's and Mathias's birthdays were. Not that anyone made a big fuss but she usually created a custom card and brought in a cupcake. Something she'd never done for Ronan because she hadn't known the date.

When she finished her filing, she went back to the work studio. She happened to know that Ronan had a video conference call with a gallery owner in London that morning, something he would do from home, which meant she could talk to his brothers without him knowing.

She found Nick sketching at his desk while Mathias polished the edges of a new light fixture he'd made the previous day. They both looked up when she walked into the studio and said, "We have to talk."

"Sure," Nick said easily. "What's up?"

"Ronan's birthday. It's next week. I never knew the date, so I haven't ever made him a card or anything. We should do something."

Nick and Mathias exchanged a look. Natalie tried to figure out what they were thinking, but there was too much brother communication for her to decipher.

"We know when his birthday is," Nick told her. "As for doing something, Ronan's not really a party guy."

There was something about the way he spoke, she thought. Not the words as much as the tone. As if he was trying to warn her not to wade out too far into the emotional pool.

She knew that, until a few years ago, Mathias and Ronan had thought they were fraternal twins. To make that story work, they would have shared a birthday, only it wouldn't have been their *real* birthday—at least not for Ronan.

"You usually celebrate together," she breathed, staring at Mathias. "You and he probably planned the parties, or at least told your mom what you wanted. But that's been lost, too, along with everything else, and you haven't known what to do about it."

Mathias set down the light pendant and settled on a stool. "Maybe."

"Have you talked about your birthdays?" she asked.

"Talk?" Nick asked. "Right. You've met our other brother, haven't you? Ronan's not exactly a chatty guy."

She pulled up a third stool, took a seat and looked at Mathias. "What happened when he found out about who he was? Did he leave right away? Did you come up with a plan together?"

"There was no plan," Mathias told her. "He didn't say anything for weeks. I mean, anything. He didn't work, didn't do much of anything. Then one day he came to me and said he was leaving. He'd found a town where he wanted to live. Happily Inc. We'd sold a lot of our work through the gallery here. It's not a huge place, like a gallery in New York or Chicago, but Atsuko has connections."

Natalie nodded. She was forever shipping pieces all over the world or collecting payments from international clients.

"Did he ask you to go with him?" she asked.

"No. He gave me the information. What I did with it was up to me. But he was my twin, no matter what our father said, so I came with him." He hesitated. "At first it was okay. We rented a place together, and Atsuko gave us this studio so we could work. I thought we were going to go back to the way it had been."

Only they hadn't, she thought sadly. Ronan had started pulling away. She'd seen that when she'd started working here. How week after week he grew less and less communicative. How he wasn't working, or if he was, he worked from home.

"If he leaves again, we're going to lose him," Nick

said bluntly. "Mathias can't go with him this time. He's got Carol and everything else."

Of course, she thought. Mathias loved his wife and Carol was tied to Happily Inc. Her work was here and it wasn't as if the animal preserve could be packed up and moved.

"He's not going anywhere," she said quickly. "Why would he? His work is here, his family."

Me. Only she couldn't say that. She and Ronan weren't involved—not seriously. They were having fun. Even if she wanted more, it wasn't going to happen. She couldn't give her heart to someone she couldn't trust to treasure their connection as much as she did. He'd turned his back on his brothers and his mother. What if he decided to turn his back on her? On their children? She hated to admit it, but she and Ronan didn't have a future. She would enjoy what they had now and be careful to keep herself from getting too emotionally involved with him.

That sensible plan in place, she returned her attention to the conversation at hand. "Whether or not he's leaving isn't the issue. What about his birthday? His *actual* birthday. Have you ever celebrated it?"

Nick and Mathias looked at each other.

"I don't think so," Nick began before Mathias interrupted him.

"No. He never wanted to acknowledge it."

"Then that is going to change. We're going to have a party."

Mathias looked doubtful. "He's not going to like that."

"He's going to *say* he's not going to like it, but until he walks into the party, he won't really know, will he? We can have all his friends there. We'll have food and cake and silly presents. It will be great. You'll see."

Mathias didn't look convinced.

She stood and walked over to him, then poked him in the arm. "You owe me. When you had your mom's dog last year, I took care of her every single day. Every. Single. Day. You said that whatever I wanted from you was mine. Well, I want this."

Mathias muttered something under his breath. "You're right. We'll have a party."

She smiled. "I knew you'd see reason." She turned to Nick. "You're helping, too."

"You think I don't know that? Sure."

"Excellent. We'll celebrate Ronan's birthday and strengthen the family bond so he doesn't want to leave."

The brothers exchanged another one of those infuriatingly secret looks.

"What?" she demanded. "You know something. What is it?"

Mathias nodded and Nick spoke.

"We're way ahead of you, Natalie. On the brother front. Do you remember the poster at The Boardroom for the outdoor challenge?"

"I saw it. The activities are all outdoor, wilderness things. The proceeds go to a kids' summer camp."

"Nick signed us up," Mathias said. "The Mitchell brothers. All five of us. Del and Aidan are flying in for it."

She clapped her hands together. “That’s so great. You’ll have a blast. Does Ronan know?”

“Not exactly,” Mathias murmured. “He’s going to say no.”

She waved that away. “Tell him at the party. There will be a bunch of people around. It’s not like he can do anything in front of them.”

Nick chuckled. “I like your style.”

“Thank you. Now about the party…” She thought for a second. “We need a venue. His birthday is midweek, so we won’t be fighting with weddings. How about Weddings Out of the Box? I could organize everything so it wouldn’t be work for Pallas.”

Nick shook his head. “Not there. Let me call The Boardroom. They’ve got that big back room we could use.”

Before she could respond, Nick pulled out his phone and searched for the number. A few seconds later, he connected the call and put in the request.

“Done,” he said as he hung up. “We’re reserved. Now about the food.”

“I’ll go and arrange the menu,” she said. “Are we splitting the costs?”

“Nick and I will handle the money,” Mathias told her. “You pick whatever you want for food. We’ll do beer and wine.”

“You’re going to trust me without a budget?” she asked, a little surprised.

Mathias grinned. “Natalie, I’ve seen you squeeze a nickel fifteen times over. Yes, we trust you.”

"Mathias and I will put together a guest list," Nick said.

"Perfect." She thought about what else they would need. Ronan wouldn't want centerpieces, so that wasn't a problem. "What about a banner?"

"I'll go talk to Wynn," Mathias told her. "I have some ideas about what I want it to say."

"Okay, so we're all set." She glanced at her watch. "It's nearly lunch. I'll wait until the rush is over to go order the food." She smiled. "This is going to be fun."

"If nothing else, it will be interesting." Mathias looked at Nick. "Or a hell of a party."

"You got that right."

Natalie wasn't sure if the brothers meant that in a good way or a scary way, but she wasn't going to ask. She just wanted Ronan to know his birthday hadn't been forgotten. Everything after that was a bonus.

NATALIE BURST INTO the studio. Ronan was at his desk, studying sketches for the next segment in his commission. He hadn't yet started back to work from his lunch break, but was still surprised when she grabbed his hand and pulled him to his feet.

"Hurry! Hurry! It's time. He's here! We have to go now. I'm driving." She laughed. "I'm driving my shiny new red car. Come on!"

"I have no idea where we're going. And who is 'he'?"

She tugged him out of the studio and toward her car. "The new male giraffe. He's arriving. Carol said we could watch. We have to get there before him and we have to be really quiet. It's going to be magical. I wish it were June instead of September. June 23 is World Giraffe Day, but still. Come on!"

Ronan wondered if he should bother pointing out that he didn't actually *care* about said giraffe, but knew that would only disappoint Natalie. Plus he had to admit he was mildly curious about the great arrival. How exactly did one transport a giraffe?

He got into the passenger side of Natalie's car and took a second to check out the paint job. The work was excellent and the color made her happy—everything had turned out. Natalie had a safe car and one that was the right color. He didn't have to worry about her or feel guilty that her car had been swept over the side of his mountain. It was the definition of a win-win.

"Is this the first male giraffe?" he asked as she drove through town, then went south toward the animal preserve.

"Yes. When Millie got her herd last year, they were only girls. Male giraffes are generally solitary while female giraffes travel in a loose herd. With all the money she's raised, Carol has been able to expand and to start breeding the giraffes." Natalie glanced at him. "There are less than eighty-five hundred giraffes of Millie's species in the wild, which is really sad."

"It is."

"The new male is genetically compatible with all the females except for one. In the beginning, all the girls will be on birth control. They'll go off it one by one and he'll do his thing."

"Interesting life choice."

She glanced at him. "Oh, please. You're a guy. Are you saying you'd consider impregnating a herd tough duty?"

"Assuming I was a male giraffe? Probably not. But as a human male, I've never been into groups."

She turned into the preserve. "Not up for it, so to speak?"

He chuckled. "I'm more into quality than quantity."

"Good to know. Regardless, our new young man will have to wait for his chance at the girls. First he has to get settled."

She parked in the small parking lot. There were already several cars there and Ronan saw a group of people standing by a chain-link fence. Apparently they weren't the only ones coming to watch the new arrival.

He and Natalie walked over to join the group. The afternoon was warm, at least a hundred degrees. No doubt familiar temperatures for a giraffe. He recognized several people he knew from town. Nick and Pallas were already there, as was Mathias.

Nick raised his eyebrows. "Didn't think this was your kind of thing."

Ronan glanced at Natalie, then back at Nick. "I hear it's a once-in-a-lifetime opportunity and not to be missed."

Nick looked between them and seemed to put the pieces together. While Ronan hadn't cared if people knew he and Natalie were seeing each other, she'd wanted to keep things quiet, so he hadn't said anything. But in a town as small as Happily Inc, word was bound to get out. He knew his brothers wouldn't say anything to anyone but him and he was pretty sure he was in for a ribbing.

Not a problem, he thought. Natalie was more than worth it.

An older woman he didn't know walked over to him. "You're Ronan Mitchell," she said.

He didn't think she'd asked a question, but nodded. "Yes, ma'am."

"Uh-huh. I've seen your work in Atsuko's gallery. It's very expensive."

"It is."

She had salt-and-pepper hair and piercing black eyes. "You think you're worth that much?"

"Some days. Not others."

Her expression didn't shift for at least three seconds. Then she laughed and cuffed him on the arm. "I like that. We all have those days. I hear you're going to be using a car to decorate the bridge. You and your brother and Natalie here. I think it's a great idea. Real interesting. This town needs a little shaking up."

With that, she walked back to her group of friends. Ronan turned to Natalie. "Do you know who she is?"

"I haven't got a clue."

A low rumbling noise interrupted them. They both turned and saw the custom truck moving toward them. The cab was normal size but the back was overly tall, with canvas sides and a frame top. As they watched, the truck came to a stop.

Carol and several assistants walked over to talk to the driver. He turned the truck and backed it toward the enclosures. As the rig got closer, Ronan could see the upper back was open and a giraffe watched as he was moved closer to his new home.

"He's so handsome," Natalie said, grabbing his hand and squeezing his fingers. "I wonder if he has a name or if we get to name him. That would be fun."

She had a zest for life that impressed the hell out of him. Next to her, he was King Dour—something that had happened gradually.

Carol worked gates and portable fencing, creating a walkway for the giraffe. When everything was in place, she opened the rear door of the truck. The giraffe looked toward the enclosure, then at the people standing around, watching. He sniffed once or twice before cautiously stepping down the ramp. Once he reached solid ground, he walked more quickly and stepped right into his enclosure. Carol secured the gate behind him.

"He'll stay on his own for a couple of weeks," Natalie said. "Once he's comfortable, the other giraffes will spend time in stalls close to him so they can all get used to each other. Eventually they'll be able to roam around together."

"And have sex."

She rolled her eyes. "You are such a guy. Yes, they'll have sex and eventually we'll have baby giraffes. They're so cute. Have you seen videos of baby giraffes? They're totally adorable. So leggy and awkward." She sighed, then dropped his hand. "All right. Back to work."

He chuckled. "Way to break the mood."

"Did you need to cuddle?" she asked, her voice teasing.

"I don't know. It would have been nice, but never mind now."

She leaned close. "I'll make it up to you later. I promise."

Which was about all the inspiration he needed.

CHAPTER ELEVEN

HAPPILY INC WAS a destination wedding town. Several venues offered wedding parties the opportunity to fulfill their wildest marital fantasies—at least when it came to actually getting married. Hotels had theme rooms, there were emergency tailors and florists, not to mention officiants on the go. The bride and groom could choose to be cowboys, royalty, pirates or become legally bound in a hot-air balloon.

Natalie had discovered the unique rhythm of the town when she'd first decided to make the area her home. Locals learned not to expect to go out to dinner on the weekends and to avoid the center of town unless you wanted to get stuck behind a horse-drawn carriage.

The previous evening Pallas had texted and asked if Natalie could attend a planning meeting for the *Batman & Robin* movie-themed wedding. Natalie had agreed. As she parked outside of Weddings Out of the Box, she wondered what on earth she could add to the discussion. Still, her friend had asked, so here she was.

She found Pallas in the main conference room. There was a long table for client meetings and a large video screen and computer set up to work as a projector. Shelves and a buffet table had been set up along one wall displaying several small cakes, unopened shipping boxes of various sizes and stacks of linens.

"Hi," Natalie said, carrying in the two vases she'd filled with paper flowers. "Do you really go through all this with every wedding? It's so much work. I had no idea."

Pallas gave her a wan smile. "Some weddings are managed remotely, so we do video conferences instead of in-person ones, but Ellen and Barry live close enough that they want to be here." She pointed to the video screen. "Both sets of parents are tapping in via Skype. It's going to be a crowd."

Despite carefully applied makeup, Pallas seemed pale. Natalie frowned in concern. "Are you feeling all right?"

Pallas hesitated, then started to speak, but before she could say more than "I do want to—" they heard someone calling out to them.

Silver breezed into the conference room, pulling a cooler on wheels behind her. "Have you searched our comic book hero on Pinterest? I can't believe how many great ideas there are. People are so creative. I have too many possibilities for signature cocktails. Seriously, we need two, not twenty, but I'm having trouble choosing."

She hoisted the massive cooler onto the end of the table. "I figured the easiest way to decide is to sample."

Natalie glanced at the clock. It was ten minutes to

one in the afternoon. "I guess it's five o'clock somewhere."

Silver grinned. "Just take a sip of each cocktail, otherwise you'll be plastered."

"Not for me," Pallas said, placing a hand on her stomach. "I'm not feeling great. I'll pass on the liquor."

Silver shot her a concerned look. "I have some ginger ale with me. Want some?"

"That would be great."

Silver's gaze narrowed. "Pallas," she began.

Pallas shook her head. "Ellen and Barry will be here any second. Let's focus on that."

Natalie felt as if she were missing something, but before she could ask, the happy couple arrived.

They were both in their midthirties, on the tall side and a little chubby. They were also obviously wildly in love and totally excited about their wedding.

"My mother is texting me four hundred times a day," Ellen said as she hugged Pallas. "I think she was afraid I was never going to get married."

Barry kissed his bride's cheek. "That's because you were waiting for me."

"I was."

They gazed at each other as if they were the only people in the room. Natalie felt a little jolt of envy—oh, to be that much in love.

Pallas made introductions. Everyone took a seat at the table and Pallas got the connected parents up on the screen.

Natalie was impressed with how quickly her friend worked the technology. The split screen allowed everyone to see who was talking. When Pallas uploaded a picture from her computer, the screen divided into three parts, keeping everyone in the loop.

"We're here to make some decisions," Pallas said, opening her tablet and glancing at a very long list. "The sample cakes are here and Silver wants to talk signature drinks. Some of the favor samples have arrived. Natalie has flowers for you to look at. We're also going to brainstorm the rest of the details for the wedding and make sure our timeline still works."

Ellen sighed. "The flowers. Can I see them?"

Natalie passed over the mason jars filled with the comic book flowers. Both Ellen and Barry carefully touched the paper petals. Ellen beamed.

"They're stunning. You'll be able to make flowers for three vases for each table? Is that too much?"

"I have a schedule and I'm already ahead. So I'm glad you like what I've done."

"We don't like it," Barry told her. "We *love* it. You're a gifted artist."

Silver leaned close and whispered, "Could they be cuter? I don't think so."

Natalie smiled.

Pallas moved on to the rest of her list. "Just to clarify, the theme of this wedding is a specific movie. Not the comic books, not the rest of the franchise. So we're going to be true to those villains and the main characters." She glanced at her tablet. "The minister marrying you will be dressed as Alfred, is that right?"

Barry chuckled. "Yes, and he's superexcited about it."

Pallas confirmed that the wedding bands had been

ordered and were on time. The rings were platinum with inset round diamonds and black onyx in the shape of a bat. Ellen would wear a white eye mask and her shoes would have tiny bats on the heels. Barry had chosen a black tux with a yellow vest and tie. The bridesmaid dresses were black with yellow sashes around their waists.

"I let them pick their own dresses," Ellen said. "That way they can for sure wear them again. All I asked was that they could tie the sash on for the ceremony."

"That's a great idea," Natalie said. "I'll bet the sashes become something fun at the reception. Everyone will want to dance with them on."

"You're right." Ellen smiled at her. "I hadn't thought about that, but it's going to be true. We're having the groomsmen wear villain T-shirts under their dress shirts."

Okay, sure. Natalie had to admit that going all out for a movie-themed wedding wouldn't be what she would choose, but if Ellen and Barry wanted that, then they should have it.

"We need to brainstorm some ideas for the reception," Pallas said. "So far all the attention has been on the ceremony."

"I just saw the movie a couple of weeks ago," Natalie said. "I'll bet we could easily get a large print of the Gotham City skyline for one wall." She looked at Pallas. "Wynn could make that, couldn't she?"

Pallas typed on the computer and pulled up a picture of the city. "This is just one option. There are dozens of others. Ellen, do you want me to send you some to consider?"

"Barry and I will find the one we like best and send it to you," Ellen said, pulling a pad of paper out of her handbag. "I really like that idea."

"I'm going to have a lot of scraps of paper left over from the flowers." Natalie fingered the petal of a flower. "I wonder if I could create table numbers from them. It wouldn't be that difficult and it would keep with the theme. I could also edge the pages of the guest book with the same paper."

"Perfect," Barry said. "Now, we're doing the groom's cake in the shape of the car, right?"

"Yes, and today you'll pick the flavors of the two cakes." Pallas put up pictures of possible cake decorations. There were the obvious black and yellow and one cake was decorated with ivy, but the one Natalie liked best was more subtle—three round layers frosted in cream with the classic bat shape in a darker ivory.

"That one," Barry and Ellen said together, then laughed.

They all continued to brainstorm. Ellen's mother wanted a photo booth with a fun backdrop of words like *Wham!* and *Pow!* Natalie and Ellen had a long conversation about flowers, with the bride deciding on black and white calla lilies trimmed with ivy. Once all the decisions were made, the parents signed off and the bride and groom tasted cake and cocktails.

Three hours flew by. When Barry and Ellen had left, still talking drinks with Silver, Natalie stayed behind to help Pallas tidy up.

"That was amazing," Natalie said. "So much work, but really fun. I can see why you love what you do."

Pallas stunned her by sinking into a chair and dropping her head to the table. "I can't do it. I just can't."

"What's wrong?" Natalie settled next to her. "Tell me what it is and I'll fix it."

Pallas looked at her, her eyes filled with tears. "It's not bad, I swear. I'm thrilled, but I just can't keep doing this." She drew in a breath. "I'm pregnant."

"What? That's fabulous." Natalie hugged her. "You're going to have a baby. Why are you crying?"

"Because I'm exhausted. I've been sick since the first day. I can't sleep. The doctor says I'm perfectly healthy but that I'm having a horrible reaction to my body's changing hormones. She swears it will get better, but so far it hasn't and I'm drowning here." She tried to smile. "My mother is over the moon, which is its own kind of weirdness, but we don't have to discuss that."

She sniffed. "The weddings are too much. Especially this one. There are a thousand moving parts. I'm in the process of hiring an assistant, but that's going to take a while. Do you think you could help me for a few weeks until I have someone in place?"

"What? Of course. I'd be glad to." Natalie hesitated. "But, Pallas, I don't know anything about weddings."

"You did great today. You have excellent taste and people like you. That's a big one. So if you're willing, I'd love to hire you. And I do mean hire. I'd pay you for your time. I'm just so busy right now and I feel awful every second of every day."

Natalie hugged her friend again. "I'm yours to command. I mean that. I'll talk to Atsuko and see about shifting my hours so I can be available when you need me. I can make the flowers for the wedding at night or early in the morning. Seriously, I can do this."

"It's not too much?"

"No. It's just enough. I want to help."

Natalie was happy to be there for her friend, but just as exciting was the thought of extra income. If she added the money she earned helping Pallas to what she made from the flowers, she might have enough to take a two- or three-week sabbatical from her day job, *and* have two or three months of paid rent. That would allow her to focus on one or two big art projects and wouldn't that be amazing!

"You're the best," Pallas told her. "I don't know how to thank you."

"We're both the best and this is going to be so much fun."

RONAN DIDN'T KNOW why everyone had a burr up their ass about his birthday. When Mathias had told him about the party, his first instinct had been to say, "Hell, no." The problem with that was Natalie had been standing right there, looking all happy and excited, and he just couldn't figure out how to disappoint her. Which was why he was now stuck going to The Boardroom for some ridiculous party that he wasn't going to enjoy.

He'd spent the day working from home so he could shower and change before driving into town. He was going to meet Natalie at the gallery and then walk over with her. At least she would be a distraction, he thought. A sexy one, but still. A party?

He had no idea who was going to be there. He supposed if things got awkward with his brothers, he would just mention Pallas's pregnancy and that would change the subject.

He got in his truck and started down the mountain. He still couldn't believe Nick was going to be a father. Elaine must have been giddy at the thought of a grandkid. He doubted Ceallach would care—not unless his grandchild showed artistic ability. As for Nick, Ronan figured he had to be two parts terrified, one part thrilled.

At one time Ronan had assumed he would have children. That he would be a typical guy, not doing enough around the house and spoiling the kids when their mom wasn't looking. He'd never thought much past that—hadn't considered who the woman might be or how many children he wanted. There had always been time. All that had changed with his father's revelation. He no longer knew who he was or trusted himself enough to have kids. That required more faith than he could muster.

He drove through town to the gallery. Natalie was waiting for him outside, practically dancing with excitement in the warm evening air. She was always so happy, he thought, feeling his tension ease. So positive and sure. And beautiful. She had on some kind of floaty dress that fell to midcalf. The colors ranged from yellow to orange to red. Her hair was loose and curly and she was smiling long before he got out of the truck.

"You made it!" she said, rushing toward him. "I

was afraid you'd come up with an excuse to duck out of the party."

"Would I do that?" he asked before he kissed her.

"In a hot minute." She gazed into his eyes. "Happy birthday. Your present is already at The Boardroom. I hope you like the food. I chose it and think I got all your favorites." She raised herself on tiptoe and kissed his mouth. "You're not mad, are you?"

"About the kissing? No. I kind of like the kissing."

"About the *party.* You didn't tell anyone it was your birthday."

"Maybe no one asked."

She sighed. "You're going to be difficult, aren't you?"

"Maybe a little."

She linked her arm through his. "That's okay. We're celebrating the birth of you. Difficult is allowed. Come on. Let's get going. I hear there's going to be cake."

Whatever irritation he'd been feeling had disappeared the second she'd started talking. He had no idea how she did that, but it was an impressive gift. With Natalie around, the darkness wasn't so grim and the good parts were even better.

"Where did you go for fun back in Fool's Gold?" she asked. "Was there a place like The Boardroom?"

"There was a bar called The Man Cave, but it opened after Mathias and I left. Despite its name and its affinity for all things male, women were welcome. Nick used to bartend there."

"What? Why?"

"He avoided his art for a while. Things were complicated."

"With your father." She leaned in closer. "I know it's wrong, but I really don't like him."

"Me, either. He has a lot to answer for." Ceallach had managed to screw up all his sons. Despite that, each of them had found happiness. Not him, but the others.

"Did you like where you grew up?" she asked. "You must have. You moved from one small town to another."

"Fool's Gold is interesting. The entire year of the town is defined by the various seasonal festivals. There are casserole cook-offs and parades and bazaars. They have an elephant now. Priscilla." He frowned. "I don't know exactly how she came to be in town, but she's much loved. Her best friend is a pony."

"We have giraffes," Natalie told him. "That's better."

He chuckled. "It's not a competition."

"It is to me. I'm Team Happily Inc all the way."

"You'd like Fool's Gold. We have the longest serving mayor in California history. Mayor Marsha knows all. It's kind of spooky, but also oddly comforting. Our house was just outside of the main part of town, on the edge of the forest. My brothers and I had acres for our playground. In the summer, we barely spent a second inside. One year Mathias, Nick and I built a fort in some trees. I looked at it a few years ago when we were home for a visit. It's a rickety thing. We're lucky it didn't fall apart and send us crashing to the ground.

Whenever our father got in one of his moods, we disappeared. We had a few places we could go to get food."

"Like where?"

"Neighbors. A couple of restaurants in town would take care of us. I'm sure they sent a bill back to Elaine and my dad."

Natalie made a little noise.

"What?" he asked.

"You do that. You call your mom Elaine."

"She's not my mother."

"She didn't give birth to you but she raised you. Of course she's your mother."

She lied to me. Ronan didn't say the words, but he thought them. Ceallach's deception had been understandable. His father was a narcissist who only thought of himself, but Elaine was supposed to have been different. He was supposed to be able to trust her.

Natalie sighed. "Sorry. It's your birthday. You get to be a butthead if you want."

"Thank you."

"You're not mad I called you a butthead?"

"Nope."

She snuggled close again. "You're the best boyfriend ever."

"Thanks."

They reached The Boardroom. The lights were on, the doors open and the sound of music drifted out. Ronan knew the party for him was in back, in the private room. He thought briefly of bolting, but knew that would disappoint Natalie. Instead he braced himself before following her through the main area and down a short hall. Another door stood open and he could see about thirty people inside.

"Ronan! Happy birthday."

People cheered and called out greetings as they entered. Nick approached and slapped him on the back. Mathias did the same. Ronan was about to say something when he caught sight of the banner on the wall.

Happy Birthday, Ronan and Mathias

Ronan glanced at his former twin. "What's up with that?"

Mathias sipped his beer. "We celebrated on my birthday for the first twenty-four years of our lives. I figure we'll celebrate on yours for the next twenty-four, then split the difference until one of us is dead."

Their gazes locked. Ronan allowed himself to remember what it had been like to really be a twin—half of an important whole. Back then he'd known what he wanted and who he was. Life had been a lot less complicated.

"Good plan," he said with a grin. "Plus, I'll outlive you."

"You wish."

More people joined them. Ronan got a beer and saw Atsuko had brought a date—a much younger blond man who looked at her as if she were the only woman alive. Carol's father and uncle—Ed and Ted—had shown up, along with several of Ronan's interns. There was a pile of presents in one corner and a buffet set out along the back wall.

Ronan excused himself to find Natalie. She was talking to a very pale Pallas.

"How are you feeling?" he asked his sister-in-law.

She waved her glass. "Living on ginger ale and crackers," she said. "The diet of champions. Or in my case, pregnant women. Happy birthday." She took a sip. "Did I know you two were dating?"

Natalie shrugged. "I'm not sure. Did you?"

Pallas groaned. "I'm in a weakened state. Please don't mess with my already shaky mental ability."

Natalie glanced at him, then turned back to her friend. "It's casual. We weren't going to mention it, but people seem to have found out."

Ronan wasn't sure he liked the description of "casual" but he was in no position to correct her.

"You make a cute couple," Pallas said. "Unexpected, but cute."

He wondered what was unexpected about them. They were both artists and had other similar interests. He supposed Pallas's surprise came from the fact that Natalie was so cheerful and always saw the positive in every situation where he did not.

Nick and Mathias joined them. "How are you enjoying the party?" Nick asked.

"It's great," he lied, although he was having a better time than he'd expected. Most likely because he was with Natalie.

"We're signed up for the outdoor charity challenge next month. You probably saw the signs out front. It'll be the five of us."

The information processed slowly. Ronan had seen

the signs—the outdoor challenge was a charity event with everything from a 5K to a tug-of-war. He had no problem with the individual events. It was the team that got his attention.

What five was the obvious question, only he had a feeling he already knew the answer.

"Del and Aidan flying in?" he asked instead.

"Yup. Mitchell brothers rule."

Nick's gaze was steady, his tone firm, as if he was doing his damnedest to make sure Ronan knew there was no getting out of this. That he was one of the brothers and expected to attend.

Ronan glanced toward the door and thought longingly of his solitary house on the mountain. How he could be alone there and happy to be so. Only being on his own hadn't been all that successful for him. He'd stopped working and he'd been lonely. He reminded himself that the best times of his life had been spent with his brothers. He should be grateful Nick was being a hard-ass about the whole thing.

"I'm in," he said quickly before he could change his mind.

His brother relaxed. "Awesome. I'll let the others know."

Natalie moved next to him and smiled. "We're going to start the dart competition in a few minutes. Want to be on my team?"

He looked into her brown eyes and saw smug confidence. "Let me guess. You're as good at darts as you are at flying paper airplanes."

"It's kind of the same thing. Aim and throw."

He put his arm around her. "You have unexpected depths."

"I know. Makes me pretty irresistible."

She was teasing, but he knew there was truth to her words. And while she was a temptation, she was one he was going to have to resist. What they were doing was fine. Anything more would cross the line…for both of them.

CHAPTER TWELVE

NATALIE WAS DEFINITELY feeling her wine. She'd had a great time at Ronan's birthday party, but even more important, *he'd* enjoyed himself, as well. She'd kicked his manly butt at darts, had watched him talk and laugh with his brothers, and then when the night had gotten late, Ronan had pulled her close and they'd danced. She was tipsy, tired and totally happy.

Ronan held her hand as they walked back to the gallery where they'd parked their cars. She was going to ask him to drive her home—there was no way she wanted to drive and it was a little too far for her to walk. She knew she needed the exercise, but the thought of getting home and just sliding into bed was way more appealing.

"What?" he asked as they crossed the street. "You're smiling."

"You had a good time."

"I did. You were right about the party."

"Ha!"

He chuckled. “I didn’t want to go and you said I had to and you were right.”

“Double ha! See? You like hanging out with people. You’re practically normal.”

“Practically.”

She laughed. “There’s still some work to do, but progress has been made.”

“You think you’re so smart.”

“I am so smart, and you have a great family. Nick and Mathias are the best. I don’t know Del and Aidan, but I’m sure they’re just as wonderful. You’re lucky.”

Some emotion she couldn’t name moved across his face and the humor faded from his eyes.

“What are you thinking?” she asked.

He shrugged. “When I was a kid, I always thought I took after Elaine.”

“You mean *your mother*?”

He ignored her. “I thought I had her sense of humor and that we thought the same way. I was wrong.”

“You weren’t.”

They reached the gallery. She turned to face him. Despite the late hour, the streetlights illuminated the parking lot.

“You weren’t wrong,” she repeated. “You have to see that. What you saw in yourself was a reflection of the woman who raised you. You saw her love and responded to it.”

“She lied to me.”

“She did what she thought was best under difficult circumstances. Honestly, you have got to get over this. You’re being ridiculous. Worse, you’re hurting her. Elaine's big crime is taking you in and loving you like one of her own. Boo hoo."

His expression tightened. "She lied about who I was and our relationship every day of my life. I have no idea who I really am. All I have is my father, and trust me, you don't want a man like Ceallach Mitchell to be all you are."

"You're nothing like your father." She put her hands on her hips and glared at him. Annoyance was turning into genuine anger—an unusual occurrence for her.

"I see you every day, Ronan. You're a good guy. You love your brothers. You do great work. You're not mean or cruel or any of those things. Get over yourself. So you have a bit of a mystery in your past. It doesn't have to be the end of the world."

She narrowed her gaze. "The reason you're having all the trouble you are is that you've cut yourself off from the one person you loved most in the world. You've cut yourself off from the woman who loved you and raised you. You have this stupid idea that just because she didn't push you out of her vagina, she's not your mother. Well, I have news for you. Adoption is a totally viable way of raising a kid."

She turned her back on him, walked away three steps, then faced him again. "You know what? You're lucky. Elaine could have said, 'Hell, no,' when she found out about her husband's affair and the fact that there was a kid. Most women would have. Then you would have been thrown into the foster care system and who knows what would have happened to you. Instead you were taken in and raised as one of her own.

According to Nick and Mathias, everyone thought you were the favorite. How is that bad? How?"

Her voice was a little louder than usual, but she no longer cared.

Ronan looked away. "You don't understand."

"You're right." She walked up to him and poked him in the chest. "I don't understand. I don't and I never will. You know why? Because you still have family. You still have people who love you. You still have a mother."

Tears burned in her eyes. "I lost mine. She was my best friend, my only family, and I lost her. My dad was killed before I was born, so she was all I had. And then she was gone. You have no idea what that was like. I thought we were going to have another fifty years, but she got sick and then she died and I was totally alone. When I met Quentin, I thought I was going to be part of a family again. In fact, it was just as hard to lose that, when he dumped me, as to lose him. I thought I was going to have it all and I ended up with nothing. I don't have family and that's what I can't forgive. You have everything."

She brushed away tears. "I got over Quentin but I will never get over losing my mom. Do you know what I would give to have just one day with her? One day. Ten years of my life. Twenty. The rest of it. Just one day to talk to her and hold her and see her s-smile at me."

Sobs clawed at her throat, but she held them back. "Damn you, Ronan. How dare you not appreciate what you have. You aren't the only one who has lost something. Everyone has. It's part of the human condition.

You could make this right. You could call her and make it right, but you'd rather sulk and pity yourself. The world doesn't revolve around you. Stop acting like it does."

She wiped away her tears. Ronan stared at her, obviously shocked by her outburst. Well, fine. She was pissed and he deserved what she'd said.

"It's all true. Every word and you know it." She sucked in a breath. "I can't be with you right now. I'm going to walk home. Just leave me alone."

"Natalie, no. It's late. I'll drive you."

She rolled her eyes. "It's Happily Inc. Nothing's going to happen to me. Just go away."

She turned and started walking. All sleepiness had faded. Anger gave her energy and purpose. She supposed she should feel bad about what she'd said, but she didn't. Ronan deserved that and more. When she thought about losing her mom and how horrible that had been, she nearly wanted to slap him. He was being selfish and shortsighted. He didn't know how lucky he was.

About halfway to her apartment, she became aware of his truck a block or so behind her, keeping pace. Because he wanted to make sure she was safe.

She thought about stopping and telling him she would really rather he left her alone and called his mother instead, but she didn't. She kept walking, and when she reached her place, she went inside without once looking back.

After washing her face and changing into pajamas,

she went into her small bedroom and sat on the floor. She pulled a box out from under the bed and opened it.

Inside were photographs of her with her mother or her mom by herself, including one picture of her mother as a bride, standing next to the father Natalie had never known.

He was a mystery to her. A figure she'd only heard about. She supposed she should miss him as well as her mom, but he was little more than a concept. Her mother had been real.

Natalie turned back to the box. There were a few pieces of jewelry, some favorite paintbrushes and the Kaleta family Bible, along with a beautifully embroidered shrug her mother had worn whenever she wanted to feel "fancy" and a tube of her favorite lipstick. Silly things, items that would have no value to anyone else. Natalie picked up the pictures and looked through them until the tears filling her eyes made it impossible to see anything. Still crying, she put them back in the box before curling up on the floor and sobbing for the one person who couldn't be with her anymore.

RONAN DIDN'T SLEEP at all. He tried for about an hour, then gave up and went into his studio. Not that he could work by himself. Anything he was doing for his commission required multiple hands and even he wasn't enough of an asshole to call up his assistants at two in the morning.

He paced for a while, then went into the kitchen and made coffee, but that wasn't an escape. He could remember what it had been like to have Natalie in his house. How easy she'd made everything. How even now he could see her everywhere.

He'd never thought of her as touched by tragedy. Her story had shocked him. He'd known she lost her mother but hadn't considered the event had been traumatic. She'd never talked about missing her, not the way she had tonight—he'd had no idea she'd suffered that much. She was so upbeat and happy all the time, yet underneath, she had her pain. Why hadn't he known that before?

He'd hurt her, he thought as he carried his coffee back into the studio. Not directly, but she felt pain all the same. She thought he was wrong and unappreciative. She could be right about both—he didn't know. But he did get that he had to make things better, not that he had a clue as to how.

He waited for the oven to get hot enough, then chose his materials. He had another of her origami pieces on his desk—a tiny lion—and studied it before trying to re-create it in glass. The sun was well above the horizon by the time he'd completed what he thought was a halfway decent piece. Then he went into the house to shower.

He got to the office close to noon and parked next to her shiny red car. It was only after he'd gotten out of his truck that he realized unless Natalie had called someone she would have been forced to walk to work. Something else he would have to answer for, he thought grimly.

He found her sitting at her desk. She looked pale and her eyes were puffy, as if she'd spent much of the night crying. As she looked up at him, he found himself hoping she wouldn't apologize. She hadn't done anything wrong.

He couldn't agree with her about Elaine, but he thought he understood how the situation would push her buttons. As for appreciating what he had, when it came to his brothers, he knew she was right. They'd always been there for him and he'd spent the last couple of years being a jackass. All five of them had been lied to and Mathias had lost being a twin. Ronan wasn't the only brother to have to deal with Ceallach's crap.

"You're late," she said by way of greeting. "It's nearly lunchtime. Do you really think you can come and go as you please?"

Her gaze was steady and he had no idea what she was thinking.

"Yes," he told her. "I'm not an employee."

"You have all the luck."

He set the small glass lion on her desk. "I'm going to do better. It's an interesting challenge. This is the best one I have for now. You still mad?"

She picked up the tiny piece of glass and put it on her palm. "I was never mad."

"You acted mad."

She stood and crossed to the shelf behind her desk. There were over a dozen small origami shapes there and the other piece of glass he'd made for her. She set this one next to it before turning toward him.

"We're going to have to agree to disagree."

"Can you do that?" he asked.

"Yes. Mostly. I'm sad about my mom."

"I know. I'm sorry for what you went through. I'm sorry she's gone. I understand that you miss her."

"More than miss her."

He nodded, not sure what else to say. "I'm sorry I upset you and I'm sorry I don't appreciate what you think I have."

"What I think you have? Meaning you don't agree with the premise?"

"Elaine is not my mother."

"You're a stupid butthead." She sighed. "But it's not my rock, so I'm going to put it down now. I believe in my heart of hearts you are as wrong as it is possible to be. You live in wrongness about your mom. You wallow in it. But it's your decision to make."

"Even if I'm wrong?"

Her gaze was steady, her expression serious. "Yes. Even if."

"So you still like me?"

"Sort of."

"Are we still…together?"

A question he hadn't planned on asking, but as he spoke the words, he felt a tension in his gut. He didn't want to lose Natalie. He liked having her around. He liked *her* and them and how things were now, as opposed to how they'd been before she'd stumbled into his life.

She walked around the desk, wrapped her arms around his waist and rested her head on his chest. He held her close, breathing in the scent of her.

"You're not easy," she whispered.

"I know."

"I'm still upset."

"I know."

"But I'm not going anywhere."

Relief was cool and sweet and happy. The bands around his chest eased as he took his first deep breath in hours.

"Thank you."

THE FLOWERS ARRIVED close to three o'clock. Natalie stared at the huge arrangement of roses, lilies, cymbidium orchids and hydrangea that stood nearly two feet high. The blooms were fresh and colorful but what most caught her attention was the vase. It was a swirl of clear and silver glass she didn't think had been sitting on the florist's shelf. She had a feeling it was a custom piece made by a famous glass artist and worth, well, way more than her car!

When her breathing returned to normal, she sank into her chair and touched one of the petals. No one had ever sent her flowers before. Not Quentin or any other boyfriend. She had always supposed she wasn't the type of woman to inspire flower-giving. At least she hadn't been before now, and wasn't it odd that despite the value of the vase, the flowers were even more special?

There was a small card tucked in with the blooms. She opened it and read the single word. *Tonight?* She recognized the handwriting and knew Ronan had written the card himself. Probably when he'd delivered the vase.

She knew nothing had changed. Ronan still didn't

appreciate what he had and she still didn't understand. The question was, could she overlook that? She supposed she already had, in a way. She understood that each of them had a different path to travel. That his inability to see what he was turning his back on made him who he was. That even though she wanted to change him, she really couldn't—he could only change himself.

On the other hand, progress had been made. He was less isolated than he had been and he was working again. While she would love to take credit for all of that, the truth was *he'd* made the decision to let her in. He could have offered her housing during the storm and then have had nothing to do with her. At least he wasn't cutting himself off from his brothers anymore.

She thought about what had happened the previous night and how upset she'd been. She thought about how much she cared about him and wished, just for a second, that she could see a future for them together. That she was one of the lucky people who could fall in love and know it would last. Then she went into the studio where she found the three brothers working on a large piece of glass together.

She waited until it had been set aside to cool before walking over to Ronan. He pulled off his protective goggles.

"Thank you for the flowers," she said softly so his brothers couldn't hear.

"You're welcome."

"Want me to come over tonight?"

Passion and relief flared in his eyes. "Yes."

"Want me to spend the night?"

"Yes."

"Want to cook?"

He grinned. "I'm not trusting you in the kitchen by yourself."

"You're judging me."

"More than a little."

She raised herself on tiptoe and kissed him. "I'll see you around six."

"I'll be there."

NATALIE DROVE UP the mountain, her zippy little car taking the steep grade with no problem. She felt more centered than she had since her argument with Ronan—happier. Yes, there had been loss, but she knew how to miss her mom and live her life.

When she pulled into the driveway, anticipation hummed through her body. She enjoyed spending time with Ronan. They never seemed to run out of things to say. There was the added anticipation of what they would do after dinner. Ronan was nothing if not thorough when it came to pleasing her.

She was still smiling as she got out of her car and pulled a small tote bag from the back seat. She'd packed a nightgown and a few skin-care items. She had her work clothes on a hanger. It would be easier to just get ready at his place and go directly into the office.

She'd barely reached for her clothes when she felt a strong hand settle on her waist. She turned and Ronan kissed her, his mouth warm and tender against her own.

"Hey," he said, nibbling along her jaw, then dipping

to her collarbone. "I'm thinking steaks and baked potato and wine, then maybe a brandy by the fire pit."

"A man with a plan. What's not to like?"

He kissed her again, lingering this time, before taking her clothes and tote and leading her into the house.

She paused in the foyer to enjoy the welcoming atmosphere. She loved everything about the house. The lines of it, the hidden studio, the light. He'd chosen well, she thought, following him to the master bedroom.

There was a surprise waiting in the walk-in closet. He'd cleared out several feet of hanging space.

"In case you want to leave stuff here," he said, sounding both proud and bashful. "There are drawers, too."

Because the massive closet had two built-in dressers. The left one was filled with briefs and socks and some brightly colored boxers, but the one on the right was empty.

There was more space for her in the big master bath. The his-and-her vanities were separated by the big shower. He used the vanity with less counter space, leaving the other one for her.

She didn't know exactly what he was trying to tell her. They'd both agreed this wasn't going to be permanent, that they were enjoying each other for the moment. Still, he'd gone out of his way to make her feel welcome and special, and she appreciated that.

"Next time I'll bring more," she said, setting her tote on the bathroom counter. "Thank you for this. I would have been happy with a single drawer."

"Now you can be even happier."

They went into the kitchen. Ronan had already pulled the steaks out of the refrigerator and made the salad. There was some kind of delicious-looking potato casserole ready to put in the oven and a bottle of red wine on the island.

"How is it working with Pallas?" he asked as he poured the wine. "She seems like she has it all together."

"She does. She has different computer applications for the various parts of the wedding that all break down into the tiniest detail. You can pull up everything from wine selections to napkin colors. There's a whole section on who can't sit together at the reception. Then she has a master program that pulls it all together. She runs the whole thing on an interconnected computer-tablet magical mind meld I can't begin to understand. It's impressive and a little scary."

"Maybe she can help you with your baby app," he teased. "You don't seem to be making much progress."

"Uh-huh. Because you want me interviewing potential sperm donors."

"I wouldn't mind if I could be there and ask questions, as well."

She grinned. "I can only imagine what you would ask. Besides, I've let that go for now. We're having a good time and me getting pregnant would mess up everything."

He looked at her for a second, then grinned. "Probably a good decision."

The evening passed quickly. They finished dinner

and sat outside by the roaring fire pit before heading upstairs. After they made love, Natalie lay in the dark, enjoying the tingles and zings that were a testament to the things the man could do to her body.

This was good, she thought, listening to his steady breathing. Being with Ronan. He was so kind and affectionate. He took care of her. She loved how talented he was and that he was reconnecting with his brothers. Everything was perfect. Everything except…

She wanted more. There, she'd thought it. She wanted what everyone else had—love and hope and a future. She wanted him to fall head over heels for her and she wanted to feel the same way. She wanted to believe it could be forever—that he would always be there. She wanted to know they could have a future. Only they couldn't. He still thought he didn't know who he was. He would never give over his heart as long as he truly believed he might one day wake up and be Ceallach and she could never trust him not to pull his heart back from her.

If only it could be different. If *they* were different. She wanted so much with him. She touched her belly and wished there was no baby app, just the promise of a family in a few years. Not that she had to worry about that now. Ronan always used a condom and she was—

Natalie sat up in the dark. Ronan stirred but didn't wake, thank goodness, because there was no way for her to act normal. Not now, maybe not ever. She wasn't on anything. No birth control. No pill, no IUD, no whatever else there was. She was on nothing.

She hadn't been with anyone since her broken engagement—there hadn't been much of a reason. And since she and Ronan had started hanging out, she hadn't once thought, *Birth control.* Although she should have.

She got out of bed and walked into the kitchen, where she pulled out her phone and pushed the button to bring up her calendar. When had she last had her period? Four weeks ago? Five? S-six?

Fear gripped her. Fear and terror and dread and a sinking sensation that made her a little sick to her stomach. She was late. Maybe by as much as two weeks. She was *never* late. Never, never, never. She clutched her phone, closed her eyes and repeated words women had been praying since the dawn of time.

"Please, God, don't let me be pregnant."

CHAPTER THIRTEEN

NATALIE WAS RULED by fear for three days. She knew that she could put herself out of her misery by simply taking a pregnancy test, but she didn't want to. Seeing the answer, if it was positive, would change everything. She would rather be scared and not know than have the truth confirmed. Because if she was pregnant…

"Don't go there," she murmured to herself as she finished logging in several new art pieces for the gallery.

She glanced at the clock and saw it was close to noon, then grabbed her phone and texted Silver.

You around? Can I talk to you?

Silver texted back almost immediately. Sure. I'm at home. Want to come by?

Natalie replied that she would be there in five minutes, then grabbed her bag and headed for the door.

"Hi." Silver let her in. "You okay?"

"No. We have to talk. Can we go upstairs?"

"Sure."

Silver locked the front door and led the way up to the second-floor loft apartment. They sat at the table and chairs by the window. Silver looked more curious than concerned.

"Do you want something to drink? Water? Tea? Vodka?"

Natalie tried to smile but failed. She'd been pretty much holding it together until right this second. Suddenly she desperately missed her mother and wanted to break into tears.

"No, thanks," she murmured as she struggled for control. "I'm sorry to barge in like this but I didn't know what else to do. I'm a mess."

"I can see that. What's wrong?"

"Remember when I went up the mountain to Ronan's house and got stuck for those several days?"

"Uh-huh."

"Ronan and I really got to know each other. He's great, you know. He's a bit of a brooding artist, but less than you'd think. And he cooks. He can pull a meal together better than I can. It's kind of—"

"Natalie, honey, get to the point. And if that point is to tell me that you and Ronan are seeing each other, the whole town already knows."

Natalie swallowed. "It's not that."

"Then what is it?"

"We've been sleeping together and I have that stupid baby app and he knows about it and he used a condom, but I'm not on anything because there hasn't been a guy in like forever and I didn't think I was anywhere close to breaking my losing streak but now we are and I didn't even think about birth control until a few nights ago and I'm afraid it might be too late because my period is late and I'm terrified I'm pregnant and that will ruin everything."

She had more she wanted to say, but she'd run out of air and had to stop to suck in a breath.

Silver's expression was more kind than anything else. "That's a lot."

"I know, right?"

"The baby app is a complication but I doubt Ronan will think you got pregnant on purpose. Finding out you're pregnant can be a life changer. That I know for sure." Her gaze sharpened. "Wait—your period is late, but you don't know if you're pregnant or not?"

"I haven't taken the test."

"Why not?"

"I don't want to know."

Silver smiled. "That's mature. You do realize that your pregnancy exists or doesn't exist, regardless of the results. Finding out for sure won't change the biology of it all."

"I know, but once I have the information, I have to deal with it. I'm not ready for that. I enjoy living in blissful ignorance."

"I'm going to lovingly disagree. If you enjoyed it you wouldn't be over here, freaking out."

Natalie wanted to say she wasn't even close to freaking out but got her friend's point. "I'm scared. I really like Ronan and being pregnant with his baby will ruin everything. I don't know that he'll assume I trapped him, but he won't be happy. How can I not be on birth control?"

"How could he not ask if you were?"

Natalie brightened. "You're right. He should have asked. So that's something I can throw in his face, but still. At the end of the day, I'm the one having the baby, not him."

"How long do you plan to ignore the problem?"

"I don't know. A few more days." She brightened. "If I don't get my period before Saturday, I'll take a pregnancy test then."

"It's only Tuesday. That's a long time to live in uncertainty. I'd want to know right away."

There was something in the way she made the statement. Had Silver gone through something similar?

No, she told herself. Silver was strong and self-actualized. She would never make that kind of mistake. Silver had her own business and controlled her destiny. Natalie was the only idiot in the room.

"I can wait."

"Then you have your answer." Silver studied her. "You're going to keep the baby, aren't you?"

"If I'm pregnant? Of course. I wouldn't give it up. I'm capable of being a single parent."

She wasn't exactly sure how but she had the memories of how great her mother had been with her. Surely she could learn from that excellent example. Plus, she had friends. Pallas was pregnant. They could go through it together. Only Pallas was sick all the time. Natalie really hoped that didn't happen to her.

"Is Ronan capable of being a father?" Silver asked. "Like you said, he's a bit of a brooding artist. Honestly, I don't get the appeal. Give me a normal guy who enjoys sports and I'm all in."

"You're so lying. You don't get serious about anyone."

Silver chuckled. "You're right—I don't. So what about Ronan? You said getting pregnant would ruin everything."

"It would. I don't even know how I would tell him. He's convinced he's like a bad seed or something because of who he is."

"Or who he's not," Silver added. "I know the story. His dad is a total dick. Remember how he was at the giraffe fundraiser last year? He wanted all the attention on himself. With a father like that, any guy would be concerned that he wasn't—" She made a strangled noise in her throat. "Now you have me doing it."

"Doing what?"

"Talking about a future that doesn't exist." She pointed at Natalie. "We don't know that you're pregnant. You might be reacting to stress, or sex. You used condoms, so it's not like there was nothing protecting you. Chances are, you're fine."

"You're so rational. It's upsetting."

"Would you prefer I panicked?"

"A little. I'd feel like you were more like me."

"Fine. Let's assume you are pregnant. If you are, what do you really want?"

Natalie didn't have to consider the question. The answer came to her without warning. *Ronan.* The image was so vivid, so real, she nearly gasped. No, not him, she told herself. Wanting him in her future would mean she'd fallen for him.

She searched frantically for something else to say only to have Silver roll her eyes.

"You obviously thought of something that made you go pale. What is it?"

"Nothing. I, ah, miss my mom."

"Really? I'm sure you do miss her, but you are so lying. It's Ronan, isn't it? You were wishing that it was real."

Natalie opened her mouth, then closed it. "No. Maybe. I guess. Yes, but could it be? I'm, um…" She searched for a plausible lie because the truth was too humiliating. "Oh, I'm unlucky in love!" There—that should work.

"That's a total crock."

So much for it working. "It's not. My fiancé broke up with me less than a week before the wedding and left me to tell everyone and pay for it all. It was horrible."

"Yes, it was, and I'm sorry you had to go through that, but it doesn't mean—"

"There's more. My mother was a wonderful woman. Beautiful and talented and so loving. My dad died before I was born and my grandfather disappeared when my mom was still a kid."

"So you come from a long line of women who chose badly or have had bad luck. Believe me, I totally get that. I have a bit of it in my past, but that doesn't mean you won't eventually fall madly in love and live happily ever after."

"You don't know that."

Silver sighed. "This isn't the movie *Practical Magic*. There is no curse."

"I loved that movie. Their hair."

"Aidan Quinn, which is not the point. You're hiding, emotionally. From finding someone great in general, and specifically this second from knowing if you're pregnant. You might want to think about why that's happening and what you're going to do to fix it."

Natalie knew that of all her friends, Silver was the most blunt and brutally honest. She must have wanted to hear the truth or she would have texted someone with a more gentle personality.

"I'm scared," she admitted. "About everything."

"I know you are. Whatever happens, you have a lot of people who care about you. You might not have biological family around but you have made your own family of the heart. Pregnant or not, we'll be here. In a time like this, support is important." Silver hesitated. "It just is."

"Thank you."

"Now go take the damn test."

"Saturday for sure. I swear."

"Do I look convinced?" Silver asked, sounding more than a little skeptical.

"No, but if I'm lying, you can slap me."

"I'll be counting the minutes. Now come on. I'll buy you lunch. I'll even order French fries so you can eat off my plate and pretend you didn't have any."

"You're the best friend ever."

"Tell me about it."

RONAN WATCHED NICK pace the length of their studio. His brother had been restless all morning. Mathias hadn't bothered to come in, so it was just the two of them. Nick had tried to work at least a half dozen times, then had given up and started walking back and forth.

"You're making it hard to concentrate," Ronan said mildly, turning his chair so he could watch his brother. It wasn't as if he was all that interested in finalizing his production schedule for the commission. He was on track and that was about all he had to know.

"Sorry." Nick kept walking. "I have a lot on my mind."

"Pallas?"

Nick nodded. He headed for his desk, grabbed his chair and pulled it over to Ronan's desk.

"She's so sick. The doctor swears she's going to be fine and Pallas is trying to convince me it's not as bad as it was, but I'm not sure I believe her. Even if I do, it's still awful. I hate seeing her like that."

"Won't it get better soon?"

"In the next month or so her hormones should calm down. Everyone tells me it's normal but it doesn't look normal to me."

Ronan couldn't imagine his brother's fear. To love someone as much as Nick loved Pallas, then watch her go through everything without being able to help would be awful.

"I didn't think it would be like this," Nick admitted.

"I can't imagine life without her and we both wanted kids. Now I'm terrified all the time. What if something happens to her?"

"It won't."

"You don't know that."

"You don't know that she won't be perfectly fine. You're borrowing trouble."

"Yeah, you're right, but it's hard not to. She's so great and she's being stronger than I could ever be. She's a little nervous, but not scared."

Ronan watched his brother. "She doesn't have memories of growing up with Ceallach."

Nick grimaced. "Believe me, I think about that all the time. When I worry about being a good dad I promise myself I'll figure out what he would do and then do the opposite."

"That's a great plan."

Nick looked at him. "Sometimes I wonder if it's all his fault. Being an asshole. You know what it was like for him."

Ronan knew what he'd been told. That his father had been the only child born to a lawyer and a stay-at-home mother. As far as anyone knew, there was no artist genius in the family, but by the time Ceallach had been three, his parents had realized there was something going on. Tutors had been brought in, and when he had turned seven, he'd been sent away to a famous academy in France.

"Don't pull the 'he wasn't parented' line on me," Ronan said. "Elaine used to say that all the time, all the while defending him from whatever crappy thing he'd done."

"It wasn't his fault," Nick said. "His parents and teachers pushed him. He never had a normal childhood."

"That might excuse not knowing how to be a good father but it doesn't excuse him being a horrible human being."

"True. I think about it. About how much of him is in me, about what I'm going to pass on to my kid. Pallas says it will be fine and I believe she's okay with it, but I worry."

Ronan understood. At least Nick had a counteracting force in Elaine.

"When it gets bad," Nick continued, "Pallas tells me that I'm an okay guy and you four are fairly decent, so whatever's going on with our dad is diluted."

"A good way to look at things." Diluted. He'd never thought of his Ceallach gene pool that way. The problem was, he didn't know about the other half. What if his birth mother was worse? He couldn't imagine any normal woman finding Ceallach appealing enough to have a kid with. He figured she had to have been young and assumed she was a partyer who liked to chase after rich, famous guys. Not exactly someone he ever wanted to meet. Not that he would be finding out. He didn't know anything about the woman—not her name or where she was from. He had a feeling that Natalie would tell him to talk to Elaine (or as she would say, "your mother") and get the answers. There had to have been a meeting when he'd been passed over. Or maybe not. Maybe he'd simply been left on the doorstep.

There was only one way to get the information and that was to ask for it. Something Ronan knew was never going to happen.

NATALIE DOUBLE-CHECKED the list she had made based on her notes from Pallas. Normally accomplishing a list of tasks was no big deal but these days she couldn't seem to keep her attention on anything for more than a second. The reason was simple enough—she was worried she was pregnant. The solution was equally easy. As Silver had said, all she had to do was take the damn test and she would know the answer.

Saturday, she promised herself. Today was Wednesday. If she didn't get her period by Saturday morning she would go out and buy a test, or three, and find out for sure. Until then, she would do her best not to worry. Which was turning out to really be easier said than done.

She returned her attention to the flowers for the centerpieces. They were relaxing for her to make—almost a Zen exercise. She tried to keep her breathing steady and even and stay focused. The process worked for nearly eight seconds and then she was worrying about how everything would change if she really were having a baby.

"I need therapy," she murmured. "With a mental health professional." Or maybe just the courage to go to the drugstore.

If only her mom were here, she thought. She would know what to say. Natalie smiled. Actually, her mother would go buy the test herself, hand it to her daughter, then wait outside the bathroom door until Natalie had peed. Then her mom would hold her tight and promise everything was going to be all right. The best part was that Natalie would totally believe her.

Funny how lately her mom had been on her mind so much. She would have thought with the passage of time the memories would get more infrequent. No doubt hanging out with Ronan was part of the reason.

She knew there were women who weren't close to their moms. How awful. She couldn't imagine what that would be like—not to have that loving advice, the shared jokes. Her mom had always been her best friend. They'd done everything together.

Her phone buzzed. She looked at the screen and saw she had a text from Ronan.

Want to hang out tonight? I can cook.

Her stomach clenched. Of course she wanted to see him and be with him and enjoy the evening with him, but there was no way she could do that and not blurt out something she would regret. She hesitated only a second before texting back that she was going to be working on wedding flowers for the next couple of hours. Then she turned back to the stack of paper and did her best to make her words true.

Nearly a half hour later, there was a knock on her front door. Natalie answered it only to find Ronan on her landing.

"Hi," she said as she stepped back to let him inside. "What's up?"

His gaze settled on her face as if he were looking for something. "I wanted to make sure you were all right. You sounded, I don't know, different when you texted."

"It was a text. How could you judge how I sounded?"

He shrugged. "I had a feeling."

One that was uncomfortably accurate, she thought. Weren't men supposed to have the emotional intelligence of a plant? Why did Ronan have to be higher on the food chain than that?

For a second, she desperately wanted to tell him the truth. That she was scared. Not only because a baby would totally change everything between them but because it would turn her life upside down in ways she couldn't begin to imagine. She wasn't ready; she didn't have her crap together. A baby would be…complicated.

But to say that was to go somewhere that couldn't be ungone. She frowned. That wasn't right. Ungone? Who said that?

"Natalie?"

"What? Oh, sorry." She led the way to her studio. "I'm okay. Just feeling swamped." She pointed to the stacks of paper, the crates of vases and completed flowers. "I wasn't kidding about working. I'm struggling to keep up my daily flower count. When I figured out my schedule, I wasn't helping Pallas with other aspects of the wedding. Of course I want to be there for Pallas, but there's more to do than I'd realized. Between that and the flowers and work and trying to do at least a little project for myself, I'm running out of hours in the day."

He put his hand on the small of her back. "You're right. It's a lot. There's also our bridge project."

"What?" The word came out as a shriek. "I totally forgot about that."

"Don't worry. Mathias and I are taking care of it."

"But we're doing it together. I need to help."

"When would you do that?"

"I don't know but I should…"

She should be doing something, but it was hard to think when Ronan leaned in and kissed her. His mouth was firm, yet teasing, as if he was simply kissing her because it was fun and not because he expected anything.

"Prioritize," he told her. "Wedding and work come first. Then your art, then the bridge project."

"Are you telling me what to do?"

"I'm suggesting."

It was a good suggestion, one that made sense. "It's just…"

He kissed her again, then turned her so they were both staring at her big worktable. "Let me help. I can hand you paper or cut things out, or glue or keep count. Or if I'd only be in the way, tell me and I'll head out."

He was being so nice. It wasn't fair. She really wanted to spend the evening with him and having help would be great. But what if she said something accidentally?

Natalie wanted to slap herself. Did she really think

she was incapable of keeping even the slightest control over herself? Was she that irresponsible? The only reason she didn't know if she was pregnant or not was her unwillingness to take the test before Saturday. There was no way she was going to say anything to Ronan before she was sure. It wasn't fair to him or their relationship. She needed to grow a pair, so to speak, and start acting like an adult.

"Help would be fantastic," she told him. "Thank you."

"Want me to start by grabbing us takeout for dinner?"

She laughed. "Yes, please. Then you can glue the little beads on the flowers for me."

"I live to serve. How does pizza sound?"

"Excellent. Everything on it?"

"I would have picked you as a roasted-vegetable kind of girl."

She rolled her eyes. "Ha, ha. Why ruin a perfectly good pizza with that? Let's do meat."

"See, you just keep getting better and better." He pulled out his phone and scrolled through the apps, then found the one for their local pizza place. Seconds later, he'd ordered it. "I'll be back in fifteen minutes. We'll eat, then we'll get to work."

"Thanks. I really appreciate your help."

"I'm happy to be here, Natalie. I hope you know that."

She nodded because she had a bad feeling that if she tried to speak she would burst into tears. Which was ridiculous. She was fine. He was a great guy and they were having a good time and absolutely nothing else. Seriously. She had her emotions firmly in check. Really. It was a done deal.

CHAPTER FOURTEEN

FRIDAY MORNING CAME damned early. Ronan was up at five so he could make a quick protein shake before heading to town to meet his brothers in the park at six. After that he would go to the studio. He'd had a full team of interns all week and was making good progress on his commission. He had a few more things he wanted to get done today. At least he was getting an early start. Even with meeting his brothers, he would still be at the work studio long before his usual time.

He drank his breakfast on the way, then realized about five miles too late he should have made coffee, as well. Now it would be at least an hour and a half before he had his first cup. He had remembered a water bottle, so he would have that when the workout was done. He arrived at the park to find Nick and Mathias were already waiting for him. Both looked far more alert than he felt.

"Good morning," Nick called. "Isn't this great? We should have started working out together years ago."

"Why?" Ronan asked. "It's too early."

Mathias looked smug. "That's right. You're a night owl. Too bad. I love the mornings. The earlier, the better."

"Bite me."

Like his brothers, Ronan wore shorts and a T-shirt, along with athletic shoes. Nick had said something about running and a few other things. The morning was cool, but he knew he would work up a sweat soon enough.

"So here's the plan," Mathias said. "We're going to start with a four-mile run."

"I thought the race was only a 5K," Ronan said.

"It is, but this way we're more than ready for it."

"Or we'll overtrain," Ronan grumbled. "You know, I have a gym at home. I could have done this there."

"No one trusts you." Nick's tone was cheerful.

"You're saying I would lie about working out?"

"Yup."

Ronan laughed. "Fine. So we run, then what?"

"Push-ups and pull-ups until one of us pukes."

Mathias groaned. "Great. I can't wait for that."

They started out at a slow jog. The path around the park was a mile long, meaning they would circle it four times. Ronan knew that jogging outside was more challenging than the run he did on his treadmill at home and he looked forward to pushing himself this morning. No way he was going to be the one to puke first.

"How's Pallas?" Mathias asked Nick when they'd found their rhythm on the run.

"Feeling better. Just like the doctor said, her hormones are calming down and she's having more time between the waves of nausea." He swore, then continued. "I don't know how she got through it. I was exhausted and all I had to do was try to help. She was the one dealing with physical symptoms. Her mom told her she went through the same thing with her pregnancies."

Mathias shook his head. "Let me guess. Libby being Libby, she was almost gleeful that Pallas was suffering, as well."

"You know it. Mothers and daughters are complicated creatures."

"But Pallas is definitely better?" Mathias asked.

"She is. The doctor is hopeful that once she gets through this stage, she'll be fine. There's a chance she could be sick at the end of her pregnancy, when the hormones step up again. We'll have to see."

They continued talking about the pregnancy, but Ronan stopped listening. He didn't want to think about children—not when he was pretty sure he wasn't going to have any. How could he? The risk was too high. Yet the thought of going through his life with no family was more than grim. He liked being with someone special. Natalie, for example. She was great. Sweet and smart and funny and sexy. There was just something about the way she pushed up her glasses that made him want to rip off her clothes every time she did it.

"This is just like track team," Mathias said as they picked up the pace. "Remember?"

Ronan nodded. He and his brothers had all run track in high school. They'd trained with Nick until he'd graduated. None of them had been state championship material, but they'd been stars at the Fool's Gold high school and that had been plenty for them.

"We were gods," Ronan said with a chuckle.

"*I* was a god," Nick told him. "You two were wannabes."

"You wish." Mathias led them around the final corner as they completed their first lap. "Ronan and I dated twin sisters."

"Which was a disaster."

Ronan had to agree with Nick. It hadn't gone well at all. He and Mathias had decided to ask the sisters out to see what it would be like. Unfortunately, the girls were identical twins and he and Mathias couldn't ever tell them apart. They were forever mixing them up, which probably made a great summer movie plot but in real life led to hurt feelings and plenty of tears.

"You grabbed my date's boob," Ronan reminded Mathias. "What was up with that?"

"I thought she was my date and we'd definitely gone further than that. I don't know. It seemed like a good idea at the time."

"Not for very long. Cindy and Mindy never forgave us."

"They probably had a point," Mathias said. "Maybe we should have called them a few years later. Look at Maya and Del. They were hot and heavy in high school, broke up, then got together ten years later and now they're married."

"You want to marry either Cindy or Mindy?"

"No. I have Carol and she's the one I love. Want me to Google them for you?"

"Thanks, but I'll pass. I doubt if I could tell them apart any more today than I could back then and that would get me into trouble." Besides, there was only one woman who interested him these days.

NATALIE WOKE UP a little after seven to a horrible, heavy cramping sensation low in her belly. For a second she lay in bed wondering what on earth was wrong with her. Then she sat up with a whoop and ran to the bathroom. Seconds later, her happiness was complete and the cramps a delightful reminder that she'd been very, very lucky.

She showered, then got ready for work, all the while profoundly grateful that she hadn't had to deal with any life-changing pregnancies or births. Just as soon as she got to her desk, she was going to call her doctor and make an appointment to get on birth control. Something easy, like the patch or the shots, would work better for her. She wasn't sure she was a pill-every-day kind of girl. But either way, she would be on something as soon as possible.

As she walked to her car, she thought about all the decisions she now *didn't* have to make. Despite knowing she would have kept and raised the baby on her own, she was happy she didn't have to. There were no regrets, no might-have-beens. In her heart, she knew she wasn't ready to be a parent. She still had to make decisions about her life and figure out what she wanted and where she was going. There were so many options right now. If she'd had to make changes, she would have, but she didn't and yay.

Thank goodness she hadn't said anything to Ronan. There would have been all kinds of drama and for nothing. Even telling him she wasn't pregnant wouldn't have taken their relationship back to where it had been before.

She had a feeling that putting off the pregnancy test wasn't the lesson she was supposed to learn. That maybe she should be thinking more about taking responsibility for her actions. That the mature decision would have been not to suffer all those days in the first place, that burying her head in the sand, so to speak, wasn't anything to be proud of.

She started her car engine, then shook her head as she realized that *was* the lesson. To be responsible—for herself and her body by being on proper birth control when actively sexual, for her mental state by dealing with the problem in the moment and not ignoring it because it was uncomfortable or scary. Which was a lot to deal with so early on a Friday morning, but still something to remember. Next time she would do better, she promised herself.

She drove to the bakery on the way to the office and picked up two dozen donuts. The guys would be done with their first training session and probably starving. She got a couple of scones for Atsuko, then went directly to the gallery. She arrived at the studio and had just finished setting out the donuts when Ronan walked out from the bathroom in back.

He looked good, she thought, her insides quivering at the sight of him. Freshly showered and pumped up from his workout.

"Morning," she said. "How was it?"

"We ran four miles and did some push-ups and pull-ups. No big deal. Mathias and Nick went home to shower. I used the one here. It's faster than driving back to my place."

"Makes sense." His house was halfway up the mountain. She motioned to the bakery box. "I bought donuts."

"We're supposed to be in training."

She laughed. "Oh, please. It's a charity event and none of you needs to lose weight. Are you telling me that a little sugar doesn't sound delicious right now?"

He ran his fingers down the side of her face, then kissed her on the lips. "What kind of sugar are we talking about?"

"The bakery kind. Nothing more. We're at work."

"We are, but your place is very close." He raised his eyebrows suggestively. "Thoughts?"

"Some of us have a boss to report to."

"You're right. I don't want to be a bad influence." He studied her for a second. "You seem more relaxed today."

"I am. There is a lot going on, but it turns out I was also dealing with some hormonal stuff. It's a girl thing."

"How come you get to say that but if I ever mentioned hormones I would get slapped?"

"I don't know. It's desperately unfair, isn't it? Poor you." She reached for a donut and took a bite. "I will leave you to your emotional pain."

He pulled her close and kissed her again. "I'm glad you're feeling better."

"Me, too."

She went back into the gallery, all the while wondering how Ronan would have reacted if she *had* been pregnant. Not well, she thought. He was dealing with so much with his father and his biological mother. Rather he was *not* dealing with it. She wished there was a way to help him. A way to—

"Don't do it," she murmured as she walked to her desk. "Don't force the issue." As much as she wanted Ronan to move on, this problem was way bigger than her or their relationship. If she got involved, she would only mess things up. Her job was to be supportive and caring and let him figure it out on his own. Although if the right opportunity presented itself...

BY MONDAY, NATALIE was on a roll. Thanks to a weekend spent working on flowers, she was well ahead of her schedule and only had one table left to go. She'd checked in with Pallas and done a walk-through for a similar wedding so she could learn the flow of events. Her office work was complete for the day and she was taking the afternoon to work on something fun just for herself.

The large mixed-media piece was still in the forming stage, but she couldn't help thinking butterflies and holly. A weird combination, but it didn't want to get out of her head, and she'd learned that when it came to her art, she had to respect that. She sketched, then went through the small storage cabinet by her workstation. It was filled with all sorts of one-of-a-kind found objects. Things she'd picked up here and there or that had been given to her. She had crystals, rocks, bottle caps, buttons, pieces of ribbon, shards of glass, metal tins, erasers, dried flowers and leaves, beads, bits of fabric, bottles of glitter, yarn, thread, jewelry wire and dozens of other options.

The butterfly wings needed to be spectacular, she thought as she crumpled up the sheet of paper on her desk and tossed it into the recycle bin and put a clean page in its place. She adjusted her headphones, searched through her iPod for the right song to inspire her, then pushed Play.

The opening notes of "Eye of the Tiger" began to play. She hummed along, moving in her seat as she quickly drew the first of three hummingbirds. Maybe the problem was the placement, she thought, drawing faster and faster. Yes, that was it. She needed to—

The music went silent. She looked up and saw Nick standing next to her.

"What?" she demanded.

"You're half humming, half singing. It's annoying."

"I was not."

She looked at Ronan, who gave her a half shrug. "You were."

"How you betray me. All of you. Fine. If that's how you want to be."

She got up and walked over to the studio sound system, then set her iPod on the docking station. Seconds later, the opening notes blasted in the huge space. Mathias looked up from the piece he was polishing.

"Were you even born in the eighties?" he asked.

"I'm ignoring you," she yelled over the music.

Ronan grinned, Nick shook his head and went back to the small piece of wood he was carving, but by the chorus, they were all singing along. After it ended, Natalie turned to pull her iPod when she saw Atsuko standing by the docking station. Her boss raised her eyebrows.

"Interesting," she murmured, "what all of you find creative."

"If it works," Natalie told her. "Did you need me for something?"

"A quick chat, if you have a second."

"Of course."

Natalie put her iPod into her desk drawer, then followed Atsuko into the gallery. When they were seated across from each other at Atsuko's desk, her boss smiled at her.

"The dragon piece sold yesterday."

Natalie did her best to look calm and not start dancing in her chair. "That's great. Thanks for letting me know."

"You're welcome. The clients were asking about other pieces you have available. I had to tell them there weren't any right now." Atsuko's gaze intensified. "They insisted I take their phone number and let them know when you have something else to sell."

Natalie had never had anyone ask about her work specifically. She'd always sold everything Atsuko took, but this was different. This was about *her*!

"I don't know what to say," she admitted. "That's really exciting."

"It is." Her boss opened a desk drawer and pulled out one of the comic book flowers Natalie had made for the wedding. "I hope you don't mind, but I borrowed this the other night. I've been thinking about it."

She passed it over to Natalie. "Do you like making the flowers?"

"They're fun. I enjoy trying different techniques." She wrinkled her nose. "I don't think I'd want to do this for every wedding coming to town, but now and then, it would be interesting."

"Have you thought of doing something like this on a grander scale?"

"I haven't," she said even as she began to consider the idea. "It's possible, of course. If the flowers got much bigger, they'd need to be reinforced. Or I'd have to use a different weight of paper. I've been thinking it would be interesting to use pages from a fashion magazine instead of the comic book paper. All the colors and the thickness of the pages could add dimension. The stems would also have to be different. Stronger. Maybe something with bamboo. I like working with bamboo." Her voice trailed off. "Sorry. You wanted a simple yes or no, didn't you?"

"Not at all. I enjoy hearing about the creative process. Your work is unique. You're starting to find your style. It's never going to be just one thing with you. Not all artists are like that. Nick likes to do different things." She sighed. "I blame myself, but he's starting to talk about working with metal again."

Natalie tried not to look guilty. The previous year Atsuko had bought some used welding equipment and had offered it to the guys to experiment with. They'd quickly realized they didn't have the training to create anything and had nearly set the studio on fire. Twice. Everyone had been relieved when the equipment had been put in the storeroom.

"I wonder what inspired him," she murmured, avoiding Atsuko's knowing gaze.

"I have a suspicion that it was cutting up your car, but we'll discuss that another time. Back to your flowers. The other day I noticed the shelf you have behind your desk. The one with your origami. There are a few glass pieces there. Ronan's work, I presume?"

Natalie nodded.

"The paper and the glass are an unexpected combination, but they work. You are familiar with his vases of flowers."

Not a question, but Natalie responded. "Of course. They're beautiful."

"I agree and they sell very well."

Despite the mid-six-figure price tag, Natalie thought, wondering what it must be like to be so talented and successful and, well, rich.

"I'd like you to create a floral piece on the same scale." Atsuko pointed to an empty pewter vase in the corner of her office. It had to be at least three feet high. It was slightly battered, but elegant, and had a beautiful patina.

"Do you think you could create flowers big enough for that?"

Natalie's mouth opened, then closed. There was no reason she couldn't scale up, she thought, eyeing the vase. As for the paper, she was starting to love the idea of using pages from a magazine. Maybe she could buy the unbound, uncut paper directly from the printer. It wouldn't even have to be a fashion magazine. Anything with colorful pictures would be great. Ooh, a travel magazine would have amazing photographs.

"I definitely could do that," she said eagerly. "You wouldn't happen to have any contacts in the printing business, would you?"

"As a matter of fact, I do. Would you like me to make some calls and see about getting you uncut overruns?"

"That would be fantastic. Thank you."

"I'll find out what I can right away." Atsuko smiled at her. "I'm glad you're excited about the project." She touched the flower she'd set on her desk. "This has real potential, Natalie. I'm not making any promises, but if it comes out as well as I think it's going to, I'd want to price it somewhere in the five-figure range."

F-five figures? Five! "That's both inspiring and terrifying," she admitted. "I'll start thinking about what I'd want to do and wait to hear from you on the paper." If Atsuko didn't have any luck, Natalie would talk to her friend Wynn and see what she had to say.

"Excellent. I look forward to seeing the final project."

"Me, too."

Natalie did her best to walk sedately down the hall.

Once she cleared the gallery, she ran across the parking lot and practically floated into the studio.

The guys had country music blasting out of the speakers. Natalie started for her desk only to be intercepted by Ronan. He was hot and sweaty, but with a satisfied air of a man who had worked hard and worked well.

"Everything okay?" he asked. "You were gone a while."

"I'm fine." She showed him the flower she'd brought back. "Atsuko took one of these and was thinking about having me do a piece for the gallery, only on a larger scale."

She told him about the vase and using some kind of magazine print for the paper. "I'll have to make a bunch of practice flowers. I need to see if they'll require supports. I don't want them to look good for a couple of weeks, then droop. Anyway, it's so exciting." She glanced around to make sure no one else was close, then lowered her voice.

"You have to swear you won't tell anyone."

"I swear," he said, his green eyes bright with humor. "What?"

"She said she thought she could get five figures!" Natalie spun in a circle, then clutched the paper flower to her chest. "Do you know what that means? If she got ten thousand dollars, I'd get five thousand. That's amazing. That's months of rent. I'd been hoping to take a minisabbatical after I was done helping Pallas with the wedding and all, but that was for maybe two or three weeks. If I could sell something for that much money, I could do two more sabbaticals. Or take a longer one."

He continued to smile at her. She knew he was thinking something, but had no idea what.

"Just say it," she grumbled. "Whatever it is. You know you want to."

"She said five figures."

"I know. That's where I got the ten thousand from." She rolled her eyes. "You know she gets half of the commission. I'm not like you. I can't negotiate a special contract or anything."

"That's not my point. You're assuming a five-figure price tag is only ten thousand. There are a whole lot more numbers you're not considering."

"What? No. Really?"

She stared at him. He was right, of course. There were all the numbers between ten thousand and ninety-nine thousand.

"But I just assumed..."

"That she was talking ten grand?" he asked, lightly touching her cheek. "Maybe she was. Maybe she meant twenty or fifty instead. You could ask her."

Natalie couldn't begin to absorb the possibility. Twenty-five thousand dollars? That would mean she would get twelve thousand five hundred. Anything higher than that was unbelievable. Anything higher than that would mean she could... She could...

The thought wouldn't fully form.

"You could quit your job," Ronan said quietly. "Be an artist full-time."

Yes, that!

She knew it would be complicated. Her job provided steady income. If she was on her own, she would have to put money away for when her art wasn't selling. It was daunting to think about but also thrilling.

"I'm scared," she admitted. "And excited, and I don't want to hope too much, but wow. It's a lot to think about, savings and planning taxes."

"It is. I'll help."

"While that's a really nice offer, you don't handle any of your own money. You have Atsuko and an accountant."

He laughed. "True, but I know the basics. It wouldn't be hard to come up with a budget for what you need to live and a plan to put money away in savings. Then you'd be able to figure out how much you'd need before you could quit."

She was about to agree when the meaning of quitting sank in. "I couldn't leave the gallery. What a horrible way to thank Atsuko for believing in me."

"I'm sorry to disappoint you, but your office skills, while excellent, are not unique, and in that respect, you can be replaced. Atsuko is smart. She knows what's going to happen. My guess is she's more interested in you as an artist than you as her part-time office manager. Don't forget she gets half. You're worth a lot more to her out here than back in your office."

"You think?"

"I know." He kissed her, then turned her toward her work space. "You probably want to get back to what you were doing."

"I do. I want to finish the wedding flowers and then start planning the piece for Atsuko. Yay me!"

She hugged Ronan, then gave herself exactly one minute to consider all the beautiful possibilities. Then she made herself focus on the job at hand. One thing at a time, she told herself. One magical thing at a time.

CHAPTER FIFTEEN

CAROL HOSTED THE next girlfriend lunch, which meant it was held out on the faux savanna. Natalie loved when they could sit on the ground and picnic while enjoying the light and heat of the sun. The animals grazed in the distance, and she appreciated that she had friends she could hang out with on a regular basis.

She'd had friends in school, of course, but after her mom had died, things had changed. She'd given up her art and had gotten a "real" job in an office. From there, she'd met Quentin and the rest was history. After settling in Happily Inc and making new friends, she'd realized that between her mom's passing and getting engaged to Quentin, she'd let all her other friendships drift away. Maybe it had been because she was so sad or maybe it had been a symptom of losing herself. She wasn't sure which but she vowed it would never happen again.

"How's the new giraffe guy settling in?" Bethany

asked as she passed out the sandwiches Carol had provided.

"He's good. Already mingling with the girls. We're going to wait until next year to take one of the girls off her birth control."

"Millie should be first," Silver said. "She has seniority."

"That's what I think, too," Wynn added.

"I'll take that into account." Carol smiled at them. "So what's new with everyone?"

"I saw Wynn and Jasper making out the other night," Bethany said with a laugh. "Let's talk about what a hot couple they make."

"We're not a couple," Wynn said. "We're just..."

"Having a lot of sex?" Pallas asked.

"Yes, but that's all it is." Wynn tucked her curly hair behind her ear. "Seriously. When Jasper and I first got together, I said Hunter was my priority. I wanted to keep things light and keep my son out of it."

That sounded kind of off-putting to Natalie.

"Was he okay with that?" Bethany asked, sounding doubtful.

"He said he was fine with the rules," Wynn told them. "I don't want to worry about Hunter getting too attached before I know where things are going. So if Jasper is willing to keep things on the down low, I'm all in."

The concept made sense, Natalie thought. In a way it was what she and Ronan were doing. Just hanging out with no expectation about the future. Only when she heard someone else describe the situation, it didn't seem quite as appealing.

"You're being sensible," Pallas told her. "I admire that."

Bethany leaned close to Natalie. "I so want to be her when I grow up."

"Me, too."

"Next subject," Wynn said, eyeing them. "So, Silver, how's it going with your trailers?"

Silver sipped her soda, then laughed. "That was subtle, but sure. Let's talk about me. I'm still drooling over the two Airstreams I found. I've filled out two bank loan applications and now I wait to see what they say." She looked at Bethany. "How's life back in El Bahar?"

Bethany looked oddly guilty for a second before throwing herself back on the blanket and staring at the sky. "My parents are making me crazy," she said dramatically. "It's the marriage thing."

"Which frequently comes after an engagement," Natalie pointed out.

"I know, I know. I get it. There is the complication that my dad is who he is."

"The king of El Bahar?" Silver asked. "Is that the problem?"

"Yes." Bethany sat up. "Where do we have the wedding? How many millions of diplomats and the like get invited? How formal does it have to be before my mother starts worrying that we're doing it wrong? It's not just that I'm his only daughter, but my brothers are so much younger. It's going to be years before we have another royal wedding. I keep thinking that eloping would be so much easier."

"That's not going to happen," Pallas said lightly. "Even my brother has accepted the reality of who you are. Maybe it's time for you to do the same."

"Is Cade going to get a title when you're married?" Natalie asked. "Will he be a prince or a duke or something?"

"A prince. At least, that's the plan. It's quite the delicate negotiation."

Pallas sighed. "I'm so glad Nick and I ran away to Italy to get married. It was beautiful and perfect and I will treasure those memories always."

Bethany whimpered. "Why are you rubbing that in?"

"A future sister-in-law's prerogative."

"How are you feeling?" Natalie asked Pallas. "You're eating more."

"I'm so much better. Thanks for asking. My body has accepted the pregnancy, at least for now, and I'm spending much less time heaving up my guts. Fingers crossed it continues."

"And with that appetizing note," Wynn murmured as everyone laughed.

The lunch went on another hour. When it was time for them all to leave, they helped carry everything back to the animal preserve offices. Natalie hung back to talk to Silver for a second.

"I wanted to let you know I'm not pregnant," she said when the others had left. "I saw my doctor and

I'm on birth control. You were great and I appreciate the support."

"Thanks for letting me know. I wondered, but then when I didn't hear anything, I figured all was well."

"It is now." Natalie shook her head. "I got off lucky. I know that. I won't make that mistake again."

"Good." Silver hugged her. "Having a baby changes everything. It's a huge decision that should be made thoughtfully."

There was something in the way she said the words, Natalie thought, then told herself she was imagining things.

RONAN STEPPED OUT of the shower in the studio bathroom. He'd put in a long day of work and was pleased with the progress being made on his commission. Things were going so well he was actually a little ahead of schedule.

There'd been a change in his work, he thought as he dried off and started to dress. He was more focused. He could clearly see what needed to be done. It had been a long time since he'd been so inspired.

He knew he had Natalie to thank for that. Not just being with her, but also being around her. She was an open, gentle spirit. She saw the best in people and somehow she'd managed to share a little of that with him. She'd made him see that he needed to be with his brothers, needed their energy to unleash his own creative forces. Which all sounded way too out there, but it was true.

He'd missed Mathias and Nick. Had missed working

with them. When they were around, he was less in his head, which was probably much better for everyone.

He hung his towel, then walked back into the studio, only to find Natalie waiting for him. She shifted her weight impatiently.

"Finally," she said, grabbing his hand and pulling him toward the door. "You took forever."

"It wasn't five minutes."

"Really? Because it felt like at least ten." She walked over to his truck and waited for him to open the passenger door.

"I take it we're going somewhere."

"Duh. To the recycling center. We have to get moving on our bridge piece."

"Nick, Mathias and I have it handled. We're using the car as the basis and the theme is 'coming and going.' You don't need to worry about it. You're busy with your own stuff."

"I finished the flowers for the wedding and I'm working on a mixed-media piece to clear my head before I start on the flowers for Atsuko, so I have time. Not to be too judgy, but what you guys have done is okay but it needs pizzazz."

"Aka junk?"

"Not junk." She settled on the passenger seat. "Dazzle."

"Uh-huh. I've seen your dazzle before and I'm not sure we should be flashing that in public."

She flushed and laughed. He circled around to the driver's side and they were off to the county trash and recycling center on the far side of the animal preserve.

Happily Inc had one of the most successful recycling programs in the country. All trash was sorted and nearly all of it was recycled, sold or composted. Only a tiny fraction went into the landfill.

The food waste was combined with the droppings from the animals at the preserve into an excellent fertilizer that was sold at cost. Many of the farmers in central California had banded together to hire a truck to deliver the fertilizer to their farms. The material was organic and of a much higher quality than anything they could buy elsewhere, and by working together, they kept costs down.

He bypassed the poo storage and circled around to the recycling center. It was a busy place. Ed and Ted Lund, two brothers interested in waste management and saving animals, had contracts with two of California's largest prisons. Through a work-release program, former inmates learned everything from the ins and outs of working at a recycling facility to how to repair small appliances and discarded furniture. The repaired items were sold in a very busy store and proceeds went back into upgrading the dump.

Natalie walked through the store without glancing at anything and passed through an open doorway with a sign saying Free above it.

Of course, Ronan thought, telling himself he shouldn't be surprised. He would guess she was also a big fan of garage sales and "free to good home" items left on curbs.

She was nothing if not methodical. Natalie grabbed a shopping basket and started on the left side of the room, slowly making her way up and down the aisles. She stopped at what looked like the wheels from a couple of old wheelbarrows and picked up one of them.

"It fits the 'coming and going' theme," she said. "Too on the nose?"

"Let's make it a maybe."

"I'm hoping for door handles or hinges."

"Why?"

She looked at him. "Because I have a feeling. I think they'd work well and the material could withstand the weather. Ronan, seriously, you have to be willing to use your imagination."

"Okay, door hinges and handles. Got it."

She eyed him. "Don't just go buy them. It wouldn't be the same."

"Hey, would I do that?"

"In a heartbeat."

She was right, of course, but he wasn't going to admit it. They found a clock face that was missing several numbers. Natalie picked it up and hugged it as if it were golden treasure.

"This is going to work really well," she told him. "We're off to a great start."

"You like doing this, don't you?"

"Sure. It's fun. You never know what you're going to find. Even if there isn't a lot of stuff for the bridge project, I may find something for my next art piece. I'm in flower mode right now but that could change."

She picked up an old pie tin and he wasn't the least bit surprised when she slipped it into her basket. He took the basket from her.

"Let me carry that for you, pretty lady."

She flashed him a smile. "Thank you. Isn't this fun? My mom and I used to do this all the time when I was a kid. We'd go to flea markets and church bazaars. Oh, and library sales. It made the teachers at school go totally insane when she would start ripping up the picture books for art projects. In the end, she had to tear them up at home so the teachers wouldn't get upset."

"I didn't know your mom was a teacher."

Natalie looked at him, obviously confused. "She wasn't. She was an artist. Why would you think she was a teacher?"

Now it was his turn to not know what they were talking about. "You said the teachers got upset when she ripped up books for an art project. Why was she at school if she wasn't a teacher?"

Natalie's expression cleared. "Oh, sorry. I didn't explain that well, did I? My mom was kind of well-known in our little community. She volunteered at the elementary school. She came in once a month and taught an art class to two or three different grades. She loved doing it."

"You enjoyed having her with you at school," he guessed.

"I did. I got to show her off and all my friends were impressed. My mom always said that art was an important way to expand the mind. It wasn't about ability but being able to think in different ways. To have tangible proof that there are dozens of ways to solve a single problem."

She rushed forward. "Look! Forks."

Sure enough, there was a pile of battered forks. Each of them had at least one tine missing. Ronan would have passed them over but Natalie sorted through them and chose five that she carefully put in the basket.

"I can't believe all the great stuff they have here," she said happily.

"Me, either."

She poked his arm. "You're lying and we all know it, but I don't care what you think. This is fun."

He looked at her. "It's fun for me, too."

Being with her, listening to her talk. He didn't care about junk except that she wanted it. But what she'd said about art was interesting. He wondered if they were still able to teach it in schools or if money was too tight. Were there still art teachers? He was a part of the local community now. Shouldn't he know stuff like that?

They continued to examine every object—or rather Natalie examined and he dutifully held the basket. She found three broken license plates that she had to have, the back of a metal chair and two sprinkler heads.

"Treasures, every one," he said as they walked to the exit.

"Mock me all you want, but you'll see."

She paused to put five dollars in a can by the doorway. Above it a sign said Donations Welcome.

Natalie looked at him. "I can't just take it. I can't. So I always leave something."

Of course she did, he thought as he pulled a twenty from his jeans pocket and surreptitiously dropped it in the can as he went by. Natalie couldn't possibly take without giving back. Even from a room where everything was free.

What she'd said about art in schools had stuck in his head and refused to budge. He reminded himself that he didn't have anywhere near the time to teach art to a bunch of kids, and even if he did, he had no idea if anyone would be interested in him helping. And if they were, he had neither the skills nor the experience to design an art project that a bunch of eight-year-olds would enjoy or learn from. He should just write a check and be done with it. Only he couldn't help thinking writing a check might not always be the answer.

"I'M RENEE."

Natalie shook hands with the petite redhead and did her best not to feel intimidated. There was something about Pallas's new assistant that made her feel instantly inadequate, not to mention slightly out of place and badly dressed.

Maybe it was the fact that Renee was, well, perfect. Her dark red hair hung perfectly straight down her back; her thick bangs were perfectly even. The black suit was professional, well fitted and conservative, as if designed not to draw attention. Even her patent leather pumps were polished, contemporary and had a killer five-inch heel. In a word—perfect.

"Pallas told me you agreed to step in and help with the movie wedding." Renee consulted her tablet before smiling at Natalie. "She's been doing way too much for a woman dealing with her first pregnancy and all that morning sickness. I know she appreciates you providing support. I'm looking forward to working with you, as well, as I settle into my new position."

There was a slight formality to her speech. Natalie couldn't tell if it was because English hadn't been her first language or if she'd gone to a really demanding high school. Maybe a private one where everyone had to use multisyllable words or risk being kicked out.

"It's been fun," Natalie said, then wanted to groan. Couldn't she have come up with something less dweeby than that?

"I've been working in wedding planning for a couple of years now," Renee told her. "In Beverly Hills. Those weddings were all very formal and traditional. I'm pleased to have the opportunity to experience events that are more relaxed and fun. The idea of a wedding based on a movie will provide great memories for the couple to share. I hadn't seen the movie myself, but I watched it over the weekend."

"What did you think?"

Renee hesitated before smiling. "Let's just say I'm glad it's so meaningful to them."

Natalie laughed. "That is a very diplomatic way of saying it wasn't your thing."

"I'm more a foreign-film kind of girl."

"Oh, really?" On purpose? Natalie tried to find common ground. "The guy I've been seeing loves action movies, but I'm willing to overlook that."

Pallas joined them. "Oh, good. You've met. Sorry I'm running a little late. I actually got hungry and made myself a sandwich. Yay, progress."

"You're looking great," Natalie said, noting her

friend had some color in her cheeks and she didn't look as tired. "I'm glad you're feeling so much better."

"Me, too. All right. The bride and groom have just pulled into the parking lot. Silver texted to say she'll be here in minutes, and the parents are waiting on the conference room screen. Shall we?"

They walked toward the conference room. Natalie hung back a little, letting Renee go ahead. Pallas moved next to Natalie and lowered her voice.

"What do you think of Renee?"

Natalie looked at the petite redhead. "She scares me a little, but she seems nice. Is she as accomplished as she appears?"

"More. I know what you mean about the intimidation factor, but she knows her stuff. Sometimes I think she knows it better than me and she's what? Two years younger. Ack!"

They reached the conference room just then and went to greet the bride and groom. Silver arrived and Pallas connected the parents for the meeting.

"Are we ready?" Pallas asked as everyone took a seat.

Ellen squeezed Barry's hand. "I'm so excited about all this," she said happily. "We're talking menus and finalizing our plans. It's starting to be real."

"Very real," Pallas told her with a smile. "Renee, why don't you tell our bride and groom what you've been working on?"

Renee nodded, then glanced at Silver. "I've been consulting with our master mixologist and we have a few more exciting cocktail ideas for you to consider.

Obviously the signature cocktail needs to be green, both for the Joker and Poison Ivy—two excellent and well-developed characters. Silver and I have been discussing infusing vodka with different flavors and then using an organic food coloring to get the shade of green we want."

"I've been trying out a few ideas," Silver said. "It's going to be really easy and we can work with different ingredients."

"That sounds great." Ellen beamed. "I'm excited to try everything."

"We'll set up a tasting right after the meeting."

"Not too much tasting," Ellen's mother said from the screen. "It's the middle of the day."

Ellen rolled her eyes. "Yes, Mom."

Natalie tried not to smile.

Renee checked her tablet. "I have a vendor who will make custom tortilla chips. I've checked and a bat shape is no problem. That allows us to consider a wonderful chip and dip station. We can have the traditional salsas and guacamole, of course, but also things like crab dip or artichoke dip. I wrote down some thoughts."

She passed around sheets of paper. Natalie blanched when she saw the neatly organized spreadsheet complete with a floor plan for the reception space and a flow for the guests. Pallas caught her eye and mouthed, "I know!"

Renee turned to Natalie. "I've been admiring your flowers. They're lovely and I appreciate that you used comic book print to make them. Taking that one more step, a trend these days is to serve finger food in rolled-up paper." She turned to Ellen. "The notes from the previous meeting mention that you're interested in a lot of finger foods. What if we used the comic book paper for that, as well? It would be so charming and fun."

Renee was on a roll. She shared over a dozen other ideas that all had the bride and groom giddy with excitement. Pallas seemed relieved and Silver was scribbling furiously every time a drink was mentioned.

Natalie realized her part-time gig as Pallas's helper had ended. The slightly mysterious and very together Renee was going to pick up any slack, leaving Natalie free to return to her art projects, especially the one Atsuko had mentioned. And she would, just as soon as she stopped being curious about who Renee was and why she'd decided to move to Happily Inc.

CHAPTER SIXTEEN

THE SALLY RIDE Elementary School was about two blocks from the Rio de los Suenos and ten minutes from the gallery. Ronan figured he'd driven by it maybe a hundred times and had never once paid attention to it. Today, he pulled into the parking lot and told himself he was an idiot. Who was he to think he could help some kid he'd never met? Or a kid he *had* met. He wasn't equipped or trained. His entire experience with children came from being a kid himself. He should cancel the meeting and go back to work. Only he couldn't.

Natalie's talk about her mother had lodged in his brain and refused to let go. He'd gone online and done some preliminary research and had found out that studies really did show that art made a difference in a child's mental development. It improved confidence, motor skills and focus. Creating art used both sides of the brain and, as Natalie had said, showed more than one way to solve a problem.

He grabbed his backpack and walked into the

school. After introducing himself to the man at the front desk, he was shown to the principal's office.

Dr. Anthony was in her midfifties. She motioned for Ronan to take a seat on a very worn sofa while she sat in an equally battered club chair.

"This is where I hang out with nervous parents," she joked. "I call it my corner of tears. Having said that, let's both try not to cry during this meeting. You'll be humiliated and that will make me uncomfortable."

Ronan chuckled. "It's a deal."

She studied him. "When I saw your name on my calendar, I thought it sounded familiar, so I looked you up online. You have an interesting reputation, Mr. Mitchell."

"Ronan, please. As for my reputation, I'm assuming it was all about my work."

"It is. Your personal life is a bit of a mystery. In this day and age, that's rare. Most people who can get their fifteen minutes of fame seem willing to do almost anything."

"I prefer to work in quiet."

"Then how can I help you?"

He wasn't sure what to say. "I understand that school budgets are squeezed these days. More students and requirements with less money. Programs get cut."

"You're talking about art programs, aren't you?"

He nodded.

She sighed. "Yes, they have been. We try. Our regular teachers fill in as best they can, but we don't have a designated art teacher anymore."

"I would like to offer a monthly program for your

students. I haven't figured out all the details and I'd appreciate some help on that, assuming you're interested. I was thinking I'd come in for the day and spend an hour with each grade. We'd do something together. If you can provide the space, I'd bring in the supplies."

Her steady gaze never wavered. "Why would you want to do that? It's a huge commitment of time and resources. Don't you have better things to be doing?"

Not the answer he'd expected. "I have never wanted for anything. My father is famous, and once he figured out I had inherited his talent, the assumption was I would follow in his footsteps."

"Which you have."

"Agreed. I have been successful by any measure and I'm grateful for that. But it's not all it's cracked up to be. Helping kids discover the joy of painting or working with clay one day a month isn't asking too much of myself."

He paused. "In the spirit of full disclosure, I have no formal teaching experience. I work with college interns a lot but I've been known to yell at them. You'd want me to be supervised."

He realized about fifteen seconds too late he probably shouldn't have said that.

"Not that I would yell at children. I wouldn't. I'm just saying, I'm not a teacher. I don't claim to be. I'm a guy who knows and likes art and I want to share that."

"Would you want the press to be around while you teach? Are you working on a documentary?"

"What? No. No press, no parents, no anyone. This isn't about publicity. I'd prefer to be anonymous."

Her expression softened. "Interesting. You couldn't possibly handle the project by yourself. There are too many children in each grade. You'd be overwhelmed."

"I'll bring the interns with me." And he would ask Natalie. He had a feeling she would enjoy helping out.

"No yelling at the interns in front of the children, Ronan. I'd have to insist on that."

He grinned. "You have my word."

"Then I think we should talk about this very seriously. Your offer is generous and I want to find a way to make it work."

"Me, too."

AN HOUR LATER Ronan arrived back at the studio. He and Dr. Anthony had come up with a plan. She was going to have to run the proposal by the school board, but she had said she doubted there would be a problem. Ronan was well-known in the community and his lack of flamboyant lifestyle was in his favor. There would be teachers on hand to provide supervision. Once she had approval, she would be in touch.

He found Natalie working on a massive floral-butterfly mixed-media piece. She'd already sketched the dozens of butterflies and had begun applying torn bits of paper. On a tray next to her desk were the broken clock faces they'd picked up at the recycling center.

"Clocks and flowers and butterflies?" he asked.

"Changing seasons. I'm not totally sure about that, though. I might just do all paper. I haven't decided." She smiled. "Atsuko heard from her friend, and the magazine paper, or whatever it's called, will arrive next week. I can't wait to get started. In the meantime, I'm doing this."

She glanced over her shoulder as if making sure his brothers weren't that close, then lowered her voice. "How was the meeting?"

"Good. She liked my idea and she's going to take it to the school board."

"Yay!" Natalie shimmied in place. "I told you it would go well. You're going to let me help, right? I've been thinking we should do a theme. Like painting one time and something with wood or glass."

"And paper," he said, lightly touching her cheek. "They have to learn to work with paper."

"They do. And they will. Are you happy? Doesn't it feel good to offer this? You're going to be so great with the kids, Ronan. You're patient and you understand how stuff works."

"I warned Dr. Anthony I yell at my interns."

"You don't. Okay, every now and then, but not really."

She was always seeing the best in him. In everyone, he supposed. Every challenge was another opportunity to try something new. Only Natalie saw the beauty in a broken clock face.

"You're amazing," he said, pulling her close and kissing her.

She kissed him back and grinned. "I am pretty special. Now get back to work. I have to create beautiful butterflies here, mister."

"Yes, ma'am."

NATALIE STOOD BACK to study her mixed-media piece. The direction had taken her by surprise. She really had been thinking maybe something with seasons but instead she found herself creating flowers within flowers. Not quite a kaleidoscope, but close, with the butterflies for accent. She'd used over a dozen different types of paper, mixing them into a swirling, living creation that seemed to sway in an imaginary breeze. She wasn't completely sure, but she thought it might be the best thing she'd ever done.

"Next up, giant flowers for Atsuko," she murmured to herself as she walked to her right and looked at her piece from that angle. She was creating those in her mind right now, playing with shapes and sizes in preparation for actually starting the work. It was how her process went best—at least on the big things. She mulled and considered before actually starting with real materials. But in the meantime, she was thrilled with what she'd created.

She walked away, then spun back to look at it from a distance. The colors blended seamlessly; the energy was positive. She felt herself smiling as she gazed at it. Yup, the best thing she'd ever made by far, she thought happily.

She was in a good place. Working hard, trying new things. She knew that success required hard work, determination and persistence. Once those three were conquered, there was often an element of luck. She'd been putting in the time and now she had her reward.

She laughed and picked up the canvas, then hurried across the studio. She wanted to show Ronan the final results of her fussing for the past couple of weeks. He'd been watching her work but hadn't offered any suggestions…mostly because he was the best boyfriend ever. Despite his wild success, he never assumed he was better or knew more or—

"Ronan!" she called as she approached. "It's done. Come look."

He turned at the sound of her voice. He'd been working and had on goggles and held a blowpipe in his hands. At the end, a blob of molten glass glowed in the late-afternoon light. Natalie found herself instantly mesmerized by the colors in the nearly liquid glass and she didn't notice the box in her path.

She kicked it, stumbled and started to fall forward. Ronan instinctively moved toward her to catch her. The molten glass touched the top of the canvas and ignited a tiny petal of paper. In less than a second, the flames spread, racing toward her hands and her chest.

"No!" she shrieked, instinctively turning the canvas and dropping it facedown on the floor.

Ronan shoved the molten glass into a cooling bucket, ripped off his goggles and rushed back to her. He stood staring at the back of the canvas and swore under his breath.

"I'm sorry," he began. "Natalie, I'm sorry. It happened so fast and I didn't mean…" His voice trailed off.

She knew he meant what he said—he would never deliberately do anything to hurt her and he would never destroy anything she'd made. It had been an accident. She'd tripped, he'd started toward her. Just one of those things. A little hiccup in the forward momentum of life.

Only… Only… Her chest got so tight she couldn't breathe. Her throat burned as tears filled her eyes. Before she could figure out how to stop them, they spilled onto her cheeks. A sob escaped.

Her work. Her beautiful, amazing piece. It was destroyed. She didn't have to see it to know.

Strong arms wrapped around her. She leaned into him and let herself cry out her disappointment.

"I'm sorry," he said again and again. "Dammit, I'm so sorry."

"I know. It's o-okay."

"It's not. I want to make it better."

She was sure that was true. She could feel the tension in his body and knew he was hurting almost as much as she was. He would live with the guilt while she would deal with the loss. The piece was gone and there was nothing she could do about that.

She drew back and wiped her face. "I'm going to go home. I need to be alone right now."

"Can I come with you?"

She looked into his green eyes and saw pain and worry and enough caring that she was able to breathe again.

"I'll be okay."

He started to speak, but she shook her head. "Ronan, it's not your fault. We both know that. I'll get through this, I swear. I just have to be disappointed for a little while."

He looked as if she'd kicked him in the gut. Natalie tried to feel bad, but she hurt too much to think past her own pain. She ignored the fallen painting and got her bag from her desk, then headed for her car. When she got home, she quickly changed into yoga pants and a T-shirt, then sank onto her bed, curled up in a ball and began to cry.

"How's Natalie?" Nick asked as they ran along the park's trail. The tournament was coming up faster than Ronan had realized and they were in a rush to get in shape.

"Not good," Ronan said, thinking about how quiet she'd been when he'd stopped by the previous night. "She says she's fine, but she's not."

"I haven't seen her since it happened." Mathias glanced at him, then returned his attention to the trail. "Has she been to work?"

"Just in the office. She hasn't been back in the studio."

"It's not your fault," Nick told him. "It just happened."

Something Ronan had told himself about a thousand times, but that didn't stop the gut-churning guilt that never left. She'd created something wonderful and he'd destroyed it. He'd been the one to pick up the piece after she'd left. The canvas was still intact but the flowers were ruined. Those at the top had been burned down to nothing while those at the bottom were singed, with the middle petals somewhere on the spectrum, depending on their placement.

For a couple of minutes, he'd had the idea that maybe he could fix it or something, but who was he kidding? He didn't have her gift. Besides, it wasn't as if what had been lost could be replaced. It was a one-of-a-kind creation and now it was gone.

"So, ah, how's that volunteer school project?" Mathias asked in an obvious attempt to change the subject. "What are you going to do for your first class?"

He figured the distraction was as much for them as for him. No one liked to think about Natalie suffering.

"I thought I'd go traditional and we'd start with paints. I'm going to work up some templates, show them how to divide their work space. Talk a little about perspective, that kind of thing."

"Want some help?" Mathias asked. "Sounds like it's going to be cool. I'd like to go with you."

"Me, too," Nick added. "I can wrangle a kid or two. It will be good practice. Plus, I was thinking about the classes. Remember when I used to play around with animation? Maybe I could work up something with that. Break it down into steps. Show the kids how to illustrate the high points of a story. With all the animation software out there these days, the students who are interested could take it to the next step on their own."

"Thanks." Ronan cleared his throat. "I appreciate the offer. I welcome any help you want to give."

They finished their last lap, then walked to the chin-up bar, where they took turns alternately cheering and jeering each other as they finished their workout.

The charity tournament was in a few days. Aidan and Del would be arriving, along with their wives. It was going to be a Mitchell brother reunion.

When Ronan had first found out he'd been committed to the event, he'd felt trapped. Now he was grateful to have time with his brothers. Natalie had dragged him back to the land of the living. Without her, he would still be moody, reclusive and without purpose.

Thinking about her reminded him of what he'd done and how she was still crushed. If only there was a way to make it up to her—but there wasn't. In his head, he understood it really had been an accident and no one was at fault. In his heart and his gut, he knew he'd hurt Natalie, and how on earth was he supposed to get over that?

"I'M WHINING," PALLAS said with a strangled laugh. "You're welcome to hang up on me if you don't have time."

Natalie was alone in her office at the gallery. She'd finished all her work and, were this any other day, she would be eager to get into the studio and get going on whatever project she had planned. But she hadn't been back to the studio since the accident and going there now seemed impossible.

She shifted her cell phone to her other ear and said, "I would love to listen to you whine. What's going on?"

Pallas sighed. "Just a bunch of little stuff that makes me insane. The villain T-shirts are printed wrong. They're going to be replaced, but they're from a vendor I really trust. Now I wonder if they're going to screw up other stuff, which isn't fair, but it's how I feel. Renee was the one to find the mistakes. Thank goodness she insisted on checking the order. I would have just left the boxes in the storage room, ready to go for the wedding."

"Are we liking Renee more?"

Pallas laughed. "Yes. I mean, I never didn't like her. It's just she's so perfect. It's unnerving."

"What else is going wrong?"

"I can't for the life of me get the whole, and I'm using air quotes here, icy lair thing right. Renee's working on it, too, and we're stymied. Oh, Silver did a midweek wedding at one of the other venues last night and she called to say she thinks she got food poisoning."

"Oh, no. That's awful. How is she feeling?"

"She had to go throw up before she could tell me, so I'm guessing not good. And that's everything here. You're coming to the dinner on Friday, aren't you? I'm looking forward to hanging out with everyone."

With all five brothers in town, a big family dinner had been planned. Ronan had asked Natalie to go with him. "I'm a little nervous about seeing Aidan, Del and their wives again."

"You'll do great. They're so sweet. I got to know Del and Maya last year when I worked on their wedding. I didn't spend as much time with Aidan and Shelby, but they seemed really nice." Pallas laughed. "I'll make sure you and Ronan sit by us. How's that? Then if you run out of things to say, you can roll your eyes at me."

Natalie smiled. "It's a deal."

She and her friend chatted for a few more minutes, then hung up. Natalie looked at the clock and knew she had an entire afternoon to fill. The past couple of days, when she finished in the office, she'd simply gone home, but she couldn't avoid the studio forever. There'd been a disaster, but no one was hurt and her next piece would be even better. The only way to get over her disappointment was to move on.

That was as much of a pep talk as she could manage, so she forced herself to her feet and walked across the parking lot to the studio.

The building was closed and dark. She knew Ronan was working from home and she wasn't sure where Mathias and Nick were. After unlocking the door, she stepped inside and turned on the lights.

Nothing looked all that different than it had before. All the workstations were just as messy. The huge oven still sat in the far corner. She turned toward her area and saw the big easel was empty, which made her wonder where her canvas was. There was no way the guys would have thrown it out. She'd just assumed it would be waiting for her, all big and burned and ugly.

She looked around the studio but didn't see it anywhere. She went into the storeroom and saw it leaning up against the far wall. Her heart stopped as she relived the horrifying moment of the first flames consuming her beautiful flowers. The sound of the canvas hitting the concrete floor replayed in her mind over and over again.

But even as the sound filled her mind, she couldn't help noticing the damage wasn't total. The top of the canvas had suffered the most and the flowers were burned down to the glue, but at the very bottom they were barely touched and three butterflies were intact. The flowers in the middle had scorched and burned petals, the black contrasting with the vivid colors she'd chosen for her piece. There was, she had to admit, a savage beauty to what was left.

She carried the canvas to her workstation and set it on the easel, then walked back and forth as she studied the canvas. While it still hurt to see the destruction, a part of her knew there might be other possibilities.

She ran her hands across the flowers. Burned bits fluttered to the ground. She did it again, faster this time, until all the loose pieces were gone. The flowers at the top were totally denuded. She would have to do something there for sure. And while she'd always thought she was only going to work with paper on this one, maybe not. Maybe it was time to add something else to the mix.

She dragged her supply cart close and began pulling out drawers and setting them on her desk. Buttons, she thought. Metal. She needed metal. More flowers on the top, but maybe not out of paper. Fabric might be better, with a huge butterfly dominating the middle.

She worked until her back and arms ached. When she finally stopped it was after six and she was exhausted. She hadn't had anything to eat or drink since that morning, but none of that mattered. Not when she looked at what she'd done.

From the ashes, she thought. In this case, literally. She still had a lot to do, but she could see where she was going. The flowers were the base, but now there was so much more. There was dimension in the piece. Determination.

Her crushed heart opened and joy rushed in. She

wasn't broken or even beaten. She'd regrouped and she would be fine. As for the canvas in front of her… with a little time and love, it would still be her best creation ever.

She put away her supplies, then left the studio, careful to lock the door behind her. She got her bag and went to her car. Nearly a half hour later, she pulled up in front of Ronan's house. He met her at the door, his gaze questioning.

"Are you all right?" he asked.

She stepped inside, dropped her bag on the floor, then raised herself on tiptoe and kissed him.

"Let's go do it," she whispered.

"You don't have to ask me twice," he said, pulling her down the hallway.

A quality she could totally respect in a man.

CHAPTER SEVENTEEN

"I'M NERVOUS," NATALIE WHISPERED.

Ronan pulled into the driveway of Mathias's house and parked behind a rental car. "We're alone in my truck. You can talk in a normal voice."

"I'm practicing for the dinner party later." She worried her lower lip. "What if they don't like me?"

"Nick, Mathias, Pallas and Carol already like you. The rest of the family will feel the same." He smiled at her. "Besides, what's not to like?"

Her eyes brightened. "That's true. I am pretty likable."

She was. They'd spent the last twenty-four hours at his place. They'd made love, cooked, flown paper airplanes off the upstairs landing and she'd talked about how she'd taken what had been trash and once again created something wonderful.

He didn't know how she kept moving forward, no matter what happened to her. He'd seen her pain and devastation when her artwork had caught fire. He'd felt sick and horrified on her behalf—because he would never want to hurt her. But he'd never felt that loss himself. He knew if some glass creation was destroyed, he would make another, or pull something out of storage. He'd always had so much—it was difficult to want for anything.

Around Natalie, for the first time, he began to see he could do better. Like what he was doing with the art classes. He was excited about the possibilities and how he might, in some small way, influence a child. What could be more important than that?

He looked at the house on the edge of the animal preserve. It was a big, sprawling place. Mathias had bought it after Ronan had purchased his place up on the mountain. Until then, they'd shared a rental. Ronan had been the one to break away, to create the first crack in their relationship.

No, he thought, determined to be honest. There had been plenty of cracks below the surface. His moving to the mountain had simply been the first that everyone could see. He'd been unable to deal with what their father had told them, so he'd escaped the only way he knew how. Over time, the distance between the brothers had gotten bigger.

Things were different now. Better. He was healing—he could feel it. He wasn't there yet and he knew he could slip away if he wasn't careful, but for now, he was connecting with his family, and Natalie was the reason.

He got out of his truck, then walked around to her side to help her down. She stared at the big house.

"You're all rich, aren't you? In my next life, I'm

going to be rich, or at least well-off. Just to try it. I think it will be fun."

"You have a different kind of richness," he said, putting his hand on the small of her back and guiding her toward the front door. "It's part of who you are and you never have to worry about losing it."

She looked at him. "That's the nicest thing you've ever said to me. Thank you."

He kissed her. "You're welcome. Now brace yourself."

"I'm braced."

He knocked once, then opened the front door and walked inside. The open foyer led to a big living room and dining room. The sound of conversation came from beyond, in the family room.

"We're here," he called.

Mathias and Carol came out to greet them. Carol hugged Natalie. "This is going to be so great. I didn't even try to cook—the thought of it was too intimidating. We're being catered and there's nothing to worry about. Oh, and I have wine."

Natalie laughed with her friend. "You are the perfect hostess."

"I'm trying. Now, do you know everyone?"

Carol led Natalie into the family room and started circulating with her. Ronan watched to make sure she was all right, then turned back to Mathias.

"She'll be fine," his brother said. "She met the family at the fundraiser for Millie's herd last year, then at our wedding. Come and say hi and then I'll get you a beer."

"A reward for good behavior?"

"Something like that."

Ronan hesitated a second before following his brother into the family room. He waited for the now-familiar tension he often felt when he was around his brothers. A sense of otherness that always drove him to the fringes. But it wasn't noticeable today. Instead he was comfortable as he hugged Maya and Shelby and slapped his brothers on the back.

In a matter of minutes, the ten of them had split off by gender. The women were in the kitchen, talking and laughing, while the brothers sat on the large sofas in the family room.

"You in any kind of shape for our challenge?" Nick asked Del. "Or are you still soft?"

Del raised his eyebrows. "I'll take you, little brother, just like I did when we were kids. Now, later or in twenty years."

"You wish."

Both brothers laughed. Ronan knew that for all their cheap talk, the truth was Del had always looked out for his younger siblings. Even when they'd been split into the artist and nonartist factions, Del had taken care of them. He'd been the oldest and all the expectations had fallen on him.

"Maya and I work out together," Del told them. "I'm going to be faster and stronger than any of you."

"Huh." Mathias sipped his beer. "I see you talking, bro, but all I hear is a buzzing sound."

Del laughed.

The women called them to help get ready for dinner. The large dining room table was set for ten. Ronan noticed a couple of bottles of champagne, along with sparkling nonalcoholic cider for Pallas. Mathias and Carol had ordered in from a local Italian restaurant. Salads were served while the lasagna and garlic bread warmed in the oven.

Mathias sat at one end of the table, with Carol sitting at the other end, across from him. The rest of them claimed seats. Champagne and cider were passed around, and then Mathias raised his glass.

"To family," he said. "And those we love."

"Hear, hear."

They'd barely started eating when Del cleared his throat. "So Maya and I have an announcement." Del glanced at his wife and smiled. "We're moving back to the States."

"Great," Nick said with a wink. "The Chinese government finally throwing you two out?"

"Nothing like that. We've finished our project and we're ready to come home for a year or so."

"Where are you going to settle?" Aidan asked. "Fool's Gold?"

"Happily Inc is much better," Mathias said. "Move here. You can do whatever you want without Mayor Marsha knowing about it."

"Dude," Nick said with a grin. "You know she still keeps track of us."

"No way."

Del and Maya exchanged a look. Ronan didn't know what they were thinking, but he caught the intimacy in the gaze, and for a second, he felt a surprising jolt of envy. He was careful not to look at Natalie—he didn't want her to misunderstand or think he'd changed his mind about wanting more than they had. But for a second, just a second, he wondered what it would be like to be comfortable enough to want more and know it was possible.

"We haven't decided where yet," Maya said, still looking at her husband. "But we're definitely leaning toward Fool's Gold. I don't have any family and I want to be close to Elaine."

Ronan's good mood started to fade. Natalie reached across his lap and took his hand in hers, as if to calm him.

"Elaine?" Nick sounded surprised. "Not that I don't love my mom, but why would she influence your decision?"

Maya flushed slightly. "I don't have my mother around anymore and, well, we're going to have a baby."

"What?"

"No way!"

"That's fantastic!"

Everyone started talking at once. Ronan looked more closely and realized Maya had taken cider, too. He could tell by the color in the glass. And Shelby's glass was—

"Us, too," Aidan said proudly. "Shelby just passed the three-month mark."

"No way," Mathias said, eyeing his wife. "Carol?"

She smiled. "We were going to wait another two weeks to make the announcement, but sure. Why not?" She shrugged. "I'm eight weeks along."

Everyone laughed and then toasted again. Ronan felt as if he'd been kicked in the gut. He was the only one of his brothers who wasn't married, let alone with a pregnant wife. What the hell was going on?

Involuntarily, he glanced at Natalie, who looked happy as she clinked glasses with her friends. He told himself he didn't see anything in her eyes, only he wasn't sure if he was simply fooling himself. Natalie wanted kids—she'd downloaded that baby app, after all. Not that she'd mentioned it much lately, but who knew what she was doing when she was alone. Maybe she was researching sperm banks or something.

He grew less comfortable by the second and thought longingly of escape. It was all too much.

Time slowed as his brothers and their wives discussed pregnancy, birth, names and hoped-for gender of their soon-to-be children. Natalie joined in the conversation, but Ronan stayed quiet.

The only bright spot was the upcoming challenge. Pallas pointed out they all needed a good night's sleep and the dinner broke up shortly after dessert.

"Are you all right?" Natalie asked as he helped her into the truck.

"I'm fine. Thinking about tomorrow. Nick's expecting us to win and we have no idea about the competition. I hate to see his competitive heart broken."

As he'd hoped, Natalie accepted his words at face value and grinned. "You're right. Someone could be bringing in a few ringers and then what? We'll just have to see." She leaned back in her seat. "All right, young man. Take me home. You shouldn't be distracted by a woman tonight. You have to save yourself for the competition."

"Yes, ma'am."

He did his best to sound teasing rather than relieved. He'd been wondering how he was going to avoid spending the night with Natalie. He needed to be alone, to process everything. The sensation of being trapped only grew and more than anything he wanted to run.

He dropped her off, kissed her once, then was on his way up to his place. At the edge of town, he hesitated. The highway beckoned and in a matter of hours he could be in another state. He could just drive until he got lost for good.

His hands tightened on the steering wheel. No, he told himself. He wasn't going to run. He was going to see this out. Although he had no idea what "this" was, nor did he know what seeing it out meant. He just knew that if he screwed up this time, if he got himself lost, he might go so far that he would never be found. And even he wasn't sure he really wanted that.

THE MORNING OF the competition was cool and clear with heat promised for the afternoon. Ronan arrived still wrestling with all the emotional crap from his family. The last thing he wanted was to endure the competition, although he told himself once he had a good, hard workout, everything would look better. He hoped like hell he wasn't lying.

There had to be at least a hundred people milling around, all wearing different-colored shirts with numbers on them. His brothers were already there and had checked him in. Aidan and Shelby had stayed with Mathias and Carol while Del and Maya had stayed with Nick and Pallas. He'd been the only one alone the previous night. By choice, he reminded himself. That was how he liked things. Quiet. Solitary.

"Wondered if you were going to show," Mathias said, handing him a bright green T-shirt with their team number clearly marked on the front.

"I'm here."

"Good."

Natalie rushed up and hugged him. "I'm so excited. You're going to do great."

Just seeing her eased the tension inside of him. His gut unknotted and he found himself thinking more clearly. He kissed her. "You're going to watch?"

"I'll be here with your sisters-in-law." She grinned. "We're going to be talking about everyone, so brace yourself."

"No bracing required. I won't be able to hear it."

She laughed. "Good luck."

She ran back to join the wives.

For just that instant he allowed himself to believe it was real, that he could figure things out and convince her they belonged together. Only he knew that was impossible. There was too much for him to overcome. He couldn't trust who he was and there was no way he would consider having children, while Natalie was born to be a mom.

"So here's how it's going to go," Nick said. "We have the 5K followed by a scavenger hunt through the wooded part of the park and then a tug-of-war. The better we do in the first two parts, the higher our ranking in the final one. The last two teams compete against each other first in the tug-of-war, with the winner taking on the next highest ranked and so on."

"The higher you are, the fewer number of turns you have to take," Del confirmed. "No problem. We've all been training for the race and Aidan will get us through the woods, no problem."

Mathias looked around. "Maybe it's just me, but doesn't that guy over there play professional soccer?"

"Ringers," Nick muttered. "I knew it."

Ronan chuckled.

"If the teams will head to the starting line, please."

The instruction came over the loudspeaker. Ronan and his brothers lined up for the race. Some of the teams were all women and others were mixed gender. There was friendly bantering at the starting line. Then the gun went off and everyone sprinted along the course.

An hour and a half later they'd completed the 5K and gotten through the scavenger hunt in the forest. Aidan had studied the map and found the shortest way through while the rest of them had worked the clues. They'd finished third out of twenty-five teams, giving them plenty of time to rest before the final event.

After a water break, they headed over to the tug-of-war area to watch the other teams. A long rope stretched over a shallow gully filled with mud. It was about ten feet wide, and while not that deep, it was going to be plenty messy, not to mention humiliating, for any team that got pulled in.

The two last-place teams took their place. A group of women easily defeated a team of guys in their late teens who were too busy laughing and joking with each other to notice the round had started.

"Never underestimate the power of a woman," Aidan said as the young guys went sprawling.

"We've got a bit until it's our turn," Del said. "We can relax. This has been fun." He made a fist and lightly socked Nick in the arm. "Thanks for arranging everything. We should do it again." He looked at Aidan. "Is there anything like this in Fool's Gold?"

"There has to be. We have a festival nearly every week. If not, we can start something."

"Why Fool's Gold?" Mathias asked, looking wary.

"Why not?" Aidan's expression tightened. "You grew up there. You have friends there. You can come back and hang with Mom. And speaking of our mother, you three need to step it up. Everything falls on me. Sending flowers for her birthday and Mother's Day doesn't mean you have an ongoing relationship."

Ronan took a step back. This wasn't his fight, he told himself. He didn't have to get involved.

Nick shuffled his feet. "It's not Mom who's the problem."

"I don't care." Aidan stepped close and glared at him. "She's your mother."

"I know." He sighed. "Fine. I'll do more. And you're right—we should do something in Fool's Gold in the next few months. Maybe before Pallas has the baby. After that we won't want to travel for a while."

Mathias nodded. "I get it. I'll talk to Carol. Maybe

we can all get together for Mom's birthday this year. Take her out to brunch."

Del grinned. "Brunch works."

Ronan knew their father hated brunch and would refuse to go.

"Besides," Del said, looking smug, "if Maya and I move back to Fool's Gold, I'm going to be golden."

"You wish," Mathias joked, and then he turned to Ronan. "You want to weigh in on this?"

"Do what you want."

Mathias's humor faded. "No way. You're not going to tell us that you're not coming with us."

"I have no reason to go see Elaine."

Nick muttered something under his breath. Del and Aidan both looked disgusted.

"You can't be serious," Del told him. "Dammit, Ronan, get over it. She raised you just like she raised us. She was there for you every single day. You've got to let this go."

"Why?" Ronan kept his voice quiet. "Tell me why I should let it go. Because it doesn't matter? Let's see—I don't know who my mother is. I don't know anything about her side of the family. The woman I thought of as my mother lied to me every single one of those days she was taking care of me. I can see keeping it quiet while I was a kid, but what about when I was older? Didn't I have the right to know?"

His brothers looked at each other.

"If you're looking for an asshole in all this," Nick said, "blame Ceallach. He's the one who had the affair."

"Believe me, I'm not letting him off the hook."

Ronan tightened his hands into fists, then consciously relaxed. "But so what? He'll always be a jerk. None of us cares about him. You're asking me to say what Elaine did is okay. You're asking me to just let it go. I'm not going to do that."

"What does that mean?" Aidan glared at him. "You're never going to speak to her again? That's the thanks she gets for taking you in and loving you?"

Ronan turned away only to see one of the volunteers approaching. She waved a clipboard.

"Gentlemen, you're up."

Ronan thought about getting in his truck and driving away. Instead he joined his brothers on the edge of the now-crumbling bank.

Nick and Aidan were in front, with Ronan in the middle and Mathias and Del behind. They all grabbed the rope.

"This isn't over," Mathias said loudly. "When we're done here, you and I are going to have this out. How come I never saw until this second our father isn't the only dick in the family? Who'd have guessed it? Ronan, you're just as bad as him."

Of all the things his former twin could have said, that was the worst.

"You don't know," Ronan started, his teeth clenched. "You have no idea."

"Fight later, focus now," Del yelled as the rope tightened.

But Mathias wasn't giving up. "Boo hoo. Poor you. Taken in by a good woman and loved as a child. How awful. You need a service dog to help you with that incredible emotional wound?"

"Asshole," Ronan muttered, pulling.

"Say that to my face. Stand up to me. Oh, wait. No. You're going to walk away. It's what you always do. Why bother fighting for something when it's just so easy to give up?"

Rage exploded. Without thinking, Ronan turned to give Mathias exactly what he was asking for. Mathias must have read his mind because his twin also let go of the rope and started for him.

"No!" Nick yelled, but it was too late. One savage tug on the rope later, all five of them were tumbling into the gully.

The mud might not be very deep but it was wet and cold and humiliating. The other team, all women, stood staring at them. Then they burst into laughter.

"I thought they'd be a lot harder to take," one of the women said as they began to high-five each other.

"We need to work on our communication skills," Nick muttered as he climbed out of the gully. "All of us."

Ronan and Mathias stood and glared at each other, and then Ronan stalked off. He didn't need any of this. Not anymore.

CHAPTER EIGHTEEN

Ellen and Barry's movie-based wedding also had the same theme for their rehearsal dinner and the party that followed. With Pallas still taking things easy so she would be rested for the wedding on Saturday afternoon, Natalie had offered to help the ever-efficient Renee get things organized for the party Friday night. She was slightly overwhelmed by the number of details that went into the evening, but as she wasn't in charge, she simply did what she was told.

She'd already started on the large flowers she was making for the "Atsuko project" and was also playing with her burned piece in addition to working, so she should have felt as if she were running flat out all the time. Instead she was grateful to be busy, grateful not to have time to think. In truth, she was mostly consumed by whatever was going on with Ronan.

Something had changed. In the past week, he'd worked from home more than he'd been in the studio. The few times she'd seen him, he'd claimed that he was in the home stretch of his commission and needed to get as much done as he could. He'd *said* all the right things, but she didn't believe him.

She knew he and his brothers had fought the previous weekend. While she hadn't heard all that had been said, she'd been able to read the body language and knew that whatever they'd been arguing about had been the reason they'd lost. She'd watched Ronan drive away, his pain obvious with every breath.

Over the past few days, she'd talked to Mathias and Nick and had pieced together what had happened. As far as she could tell, Ronan was once again dealing with his past and everything he didn't know about himself.

She wasn't sure how sympathetic she was willing to be with him. On the one hand, he had been dealt a hard blow. On the other hand, really? Really? Wasn't it time to either find out what he could or start to deal? Did he plan to spend the rest of his life moping?

She wasn't sure if thinking that made her a bad girlfriend or not. She also wasn't sure how much she could understand about his situation and his feelings. She tried to imagine what it would be like if she'd found her mother wasn't her mother—that she'd lied to her all her life. She would be devastated to think all that love and caring and support had been shielding a lie. So maybe accusing him of moping was a bit harsh.

Natalie finished setting the table and looked around the room. Renee had created a movie-based wonderland with posters and comic-themed objects. There were cityscapes made from cardboard and bats on everything. Banners, and a flock (or colony) of paper bats, compliments of Natalie. There were eye masks for the guests and a small but beautiful bat-themed cake for dessert.

"Looks good," Silver said from the bar she'd set up in a corner of the room. "I'm really excited about tonight. Tomorrow will be the real thing and more serious, but this is all fun."

Natalie walked over and looked at the menu written on the chalkboard Silver had set up.

"Went a little crazy, did we?" she asked with a laugh.

Silver grinned. "I might have."

The drinks were charmingly named with a brief description. Sweet Poison—two kinds of rum. Boy Wonder—tequila and champagne. Joker—infused vodka. Poison Ivy—gin. Gotham Chill—Wild Turkey.

"Have you tasted them all?" Natalie asked, thinking work like that would give her a really bad hangover.

"In very small amounts and not on the same day. I've learned to be careful."

"I'll bet."

Silver set out glasses. "You okay?"

"Sure. Why do you ask?"

"I heard some things about last weekend. That Ronan and his brothers got in a fight."

Natalie wondered who had talked. Most likely Carol or Pallas. They were all close and there weren't a lot of secrets between them.

"I think things are all right," she said, hoping she wasn't lying. "Honestly, I can't tell. Ronan says he's busy with work, so I've let him be."

"Do you believe him? About the work?"

"I want to. I hope he is. Otherwise he's withdrawing and that scares me. What if he runs again?"

"I thought things weren't serious. I thought you didn't believe in happily-ever-after. What happened to you being unable to find a good guy?"

"This isn't about me," Natalie said quickly. "I'm just worried about Ronan."

Silver set out several more glasses. "I get that and I think it's really great you care about him. I would also like to point out that there's more going on here."

Natalie didn't like how the conversation had shifted. Things were so much better when she was talking about someone else.

"Maybe."

The corner of Silver's mouth turned up. "As long as you're not trying to deceive yourself." The smile faded. "Natalie, whatever Ronan has going on, he has to deal with. I like him, but you're my friend, so I'm on your team. I can't help wondering if all this fuss about him is really about distracting yourself from the truth. You're falling for him in a big way and for whatever reason you can't or won't accept that."

"No." The word was automatic. "I haven't. I can't. He's wrong for me, so I wouldn't let that happen."

"Famous last words." She held up both hands. "I'm not saying you have to do anything. It's your life. I'm simply suggesting you might want to be honest with yourself. You're not hurting for Ronan because of his past. You're hurting for Ronan because you're in love with him. That's why you don't want him to run away.

That's why you think you need to fix this problem—so he'll want to be with you."

"What? No. No, I wouldn't…" She took a couple of steps back. "That's silly. I'm not in love with him."

She continued to back up until she bumped into the table. Then she turned and raced for the door.

"I'm going to check on the food," she said. "I'll be right back."

Silver only smiled. "I'll be here."

Natalie waited until she was alone in the hallway, then crouched down and wrapped her arms around her stomach.

She wasn't in love with Ronan. She refused to be! No. This was just them having fun. It was easy and great and she liked being around him, but anything else wasn't going to happen. It couldn't. He didn't want a relationship that would last forever and she couldn't accept anything else. So there would be no "in love" for them. Just this fun stuff, and then, well, she wasn't sure what the "then" was, but it wasn't love. It couldn't be. His hiding from his brothers proved her point.

She forced herself to her feet. She had a rehearsal dinner to help with and then the wedding tomorrow. For now, she would let it all go. Ellen and Barry needed her. As for the rest of it, chances were her problems would be patiently waiting for her after that.

THE WEDDING STARTED on time exactly at three. By five, it was a party.

"What is it with zip lines at weddings?" Natalie

asked Pallas as they paused in the kitchen to grab a glass of water before heading back to work.

"I know, right? We had that one last year and I honestly never thought I'd have reason to call the guy again. Still, it's a fun and memorable addition." She sat on a chair in the corner, leaning her head against the wall. "I feel so much better. Still tired, but better."

"You look good."

Pallas smiled. "Thanks. In a couple of months, I'll be a whale, so I'm trying to really enjoy all the compliments I'm getting now."

"First, you will never be a whale. Second, you're having a baby. It's worth it and you know it."

"I do. I'm so happy." She touched her stomach. She looked at Natalie. "Have you talked to Ronan?"

"Not today. But I saw him Thursday. Why?"

"I don't know. Nick's worried. Everything was okay and then it all blew up at the tournament." She got up. "Sorry, I shouldn't have said anything. We have a reception to get through. Have I mentioned how much I appreciate your help?"

"About a thousand times," Natalie said, pretending to be totally fine with what they'd just talked about. "Renee is going to be jealous."

"You think? I'm still having trouble reading her, although I certainly can't complain about her work. She's amazing, but sometimes, when she doesn't know I'm looking, I would swear she's…" Pallas hesitated. "I'm not sure. Sad, I guess. Not that it's any of my business. Okay, I'm rested. You ready to go back and deal with our slightly drunk guests?"

"I'm here to do whatever makes your day easier."

Pallas chuckled. "That makes me love you even more!"

NATALIE MADE HER escape close to eight o'clock. She wasn't sure how long the party would go, but Pallas was heading home, leaving Renee in charge, and she'd told Natalie she was free to go, as well. Natalie sat in her shiny red car for a couple of seconds as she tried to figure out what she was going to do. Going back to her place was one option. She was tired and wanted to just sleep the whole night. But she couldn't stop thinking about Ronan and all that had, or hadn't, happened in the past week.

He was pulling away from her. She could feel it, and while she tried to understand why, she found herself getting more and more pissed. He'd come so far and now he was retreating and she knew exactly what would happen then. He wouldn't be able to work, he wouldn't be happy and he wouldn't want to be with her.

Her anger gave her a burst of energy. She pulled out of the parking lot and headed up the mountain. She pulled into the driveway and gave herself a second to really get her juices flowing, then stomped up to the front door and rang the bell.

Ronan answered quickly, looking surprised. "Hi. Did I know you were coming by after the wedding?"

"No." She pushed past him, then waited while he closed the door behind her. "You didn't. I want to talk."

His expression turned wary. "Okay," he said slowly. "Should we go into the—"

"No," she interrupted. "We should stay right here. I don't want to be comfortable and I'm not staying long." She tried to think of something rational to say, but all that came out was "You're a butthead. A complete and total butthead."

Ronan's mouth tightened, but he didn't speak.

She glared at him. "Worse, you're stupid. You know what you're doing and you know the consequences, but here you are hiding out, anyway. You're probably thinking about leaving. Am I right?"

She didn't bother waiting for an answer. "But here's the thing. You like what's been happening to you. You like it a lot. You like hanging out with me. You like what we have. You also enjoy being with your brothers and working in the gallery studio again. You're creating and that's got to feel like you can finally draw in a full breath. But is it enough? Of course not."

She put her hands on her hips. "You know what's going to happen. You're going to cut yourself off from everyone and then what? You won't be able to work anymore. You'll be stuck, like you were before, only it will be worse this time because you just had everything you wanted and you lost it because you're a stupid butthead."

"You have no idea what I'm dealing with."

He spoke between clenched teeth, which made her wonder how mad he was. She supposed she should have been afraid, but it was too late for that.

"You're right. I don't. So here's the thing—you're not dying. You're not sick. You haven't lost a child, or your job or your house. You're not worried about how to deal with your mom's Alzheimer's when you can't afford care and you have to work and she's started wandering around the neighborhood. You have as much money as God, a family who loves you and a hell of a cute girlfriend."

Her voice was getting louder, but she couldn't seem to stop herself. "I'm sorry about your dad and what he did and I'm sorry you don't know who your biological mother is, but you know what? You have a mom who loves you and you don't care. That is wrong. People care about you and you're going to throw it all away because you're a stupid butthead and you liked being in the world again."

She drew in a breath, then realized she'd said all she wanted, so she walked past him to the front door. Once she was in the car, she started it and headed down the mountain.

By the time she got home, she was shaking. Possibly from fatigue, possibly from emotional overload. She forced herself to eat some cheese and crackers and drink some water before pulling on yoga pants and a T-shirt. She would veg out in front of the TV until she felt sleepy, and then she would go to bed. As for Ronan, she honestly didn't know what was going to happen. She'd told him the truth. She didn't have anything else to give.

She'd barely settled on the sofa when she heard a knock at her door. Her heart fluttered and ridiculous hope flared. She had it bad, she thought grimly as she walked to the door.

Ronan stood on the landing. She couldn't read his expression and had no idea what he was thinking.

"You're right," he told her. "I do like it. All of it. You, my brothers, working again. That scares the hell out of me because it could all be gone in a second."

"Only if you walk away from us," she told him. "Otherwise we're just here."

"I'm sorry."

"I know."

She motioned for him to come inside. He walked into the living room. When she'd closed and locked the door, he reached for her, pulling her close. Then his mouth was on hers and his hands were everywhere and absolutely nothing else mattered but the man and how he made her feel.

MONDAY MORNING RONAN was back in the gallery studio. He hadn't been sure of his reception but both his brothers greeted him as if the previous week of angst hadn't happened. His work went well and his demons receded. It turned out Natalie had been right—he was a stupid butthead.

Around eleven, his cell phone rang.

"Where are you?" he asked by way of greeting. "I thought you were working in the office today."

"I was." Natalie sounded like her normal happy self. "I had to run some errands. Then Ted called from the recycling center and told me they had something for me." She laughed. "It's amazing and you have to come right now. I mean, right now. This second. Bring your truck. You're going to be so excited."

"Uh-huh. What is it?"

"I'm not going to tell you. It's a surprise."

Which could mean anything from a bag of recycled cans to he had no idea what. "Give me five minutes and I'll head out."

"I'll be waiting."

He hung up. "I have to go to the recycling center."

Nick chuckled. "Did she say what it was?"

"No."

"Good luck with that."

"Whatever it is, I'm bringing it back here. I'm not going through this alone."

Nick was still laughing when Ronan left.

He drove to the recycling center and parked. Natalie danced out of the main building and raced over to him.

"It's so great. We're so lucky Ted called. What a nice guy."

"Uh-huh. What is it?"

She grabbed his arm and pulled him inside. At first all he saw was the normal clutter of refurbished left-overs for sale, but then he noticed a battered item on the floor.

He stared at the old, beat-up bowl with a flat disc in it, all supported on a slightly tilted table. What on earth?

"Isn't it great?" Natalie asked, beaming at him. "I'm so excited. The second Ted saw it, he thought of me."

"Of course he did. What is it?"

She looked shocked. "It's a pottery wheel."

He looked closer and recognized the components.

The table could be adjusted up and down, and he saw a foot pedal, no doubt to control the speed.

"I've never thrown pottery," he said cautiously, knowing it wasn't going to matter. Natalie had made up her mind.

"I haven't, either, but come on. It's only twenty-five dollars and it's in great shape. Ted said the motor still works. What's not to like?"

He knew he shouldn't bother, but he couldn't help asking, "Why do you want this?"

She stared at him in disbelief. "For the school. Your art classes. The kids will love it and it's small enough we can take it to them!"

"Sure, but that brings me back to my earlier point that neither of us knows what we're doing."

Her expression turned pitying. "Ronan, we're artists. We'll learn how to work with the wheel. We have time. I'm not saying we'll be great, but we can study the basics and then teach the kids. We can fire their work and bring it when we come back."

He knew better than to fight her. "Okay, then." He pulled out his wallet and dropped two twenties into the cash tin on the counter. "Let's get it back to the studio."

They wrestled the table and wheel into the back of his truck. When they got back to the studio, both Mathias and Nick came out to see what they'd bought.

"Is it alive?" Mathias asked hopefully. "Is it a baby gazelle?"

"I knew you were missing Sophie," Ronan muttered, remembering how his brother had looked after their mother's dog the previous year. "Get a puppy."

"I want to but not until Carol has the baby. That way they can grow up together."

Nick shook his head. "Sure. A newborn and potty training. That's smart." He peered over the side of the truck. "Cool. A pottery wheel. That's a great idea. You can take it to the school and teach kids how to use it."

Natalie's expression turned knowing. "See?"

Ronan held in a sigh. "I've heard that one already."

"What he really means," Natalie said as the guys easily lifted the wheel down, then carried it into the studio, "is that we don't know how to work with a wheel."

"That's why they have YouTube videos," Mathias said as he walked to his computer. "We already have clay. This is going to be fun."

In less time than he would have thought, they were all covered in clay and laughing over their disasters. As with many techniques, it was harder than it looked. Natalie had produced a passably acceptable bowl. Nick turned everything he touched into an oversize penis and Mathias kept pressing too hard to the left, creating lopsided, undefinable blobs.

"I would have thought you'd be the best of all of us," Ronan admitted. "You make dishes and vases all the time. Shouldn't you be able to translate into clay the easiest?"

"I'm ignoring you," Mathias said cheerfully, taking his turn at the wheel. "At least I'm not advertising my inability to satisfy my wife." He nodded at Nick's long and bulbous creation.

“Hey, Pallas is perfectly satisfied. I was trying to make a tall vase.”

“Sure you were.”

Ronan caught Natalie’s gaze and winked at her. She laughed. He felt the weight he’d been carrying lighten a little. She was good for him, he admitted, knowing it was equally important that he be good for her, as well.

CHAPTER NINETEEN

NATALIE STUDIED THE CANVAS. It was the second time she'd finished the piece—the first had ended with it going up in flames. She still had to struggle not to wince when she thought about how horrible that had been. Although now, stepping back and looking at what she'd completed, she had to concede this one was even better.

She liked the different textures from all the items she'd used. Found bits and buttons and ribbon and fabric all blended perfectly with the paper flowers and butterflies that made up the foundation. There was something alive, a sense of hope. Or maybe that was just her. Regardless, it was finished and now she had to suck it up and show Atsuko.

She should have done it yesterday, she thought. Or the day before. But fear was a bitch and she'd had to work up the courage. Not that her boss would ever be anything less than supportive. She had a feeling Atsuko would take the piece and put it in the gallery. It was the price that was the reckoning.

She grabbed the canvas in both hands and started for the door. Nick beat her to it and held it open, then murmured, “Good luck.”

“Thanks.”

She glanced back at Ronan, on the far side of the room. He was working with his team today, already dripping sweat from too much time spent near the fiery ovens. He spotted her and gave her a quick thumbs-up.

She went into the gallery and set the canvas on an easel in the back room, then knocked on Atsuko’s open office door.

“Natalie. I thought today was an art day for you.”

“It is. I finished something.”

Her boss immediately rose. “I’m excited to see whatever it is.”

“It’s not the flowers. I’m still working on those.”

“That’s fine. I know better than to push one of my artists.”

Natalie nearly stumbled. Was that how Atsuko thought of her? As one of her artists? Nick and Mathias and Ronan were her artists. Natalie had always thought of herself as, well, not like them.

She mentally paused to remind herself that getting a lot of money for something didn’t mean someone was better or worse than anyone else. Art was about creation and drive and vision, not a check from a gallery. And while she mostly believed that, she had to admit there was an element of legitimacy that she craved. Not to mention a few dollars in her hiatus fund.

They walked into the small back room where they stored tables and chairs and linens for their special events. Atsuko paused when she saw the canvas.

"I saw this before, when you first started it. You made a lot of changes."

Natalie shook her head. "They weren't voluntary. At least not at first." She explained about the fire.

"Once I recovered from the shock, I kept going back to it. One day I knew what to do." She touched a ribbon petal. "I'm thinking I might try burning a piece again. In a very controlled way, of course. There's something very freeing about the whole rising-from-the-ashes concept. I can't really explain it."

Atsuko walked back and forth, examined the canvas, moved close, then moved back. "I would suggest you start working on being able to explain it. We have a gallery event in a couple of weeks and you might be asked a few questions."

"Wh-what?"

Asked questions? Why would that happen? While she'd had her pieces in the gallery during events before, she'd never been one of the featured artists. She'd attended the fancy evenings, but only as staff. The important artists, the ones displayed on the gallery walls, were the featured talents. They were expected to mingle with potential buyers, make small talk and explain their art.

Before she could think about breathing or ask any questions, Atsuko picked up the canvas and carried it into the gallery. She leaned it up against the far left wall, considered it, then shook her head.

"No, not on the end. I think I want it more toward the center. I'm going to need to do some rearranging." She glanced at Natalie. "Assuming this is mine to sell."

"Of course."

"Good. Draw up the standard contract." Atsuko smiled. "I'm going to price this at twenty-four thousand dollars."

Natalie did her best not to gasp or faint or scream. Rather than risking speech, she simply nodded. "I'll get to it right away."

"Good. I'm going to need a little time to figure out how I want to rearrange the gallery, but I should have your piece up by tomorrow."

"Thank you."

Natalie left her talking to herself about space and display, and slowly made her way back to the studio. Her heart was pounding and she was having trouble doing the very simple math. The gallery took half the sale's price, which meant Natalie got the other half. She was almost sure that meant she would get twelve thousand dollars.

If it sold, she reminded herself. That had to happen first. Except all her pieces had sold so far and Atsuko had an excellent eye and if she were even slightly featured in the next gallery event, then… Then…

She came to a stop and closed her eyes. Twelve thousand dollars. That was huge! That was five figures. That changed everything.

Okay, not *everything*, but close. Between what she'd earned helping Pallas and making the centerpieces for the wedding, she had three months' rent. Even after taxes, the commission would maybe cover another three plus her living expenses for nearly half a year. She could afford to take a couple of weeks off a month to really focus on her art. She was nowhere near ready to stop working completely, but she was on her way.

She drew in a breath and thought longingly of her mother, who would be so proud of her. She thought of all the work, all the small projects that had sold for fifty or a hundred dollars. She thought of how life was quirky and unexpected and surprising all at the same time. Then she thought of Ronan.

He would be so happy for her. So excited. He would want to celebrate and tell everyone. On the night of the event, she had a feeling the usually famously reclusive Ronan Mitchell would make an appearance. All for her.

He was good to her. So supportive and affectionate. She enjoyed his company, his laughter, his brilliance. Even his struggle made her care about him more.

She reached for the studio door only to stop. The truth she'd been avoiding, the truth Silver had so bluntly shared, couldn't be ignored anymore.

She was in love with him. She was in love with Ronan. She'd assumed she would be sensible and not fall for him but she'd been wrong. She loved him and she honestly had no idea what that meant or how to deal with the fact that there was a very good chance he would leave her. But for the next however long the guys wanted to talk about her meeting with Atsuko, she was going to have to fake it.

She pushed away thoughts of love and what it all

meant, remembered how it felt when Atsuko had said she would be on one of the center walls and walked into the studio.

All three of them were waiting there, looking expectant.

"Well?" Ronan asked. "Tell us."

"She took it! It's going up in the next couple of days." She paused for effect. "On one of the center walls."

Mathias and Nick cheered. Ronan wrapped his arms around her waist and spun her around.

"I knew it," he told her as he held her close. "Good for you, Natalie. Congratulations."

Her heart swelled a little and her eyes filled with tears. Happy tears, she thought as he kissed her.

This was what she wanted. As for the loving part, she would deal with that later. Or maybe not at all.

"I'M IN LOVE with Ronan," Natalie said plaintively.

"Well, duh." Silver was sprawled in the club chair in her living room while Natalie sat on the sofa. "You're just now getting that?"

"You were right. I was wrong. Better?"

Silver grinned. "As nice as that is to hear, this isn't about me." Her smile softened. "Are you okay?"

"I don't know. Maybe. I hope so. I'm trying. It's just I never expected this to happen."

"Why not? He's a good-looking guy. Successful, talented, and he treats you like gold. How could you *not* fall in love?"

"I thought I was immune."

"No such luck."

Apparently not, Natalie thought. "Do you think anyone knows?"

"Your friends might be suspicious but no one will say anything. If you're asking if Ronan knows, I wouldn't worry about it. Men don't see that kind of stuff. I'm not sure if that's a blessing or a curse."

Natalie wondered if they'd stopped talking about her and Ronan and had shifted to Silver and Drew. Not that there was anything to talk about.

Natalie didn't know all the details but she'd heard that the couple had been hot and heavy back in high school. Things had gone awry, and while they'd never gotten back together again, there were rumors that Drew was more than a little interested in winning back the platinum blonde he'd once sworn to love forever.

Silver shook her head. "Let me be clear. I was not talking about myself."

"If you're sure."

"I am. Now what are you going to do?"

"I don't know. I'm scared on so many levels."

She'd never thought she would fall in love. She'd even been considering having a baby on her own. Okay, not *considering*, but toying with the idea. Now she knew that wasn't possible—at least not for a long time. She loved Ronan—she wanted to be with him. She wanted him to be "the one" and have them get married and start a family together. She wanted the fantasy. But she needed him to want it, too, and right now he wouldn't even admit Elaine was his mother.

"He won't love me back. He doesn't trust emotionally because he's too closed off."

"He's changing."

"Not enough." Of that she was sure.

"How do you know?" Silver asked. "Maybe your love is what he needs to push him over the edge." She smiled. "In a good way."

Natalie was having a little trouble in the faith department. "You're saying I should just walk up to Ronan and tell him I love him and everything will be fine?"

Silver shrugged. "Yeah, I'm not sure Ronan is that guy, but that's about him, not you. But maybe you should try."

Maybe, she thought, trying to imagine the moment. What would he do? Accept her love? Walk away? Maybe it was better not to know.

Like with the pregnancy?

The voice was so soft she barely heard it, but the words resonated all the same. Natalie had promised herself to do better next time. Was she going to keep her word or not?

"I'll tell him," she said aloud, so the words had more power. "I'm going to trust him to be okay. I should tell him how I feel and that I believe in him. Then he can make his own decision."

"That's very mature of you."

Natalie drew in a breath. "I hope so. Regardless, it's right. I'm hoping that my believing in him is going to help him believe in himself."

"You really are an optimist."

"I'm in love. What else would I be?"

It took Natalie three days to internalize the whole concept of being in love with Ronan. She had to think about her past and what she'd done both right and wrong before she could accept that when she hadn't been looking or paying attention, she'd made the most significant decision of her life.

Once she'd accepted the truth of it, she had reveled in knowing her heart was open and happy and ready to accept the one man meant for her, she knew the next step was telling him. She needed him to hear the words—for his sake and for her own. She wanted to declare herself, to be honest and open. He'd had so much deception already. She sensed in her gut that the way to connect with him was to bare her soul…or, in this case, her heart. What he did after that was up to him.

With that in mind, she invited him to dinner, then picked up takeout from the Italian place they both loved.

"Hey, you," Ronan said when he arrived. He kissed her. "I feel like I haven't seen you in a while."

"There's been a lot going on." She stared into his green eyes and saw the affection there. Her worry faded. He'd come so far. He was realizing how much love and family mattered. Maybe this would be okay.

They walked into the kitchen and he opened the wine he'd brought. "Tell me what's been going on."

She smiled. "Different things. I'm trying to keep my expectations low on selling the burned piece while at the same time planning for what to do if it does sell. I've been working on a budget, figuring out exactly how much I need to pay my bills. I'm nowhere near ready to quit my job, but I'd like to take off a couple weeks at a time. I don't want to waste the days, so I need to know what I'm going to be doing. Obviously the big flower project for Atsuko, but there are other things, too."

"You have been busy." He handed her a glass of wine and they went into the living room and sat facing each other on the sofa. "I'm so proud of you."

"Thank you. Like I said, I'm trying to manage my expectations."

"You've never had trouble selling anything before."

She wrinkled her nose. "I've never had a piece priced so high."

"It'll sell. Trust me. I have total faith in you."

She believed him yet wondered if total faith was the same as love.

"Enough about my still-uncertain future. How are you doing? Last I saw, great progress had been made on your commission."

"That's still the case. I'm starting to think about shipping and installation. Both are going to take some time." He touched her face. "You should come with me. We'll have a great time."

"You'll be busy, working sixteen-hour days to get the installation right. You won't have time to miss me."

"You're wrong."

She felt her stomach tighten. Did he mean that? Because if he did, maybe she wasn't the only one to realize what had happened. Maybe it was all going to work out.

He chuckled. "What are you thinking? You have the strangest expression."

"I want to show you something."

She grabbed her laptop keyboard and opened the slide show she'd prepared, then brought the laptop back to the sofa and sat so Ronan could see the screen.

"What is that?" he asked, staring at a color photograph of his father's work. "If you're trying to break the mood, you're doing a really good job."

"Just look. Don't think about the artist—he's not important. Think about the art. That one." She stopped the slide show on a massive glass wave that was all the colors of the sea. She half expected to see a dolphin jumping out of the water at any second. She would swear she could see the shadow of it, deep in the glass.

"He has a gift," she said. "What he creates can be beautiful." She started the show again and the pictures showed the darker side of his creations. Sharp, angry pieces that seemed to suck in all the light and happiness appeared on the screen.

"Some of his pieces are more to be appreciated rather than admired," she continued. "But love it or hate it, his work inspires emotion."

"If you say so."

"You know I'm right."

Ronan put down his wine. "Why are you doing this, Natalie? What's the point?"

"If he wasn't who he is, you wouldn't be who you are. You get your ability to create from him. Can you imagine who you would be without that?"

"No."

"So there is a plus side to having him as your dad."

He looked at her. "And?"

She put the computer on the coffee table and faced him. "Like all of us, you're the sum of your parts. I never knew my dad, but my mom loved him. I guess what I have inside that I didn't see in my mom comes from him. I have no idea what kind of man he was, but I trust her and I trust who I am."

"It's different," he told her. "The parent you knew was a wonderful person who loved you and nurtured you. It's not the same for me."

"It's true that you don't know who your biological mother is, but I disagree about it changing who you are inside. You are good and funny and smart and gifted and an amazing man." She took his hands in hers. "I've fallen in love with you, Ronan. I've been so afraid to risk my heart. I lost my mom. Then I lost Quentin and, more importantly, his family. I was afraid to believe." She smiled. "Until I met you. I love you and I wanted you to know."

She tried to keep her voice light and hopeful but it was difficult as she watched his expression tighten and all emotion fade from his eyes.

"You're all I've been looking for," she went on. "I didn't know it, but you are. I understand if you're not ready or you don't feel the same, but I needed to tell you. It seemed the right thing to do."

At least, it had in the safety of her bedroom. Now, facing him, she was less sure about anything.

He stood up abruptly and glared at her. "Why did you have to do this? Why did you have to change everything? This isn't going to work. What are you thinking? Look at you. You're light and whole and happy. You think I want to be responsible for destroying that? Look at what I did to your canvas. I destroyed it."

She stood. "You didn't. It turned out even better."

"You were lucky. I could have ruined it. I could ruin you. Do you know how that thought terrifies me? I could destroy you."

"No. I'm stronger than that, Ronan. I always have been."

"Do you know what's inside of me?" he asked, his voice low and filled with fury. "Do you? Because I sure as hell don't. I have *him* and that's all. All the selfish, narcissistic evil in that man is in me. Every single day I think about that. When will I become him? When will I start hitting my kids and destroying their creations? When will I cheat on my wife and become an asshole? It's just a matter of time."

"You're not him," she protested. "You never have been. The fact that you worry about it proves the point. If you were like him, you wouldn't care."

He stared at her. "I won't risk it. Not with you. Never with you."

She reached for him, but he'd already pulled back too far. Her fingers grasped only air, and before she could stop him, he was gone.

CHAPTER TWENTY

Ronan wanted to throw the cooled piece of glass against the wall, but knew that would make too much of a statement. Instead he dropped it into the large trash bin in the corner and tried to find satisfaction in the sound of it shattering into a thousand pieces.

He'd already sent his interns home. In the past two days he hadn't made any progress. Everything he touched was a disaster. He couldn't think, couldn't sleep, and he wanted to run so far the gnawing ache in his gut couldn't find him.

He ripped off his goggles as he tried to decide what to do. Working from home hadn't helped. He'd tried that only to end up here. Maybe if he ate something, or got drunk, but neither sounded appealing.

Damn it all to hell, what had she been thinking? Showing him pictures of his father's work, then telling him she loved him. Who did that? What was her point? Reminding him who his father was didn't exactly get him in the mood. Ceallach was everything he didn't want to be. Why couldn't she understand that?

And how could she love him? He was a moody SOB who was barely holding it together. He was a bad risk—she had to know that. He lived in fear that he would hurt her. Things had been difficult enough before, but now that she wanted him to know she loved him, it was so much worse.

Mathias glanced across the studio. "What has your panties in a bunch? You've had something up your ass for a couple of days now."

Ronan ignored him and the mixed metaphor. Unfortunately Natalie chose that moment to walk into the studio. Ronan wasn't sure she'd heard the exchange until she said, "That would be my fault."

All three brothers looked at her. Nick and Mathias were both curious, while Ronan was filled with dread. She wouldn't… She couldn't possibly…

"He's dealing with the fact that I told him I'm in love with him and he has no idea what to say back."

Her courage knocked the wind out of him. Her voice was strong and the only evidence of what she'd been going through was in the slight puffiness around her eyes. Because she'd been crying? He didn't want to think that, didn't want to know if she'd been hurt. He never wanted to hurt her. She was everything to him, only he couldn't—

He realized the room had gone totally silent. Everyone was staring at him. His brothers looked shocked, Natalie was in obvious pain and they all appeared to expect him to say something.

"No," he said, more to himself than them. "Just no."

He stormed out of the studio and got in his truck. There was only one place he could go and that was home. Halfway up the mountain he realized he didn't want to be alone, but where else was there? He couldn't go back to town and hang with his brothers. Natalie was totally off-limits. He'd hurt her enough already.

Without wanting to, he remembered what it had been like when he was a kid. How his father would casually backhand whichever of them was closest. They'd all learned to duck and weave until Del had gotten big enough to hit back. After that, Del had stood between his brothers and his father. When Del wasn't around, Aidan took over, then Nick. By the time he and Mathias had been about sixteen, Ceallach had stopped trying to slap them around, but he'd worked his darkness in other ways.

He'd belittled them, had destroyed their work, mocked their abilities and generally made their lives hell. He'd dismissed his two older sons for not having any artistic ability and had convinced Mathias, the most gifted of them all, that he was worthless. Nick had stopped working with glass altogether, preferring to be a bartender than having anything to do with their father's world.

There had been so much pain, so much regret, so much hiding and defending and not wanting to be like him.

He reached his house and leaned his forehead against the steering wheel. He missed Natalie so much he wondered if he could keep breathing without her. He knew she trusted him completely, that she believed she would be fine and that he would never do anything bad. But she was wrong—her current pain was proof of that. And even if she wasn't, her belief in him wasn't enough. He had to believe in himself and he couldn't.

"HEY."

Natalie looked up from the paperwork on her desk, paperwork she couldn't see because her eyes were filled with tears.

Nick stood in the doorway. "I just wanted to check on you."

"I'm fine."

"Liar."

She tried to smile and failed. Nick pulled her to her feet, then wrapped his strong arms around her.

"Damn," he said gently. "That was about the bravest thing I ever saw."

She gave in to the tears she'd been holding back. "You th-think?"

"I know. He's an idiot. Want me to beat him up for you, because I will. I'll need to take Mathias with me, but between the two of us, I'm pretty sure we can give him a black eye and maybe crack a bone or two."

She cried harder, not only because she knew she'd lost Ronan but because of deeper, sadder pain. As Nick held her and tried to make her feel better, she realized that Ronan wasn't the only Mitchell brother to gain a place in her heart. She'd fallen in love with all of them. Nick and Mathias, Pallas and Carol. Loving Ronan wasn't *just* about him; it was about his family. Once again, she'd allowed herself to belong and to believe that she could be a part of something bigger than herself. Yes, they would still be her friends, but that wasn't the same. She wanted them as her family.

"I w-wish it could have been different," she whispered.

"Me, too."

"I'm crying on your shirt."

"Pallas is having a baby in a few months. I'm pretty sure after that a few tears are going to seem downright sanitary."

She tried to laugh, but her throat was too tight. "Don't be mad, but I hoped we'd be a family," she admitted.

He touched her chin, forcing her to look at him. "We are," he told her. "No matter what, we'll be here for you. I've got your back and so does everyone else you know, Natalie. You're not alone."

"Thank you." She knew in her head he was right—it was her heart that was going to take some convincing.

He studied her for a second. "You know what, kid? I have an idea about how to fix all this. I should have thought of it before."

"Don't. Whatever you're thinking, don't. You can't shame Ronan into loving me. I wouldn't want that."

He kissed the top of her head. "No shame, I promise. Just trust me. It's a really good plan."

Natalie wanted to believe him, but she couldn't. She'd run out of faith—at least for the moment.

RONAN'S WEEK ONLY went downhill. He missed Natalie more than he would have thought possible. Sure, he saw her at the gallery, because he couldn't seem to stay home, where he wouldn't see her. Every morning he told himself to just stay put and he would be fine and within the hour he was driving down the mountain.

He wasn't sure why he bothered. He wasn't working, couldn't work. He couldn't sleep or do anything but think about her and what she'd said. She was possibly the bravest person he'd ever met.

He knew what he wanted. Plain and simple, he wanted her. All of her—heart and soul. He wanted to be with her, love her, spend the rest of his life with her. He needed her, ached for her, dreamed about her the few hours that he slept. So he existed in a hellish world where he saw her, heard her voice and yet wasn't with her.

The once-burned mixed-media piece sold in three days. He left a bottle of champagne on her desk, but couldn't stand to speak to her. She was already hard at work on another piece like it. No doubt she would ask either Mathias or Nick to burn it for her. Not him. Never him.

He kept waiting for his brothers to call him on his shit, but they avoided him instead, acting as if nothing had happened, as if everything he'd ever wanted wasn't crumbling around them. And so it went on until he couldn't stand it anymore.

Nearly a week after Natalie's heart-wrenching confession, a woman walked into the studio. She was tall and slim, with blond hair and green eyes. He'd never seen her before and would guess she was in her early forties, although she could have been older.

Natalie was in the office, so it was just him and his

brothers. When no one else looked up at her, Ronan walked over.

"Can I help you?" he asked.

She smiled at him, the corners of her mouth trembling slightly. "Ronan Mitchell?" she asked, her voice shaking.

He nodded, hoping she wasn't some buyer who wanted to have a personal experience with him. He wasn't that kind of artist. He should direct her to the gallery and tell her—

He felt a prickling sensation start at the back of his neck, then work down his spine. She wasn't a fan or a collector of art. At least, that wasn't why she was here. He had no idea how he knew that, but he was as sure of it as he was of—

The woman cleared her throat. "This is much harder than I expected, although I don't know why I would have thought it would be easy. It's not, is it?" She gave a hollow laugh, then pressed her fingers to her mouth. "I swear, I'm not going to cry. I wouldn't do that. It's just so much to take in."

She swallowed and held out her hand. "I promise, I'll start making sense now. I'm Pippa Waddell and I'm your biological mother."

The room went completely quiet. It was as if the ovens had shut off and his brothers stopped working and there was only stillness as her words echoed over and over again until they were all he could hear.

"I can see by the look on your face this is a complete surprise," she said before reaching for a chair by his desk. "I'm feeling a little light-headed. Do you mind if I sit down?"

He held the chair for her. As she sank down, Mathias went and got two glasses of water. Ronan took them and offered her one before sitting across from her. His brothers disappeared into the break room. He doubted they were out of earshot, but that was fine. He didn't have any secrets from them.

She sipped the water. "Thank you. I took the red-eye last night and drove in from Los Angeles. I'm a little tired." She tried to smile and failed.

He wanted to ask why she was here. How had she found him and why now, only he couldn't seem to speak.

She set down her glass. "I met your father at a gallery in New York. I was young, barely nineteen, and totally art struck. I was an art history major." She wrinkled her nose. "Yes, so very practical, but I couldn't help it. I loved all forms of art, and when it came to your father, I was a devoted fan."

She pressed a hand to her chest. "Meeting him was unexpected. He was so funny and charming, so handsome." Color flared on her cheeks. "I knew he was older and married, but none of that seemed to matter. I thought of myself as so very worldly and believed I was ready for a man like him."

She picked up her glass, then put it down again. "We started an affair. It was very torrid. Looking back, I realize I was completely out of my element. I was a silly girl from a small town who didn't understand what she was doing. I didn't think about the consequences of my actions or the pain they would cause others. All I knew was that for those brief months, Ceallach was my world."

She paused as if expecting Ronan to say something. He nodded, because that was the best he could do. There was no way he could string together words that made sense. Just hearing what she was saying was difficult enough.

"I moved to Sacramento to be close to him." She pressed her lips together. "I lied to my parents, who had no idea what was wrong with me. I didn't tell anyone. I couldn't. I knew our relationship was wrong, but I couldn't seem to stop." She looked at him, then away. "I'm the oldest of three girls. My dad was a plumber and my mother was a schoolteacher."

"Normal," he said quietly.

"Yes. Normal and boring and a thousand other things I didn't appreciate. All I thought of was your father. He said I was his muse and I couldn't imagine anything more wonderful."

She would have seen a side of his father he wouldn't recognize, he thought. She would know things he couldn't imagine. It was as if she were talking about someone he'd never met.

"When I found out I was pregnant, he wanted me to have an abortion. I was shocked and devastated. You were the symbol of our love—how could he want me to get rid of you?" Tears filled her eyes. "We fought and he said he never wanted to see me again. Not knowing what else to do, I called my mom and she came and got me."

Ronan tried to make sense of her story. She was

nothing like he'd pictured. Pippa had been a regular teenager who got caught up with a man so far out of her league as to be from another planet. She didn't seem jaded or manipulative. Just sad.

"My parents were wonderful," she continued. "They said they'd help me with my baby or help me find a couple to adopt you. I decided to keep you and raise you myself."

She twisted her fingers together. "I was barely twenty and so scared, and having a baby isn't easy. My mom was still working and there were so many hours I was alone. I wanted to go back to college and hang out with my friends." She bit her lower lip. "I'm sorry. I know that sounds selfish."

"No," he said, his voice thick and low. "It sounds like you were twenty and trying to raise a kid on your own."

"I hope you believe that. I couldn't just give you away, so I called Elaine."

Ronan stiffened. "Not Ceallach."

Her mouth twisted. "He'd already made his feelings clear. I knew he wouldn't take my call. But your mom was different. Obviously I'd never met her, but he talked about her all the time, about how wonderful she was. I felt as if she was someone I could trust. Looking back, I realize how naive I was and how fortunate you are to have been raised by her. When I told her who I was, she didn't hang up. She listened, and when I told her about you, about how overwhelmed I was, she told me to come to Fool's Gold, to meet with her. She wanted to see you."

Ronan couldn't believe it. How had Elaine done

that? How had she been so generous? Where was the anger at what her husband had done?

"I flew out with you the next day. When I got to the house, I was so scared. But your father wasn't there. I'm not sure where your brothers were, but it was just the three of us. She took you from my arms. I remember how she held you and smiled." Pippa looked at him. "That was it. She looked at you, and then she said she would take you and raise you as her own. She told me about her youngest. A baby only a few weeks older. She said she would tell everyone you were fraternal twins. She arranged the paperwork and that was it."

"I always thought Ceallach made her do it," he admitted, still trying to absorb all he'd been told.

"I never saw him," Pippa told him. "I don't know how she explained you or what was said. I just handed you over and left." Her smile was shaky. "She and I keep in touch. Not often, but every year or so I get an update. It's nice to know how well you're doing."

She reached in her handbag and pulled out a large envelope, then handed it to him. "My contact information is in there, along with my family's medical history. We're a pretty ordinary, healthy bunch. My parents are still alive and would love to meet you, if you're interested."

She hesitated. "I'm married. My husband is a radiologist and I'm a stay-at-home mom. I volunteer at a women's shelter and the local library. Nothing very exciting. My husband knows. I never told my kids, although I think they'd find it kind of exciting to know they have an older brother."

She leaned toward him. "I want to be clear that I don't think of myself as your mother. That's who Elaine is. But I do think of you a lot and I wanted you to know that.

"I guess that's all. I'm going to drive back to the airport. I have a flight leaving later tonight." She smiled. "There is a very big science project due in a few days, and if I'm not there things will go awry, believe me."

Everything about the moment was surreal. He didn't know what to think or how to react or what he was supposed to say.

"Why now?" he asked. "Why show up now?"

"I thought you knew." She sounded surprised. "I'm here because Elaine called me and asked me to get in touch with you as soon as possible. We agreed that speaking on the phone wouldn't be right, so I flew out first thing."

That made no sense. None of it. Not her or the fact that he now knew about the rest of his family. Not how she looked or the life she lived or that she'd shown up with no warning.

He rose. "I have to go." He got halfway to the door before returning to the table and taking the envelope. "Thank you for telling me all of this. I'll be in touch. I just need..."

She smiled. "You need time. I understand, Ronan. It was good to see you."

He nodded and then left. He drove directly to his house, then sat in the truck in his driveway and wondered what on earth he was supposed to do now.

CHAPTER TWENTY-ONE

NATALIE COULDN'T BELIEVE she'd missed it all. Ronan's birth mother showing up, the conversation, everything. She'd been in her gallery office the entire time and hadn't heard a thing. It was totally unfair.

On the bright side, speculating about what had happened was a great distraction from her broken heart. She was curious and concerned and hopeful and confused all at once. There was also the fact that getting information from Mathias and Nick was next to impossible. They told her facts. She wanted to know how Ronan had felt.

Twenty-four hours after the unexpected visit, Natalie was doing everything she could not to drive up the mountain and talk to Ronan. After their last disastrous encounter, she knew she just didn't have the strength to face him one-on-one. It was hard enough to go to the office every day and do her job. There she got to pretend she wasn't devastated, wasn't missing him with every breath, wasn't feeling as sad and crushed as shattered glass.

She'd told him she loved him and it hadn't been enough. While in her head she could admit that his healing or not healing wasn't about her and that she was wrong to think that just by falling in love with him, everything would be fine. Only that was how she wanted it to be. Her heart ached for him and demanded to know why her love wasn't enough.

She knew that what he wrestled with had nothing to do with her—that his issues had existed long before her. The fact that she had finally figured out that she loved him was great, but not life changing for anyone but her. He had to get through his past on his own.

But she still needed to see him, be held by him. She was desperate to inhale the scent of his skin, watch him move, touch him and hear his voice. She missed everything about him.

Worse, she knew he was dealing with so much all on his own. She wanted to be there for him, to help him through it, to just listen while he went around and around with the new information his birth mother had given him. Only she and Ronan weren't talking, at least not as far as she knew. She'd told him she loved him and he'd walked away. That wasn't exactly an invitation for more time together.

So she stayed home. She grabbed her keys three times, then dropped them back in her bag. Once she got as far as her car before turning around and retreating to her apartment. If Ronan wanted her or needed her, he knew exactly where to find her. She wasn't going to push herself on him. What he was going through was too important.

She tried to focus on work, but that wasn't happening, so she found a *Big Bang Theory* marathon on one of the cable channels and settled in to be distracted by the antics of Leonard and Sheldon. Somewhere close to nine o'clock, there was a knock on her door.

Natalie's heart immediately started pounding. She told herself that it wasn't going to be Ronan, that she shouldn't get her hopes up. But she couldn't help wishing and praying all the way to the door.

He stood on the landing, looking tired and confused. His expression was weary, his shoulders slumped.

"Is it okay that I'm here?" he asked.

She took his hand and pulled him inside, then wrapped her arms around him and hung on tight.

She told herself that he was here as a friend and that she shouldn't read too much into his visit. She promised that she wouldn't say or do anything cringe-worthy. That she would remember she was his friend first, and the woman who loved him second.

He hugged her back, his strong arms holding her so tight she could barely breathe. God, that felt good. All warm and safe and just like she remembered. If only he would never let go.

But he did, stepping back. "I didn't know where else to go."

"It's fine."

She led him into the kitchen, then began pulling out leftover take-out containers. Since her confession, she'd been living on Chinese, Thai and Italian, with a little Mexican thrown in. When there was a problem with her life, carbs and cheese were always the answer.

"What are you doing?" he asked, leaning against the counter.

"You haven't eaten in at least twenty-four hours. You'll feel better with food in your stomach."

His eyebrows drew together. "How do you know I haven't eaten?"

"Have you?"

"No."

She turned on the oven, then dumped fried rice, Thai basil chicken and a cheese enchilada on a plate and stuck it in the microwave. While they heated she put two slices of pizza and three egg rolls onto a cookie sheet. They could be his second course.

She poured a large glass of water and handed it to him. He took a drink. After setting the table, she opened a beer and set it by the place mat, then put the small cookie sheet in the oven and pulled the plate from the microwave. She set it in front of him.

"Eat."

He picked up his fork. "Are you sure you don't want some of this?"

"I already had plenty. Don't worry about talking. Just eat. We'll talk after."

She softened the words by putting her hand on his shoulder, then stuck her phone into a small docking station so she could put on some music. Once he'd started on his impromptu meal, she made herself some herbal tea. By then his plate was clean and the pizza slices and egg rolls were warm.

"I was starving," he admitted as she took the seat across from him. "I didn't realize. Thanks, Natalie."

"No problem." She smiled. "Think of my place as the international buffet of leftovers."

"It's more than that."

She told herself not to read anything into his words. He was here and for now that was enough. Yes, her heart was broken, but she was dealing. Just being around Ronan made her feel better. Maybe they could figure out how to get back to being friends. They'd started out as friends, and now that she knew him better, she liked him even more. Not having him as the man in her life was awful, but to lose him in every way was unthinkable. Unless she quit her job and left town, they were going to see each other all the time. Wouldn't it be better to stay friends instead?

But first, his past.

She waited while he finished eating, then drank about half the beer. Only then did he lean back in his chair and look at her.

"You heard what happened."

A statement, not a question, she thought. "Nick and Mathias told me about your birth mother."

"I didn't know if she was alive or not." He shook his head. "I still can't believe it. She was…nice. Nothing like I expected. She told me about her relationship with my dad." His mouth twisted. "Not something I want to think about. He's such a jerk."

"To you, not to her. Plus, it was a long time ago. I'm sure in his time, he was…different."

One corner of his mouth turned up. "I'm sure he

was, too. Especially around other women. She talked about meeting him and what it had been like to fall for him." He leaned forward and wrapped his hands around the beer bottle.

"She was just a kid. Nineteen. She was from some small town. He played her."

"I'm glad you're not mad at her for what happened."

"How could I be? She wasn't ready for the likes of him. I've known him my whole life and he still pushes my buttons. He doesn't believe in rules, so he nearly always wins."

He closed his eyes for a second, then looked at her. "My head hurts. I've been going over it and over it. All she told me about herself… She's married, with a couple of kids. I guess they're my half siblings, as well. She left me a letter saying she would like to stay in touch, if I'm interested."

"Are you?"

"Hell if I know."

"It's a lot to take in."

She wanted to reach across the table and touch him to offer support and reassurance. She wanted to take him to her bed and help heal him that way. Only she couldn't do either. Things were different now. Her confession stood between them—a giant elephant neither of them would acknowledge.

"Nick called Elaine," he told her.

"What?"

"Nick told her what happened with you and me and asked if she knew how to get in touch with Pippa. Nick set the whole thing in motion."

Natalie remembered Nick promising her he would fix things. She'd thought he'd meant that he would talk to Ronan. "Are you mad at him?"

"No. Why would I be? He had no idea if Elaine knew Pippa. She never said anything about her to me, but they've been communicating all this time." He looked at Natalie. "Elaine called Pippa and told her there was a problem and within twenty-four hours she was here. What does that mean?"

"That they both care about you, Ronan. They've always cared. I guess they were just waiting for permission to help."

He swore under his breath. She wasn't sure why, but told herself to keep quiet. That he had to work through it all.

She wanted to hope, wanted to believe that now everything would be all right. He would start to see that there was more in him than Ceallach, that he had a light side to counteract the darkness. Maybe then he would realize how much he needed her in his life. Maybe, just maybe, he would fall desperately in love with her and they could live happily ever after.

Or maybe not. She couldn't tell what he was thinking or feeling. While she appreciated that he'd sought her out, she didn't know what it meant.

"It was Elaine's decision to take me in," he said unexpectedly. "I thought my old man forced me on her, but it was her choice. He didn't even know. Once I found out the truth about my past, I assumed she'd been coerced and that acting as though I was her favorite was her way of overcompensating. I thought she'd been lying to me."

"But it wasn't like that," Natalie whispered.

"It wasn't. All the times she made me crazy, siding with Ceallach over her sons, that was part of it. The heart that allowed her to take in her husband's bastard was the same heart that couldn't help loving him that much. Loving all of us, I guess."

"She's flawed, Ronan. Everyone is. We make mistakes. I'm sure if she could go back, she would do things differently. Wouldn't you?"

He nodded.

"You need to go talk to her. Tell her what happened."

He looked at her for a long time. Silence stretched out between them. For a second she was terrified she'd gone too far and that he was going to get mad at her. Then she told herself to suck it up. If Ronan got mad, she would tell him he was wrong and they both knew it. The break with the woman who had raised him had gone on far too long and it was time to fix things. If he couldn't see that, he was a stupid butthead, which she had told him before.

Before she got much mad going, he smiled. "You're right. I need to go to Fool's Gold. Want to come with me?"

"What?"

"I'm going to drive up there tomorrow. Come with me. We'll take a couple of days off and see the sights." He reached across the table and took her hand. "If you don't want to, I understand, but I'm hoping you'll go with me. We have things to talk about."

Hope fluttered insistently. Natalie supposed the smart thing would be to protect herself, but she didn't know how to do that. Not when she loved Ronan as much as she did.

"Of course I'll go with you. How long will we be gone?"

He thought for a second. "If we leave early tomorrow, we can be there by the afternoon, then cut across to San Francisco. Let's spend a couple of nights there. We can hang out in the city."

She smiled. "I'd like that. Let me text Atsuko and tell her I won't be in. Oh, and I need to pack and…"

He rose and pulled her to her feet, then kissed her. "You have a lot to do. Let me get out of your hair. I'll be back tomorrow. How early is too early?"

"Does six work?" Which was early, but she doubted she would be sleeping much that night.

"Six is perfect. See you then."

Ronan kissed her again before letting himself out. Natalie stood in the middle of the kitchen, her thoughts swirling. He was going home to talk to the woman who had raised him. That was good, right? He was making peace with his past *and* he wanted her along. Maybe he was thinking they could have a future together. Ronan was many things, but he wasn't cruel. He knew exactly how she felt and she trusted him not to lead her on.

She told herself she would find out when she found out, then tidied the kitchen before going into her bedroom to figure out what she should pack. San Francisco was a beautiful city, but slightly more upscale than Happily Inc. As for Fool's Gold, she was totally flummoxed about that. There would be a long car ride, so comfort was important, but at the other end would be Ronan's mother! Not that they would necessarily meet, but still. She needed a plan.

By two in the morning, she was as ready as she was going to be. Now she simply had to wait and see how the events unfolded and hope that when it was all over Ronan would be willing to admit that he needed her in his life.

"THANKS FOR COMING with me," Ronan said as they headed north on I-5 toward Business 80. He'd told himself everything was fine, but couldn't help the sense of apprehension that weighed on him.

Natalie shifted in her seat. "You've already thanked me like a thousand times. I'm happy to be here with you. I mean that."

"A thousand times? Really?"

She laughed. "Okay, maybe more like four hundred, but still."

He reached across the console of the truck and took her hand in his. She squeezed his fingers. So far they hadn't talked about their relationship, but he knew that time was coming. She deserved to hear him tell her about his feelings and she would. Just as soon as he cleared things up with Elaine.

He hadn't slept in a couple of days, but he wasn't tired. More on edge, he thought. Running on adrenaline. He would have to sleep at some point, but not until all this was resolved.

"I made reservations at a hotel in San Francisco,"

he told her. "For tonight and tomorrow night. That will give us a day to sightsee."

"I'd like that. Did you tell Elaine we're stopping by?"

He nodded. "I texted her last night. She said she would be home all afternoon."

He wasn't sure about Ceallach. He had no interest in seeing his father, but if the old man was there, Ronan figured he would deal as best he could.

"You said your hometown has a lot of festivals," Natalie said. "What do you mean?"

"They celebrate everything. There's a waterskiing festival and a casserole cook-off in the winter. Parades all the time." He grinned at her. "Christmas is the best. From Thanksgiving until New Year's, there's something going on. Right after Thanksgiving, a huge tree goes up in the center of town. There's a Day of Giving, when all the local charities have booths and there's an animal adoption. Every Christmas Eve we went to see the *Dance of the Winter King* put on by the local dance school, then to midnight services."

"You were busy."

"Always. Growing up there was great. We were able to run around as much as we wanted. The town is safe and friendly. If one of us got into trouble, someone called home to rat us out."

"That's nice. You must have been happy."

"I was. I had my brothers." Especially Mathias, he thought. Back then, they'd been twins. Part of a unit—them against the world. He missed that.

"You were close," he said, changing the subject. "Just a few miles away in Sacramento. I never knew."

"You mean what if we'd met back then?" She smiled. "I don't know what would have happened."

"I would have liked to meet your mom."

She squeezed his hand. "I would have liked that, too. Although I think she would have warned me about you."

"Why is that?"

"You're kind of a bad boy."

"Never."

He took Forest Highway off Business 80 and pointed out several familiar buildings. The library and police station. He told her about his favorite restaurants, and when they turned north on Mother Bear Road, he motioned to the offices of Score PR.

"It's owned by former football players," he said.

"I'm not really a sports fan," she admitted.

"What a surprise."

She grinned.

But as he got closer to the house where he'd grown up, they both got quiet. He had a feeling Natalie sensed his tension. After all this time, what was he supposed to say to the woman who had raised him?

He still hadn't worked out how he felt about everything. The information was too new, too surprising. He was happy she'd taken him in and kept him out of the foster care system. More than that, he was grateful she'd made him one of her own. Growing up, he'd never once guessed he wasn't hers by birth. She'd raised him as her fifth son, had loved him, disciplined him, supported him and been there for him exactly as she had his brothers. Yes, she'd kept the truth from him, but he was starting to understand how that had happened. Once concealed, a secret tended to take on a life of its own, growing bigger and bigger with time.

He knew he could complain about what she'd done, but the truth was, there was no good time to shatter his world. Being who she was, Elaine would have also wanted to protect Ceallach—a flaw that was unlikely to change after all these years. She was who she was and he was the man he'd grown into because of her.

He pulled into the long driveway. Their house was on the outskirts of town to give Ceallach quiet and space to work. As a kid, Ronan had loved the freedom of the forest only a few yards from the edge of the backyard. Now he saw that the house was isolated and wondered if Elaine ever missed being closer to town.

He parked by the garage and turned off the engine of the truck.

"I have no idea what to say," he admitted.

"It'll come to you. I'm going to wait out here. You two need some time to clear the air." She pointed at her bag. "I've brought a book—I'll be fine. You can come get me when everything is settled."

He wanted to tell her that he needed her with him, but knew she was right. As always. Later, when this was behind them, he had a lot of things he wanted to talk to her about. But not until then.

"I won't be long," he told her, before kissing her, then stepping out of the truck.

He faced the house. The front door opened. Sophie,

Elaine's beagle, ran out onto the porch, barked when she saw him, then raced toward him, her tail wagging happily. He crouched down and greeted her before starting for the house.

Elaine stood on the porch. She looked as she always had—maybe a little older with more gray in her dark hair, but otherwise the woman he remembered always being there for him. She smiled when she saw him. There was no anger, no recriminations or judgments, he thought as he approached. But then, with her, there never had been.

A thousand thoughts raced through his mind. As he'd told Natalie, he didn't know what to say, how to explain all that had happened. Not just with Pippa, but the rest of it. How he'd felt and the anger and fear and worry. She might not understand, but he sensed she would want to talk about it and heal what she could. He also wanted to thank her for being there for him, for loving him, for making him believe he could do anything. So how on earth was he supposed to say all that when he didn't know how to begin?

They faced each other. Her smile widened as tears filled her eyes.

"You made it."

"I did." He opened his mouth, closed it. Finally he reached for her as he figured out exactly what he wanted to say. "I've missed you, Mom."

"Oh, Ronan. I've always been right here, waiting for you. I thought you knew that."

"I do now."

NATALIE WAS ALL cried out. Happy tears were still exhausting, she thought contentedly as she hugged Elaine one last time before they left.

Order had been restored. Natalie knew there would still be bumps in the road, but Ronan and his mother had talked—probably for the first time ever—about the past and what it meant to both of them. She'd apologized for not telling him about Pippa and he'd been sorry for simply walking away. They had a lifetime of love to fall back on, she thought happily. That would cushion any fall.

"You'll stay in touch?" Elaine asked anxiously as she walked them to the door.

"I promise," Ronan told her. "I'll call. I'll text. You'll be sick of me."

"Not likely."

Elaine turned to Natalie. "Thank you for coming with him. He needed the support."

"I was happy to be here."

They petted Sophie, then walked out to the truck. Ronan held open Natalie's door before glancing back at the house.

"What are you thinking?" she asked softly.

"That I've been an idiot. I thought I didn't need this, didn't need her. I thought I wasn't a part of anything." He turned to her. "Thank you for telling me I was stupid to turn my back on all I had."

"You're welcome." She got in her seat.

He watched as his mother went back in the house. "I stopped seeing who she was and all she did for me. I forgot what was important and only focused on a single lie. I should have remembered everything else, only I didn't." He looked back at her. "I remember now."

"Good. You're not mad at Nick, are you? For getting in touch with her?"

"No. He did the right thing." He touched her arm. "I'm sorry you got caught up in all this. I hurt you and I never wanted that to happen."

"I'm tougher than I look."

"You are."

His gaze settled on her face. She tried to read what he was thinking. There was still so much they hadn't talked about, hadn't cleared up. She wasn't sure what to say, so thought maybe he should be the one to initiate the conversation. Which sounded smart and mature but was so not her style.

"San Francisco?" he asked.

"I can't wait."

The drive into the city was relatively quick as they caught one of those rare traffic lulls. Before she'd really had a chance to decide what she was going to say, or not say, or if she was going to insist on her own room, they'd pulled up in front of the Ritz-Carlton. She took in the beautiful entrance and knew that once again Ronan was going to dazzle her. The man was good at that.

The check-in process was quick. In a matter of minutes they were in an elevator, then on their floor. Ronan opened the door to their room and let her step into what turned out to be a beautiful suite.

It was close to sunset and the first thing she saw was the view of the city with the bay beyond. There were a couple of sofas and a doorway leading to what she assumed was the bedroom, but none of that mattered. Not when she saw the bottle of champagne chilling in an ice bucket and rose petals scattered on the floor.

She looked back at Ronan, who crossed to her. He led her to the larger sofa and drew her down next to him.

"When you told me you loved me, I couldn't handle it," he said, staring into her eyes. "You overwhelmed me."

In a good way or a bad? But before she could ask, he was speaking again.

"You are the most amazing woman I've ever met. Your spirit, your optimism, your beauty. You have the most giving heart. You're smart and stubborn, and I am grateful every day that I've had the chance to get to know you."

He touched her cheek and smiled. "I, on the other hand, am a moody bastard who dislikes everyone and rarely sees good in the world."

"That's not true."

"It's a little true, but I'm changing. I'm becoming a better person." His expression turned serious. "I was so afraid of who I was. No, that's wrong. I was terrified of turning into my father. The idea obsessed me, even as I told myself focusing on what I didn't want was sure to make it happen. I needed a better role model. Running *from* something wasn't going to be enough. Then you tumbled into my life."

"I didn't tumble," she whispered, hoping, barely breathing and loving everything he was saying.

"You crashed your car into a tree."

"It was raining and not my fault. If you'd bothered to take your cell phone home, none of this would have happened."

"I know. I think about that. How if I'd just remembered, everything would be different and what a tragedy that would be." He cupped her face and kissed her. "You're my miracle, Natalie. You are the best person I know and I'm grateful to you for everything you've done for me. I have no idea why you'd bother to love someone like me but I'm going to accept the gift and hope you never change your mind."

He slid to the floor. She was confused for a second, then realized he was on one knee.

Her heart actually stopped beating. She couldn't breathe and desperately didn't want to start sobbing because she was not a pretty crier.

Ronan reached around her and withdrew a ring box from behind the cushion, then opened it, revealing a stunning, incredibly beautiful diamond solitaire ring.

"Natalie, I love you. I have for a long time. Being with you is the best part of my day. I want us to share our lives. I want to have children with you and grow old with you. I want to stand in the crowd as you accept awards and accolades for your brilliant art and I want to spend the rest of my life making you happy. Will you marry me?"

"I don't know what to say," she admitted, then laughed. "Yes. Yes! I love you, Ronan. Of course I'll marry you." She flung her arms around him and hung on as if she would never let go. He held her just as tight before he slid the ring on her finger. It fit perfectly and just looking at it made her heart race. Or maybe that was being so close to Ronan.

"I love you," he whispered. "For always. I promise."

She knew in her heart that he would keep that promise. That he would protect her and care for her and be an amazing partner for the rest of their lives.

He kissed her, then led her to the window. They watched the last of the sunlight fade and the city come alive with sparkling light. The view was beautiful, bright with possibilities.

"There's a balcony," he whispered in her ear. "I brought some eco-friendly, biodegradable paper with me."

She grinned. "Paper airplane contest?"

"You know it. I've been practicing in secret."

"You think you stand a chance?"

He stared into her eyes before kissing her again. "Not from the first second I met you, and I'm grateful for that."

"Me, too. Always."

* * * * *

If you loved the charm and romance of Happily Inc,
turn the page for an exclusive peek at how other
locals found their happily-ever-afters!

Then, for the full story, pick up the books you've missed:

☙❧

YOU SAY IT FIRST
SECOND CHANCE GIRL
WHY NOT TONIGHT
NOT QUITE OVER YOU

Pallas Saunders
&
Nick Mitchell
2/7/2018

As the owner of Weddings in a Box, Pallas had attended more weddings than she could remember, but this was her first time as the bride. She had a new understanding of the word "jitters." It wasn't about being nervous. She was so excited to marry Nick that she felt on edge. Unfettered energy zipped through her body. She couldn't sit still, and yet, she had nowhere to go until it was time for the wedding. In less than an hour, she would be married to the man she loved, in what had to be one of the most beautiful places on earth: the isle of Capri, Italy.

She stepped onto the balcony of her luxury suite and tried to soak in the moment. They were staying at the Amante del Mare, the five-star hotel that had purchased Nick's stunning sculpture of Neptune for the lobby. The linens on the bed probably cost more than she made in a month. Although it was February, it was an unseasonably warm sixty degrees outside, and yesterday's rain had left the sky the purest, deepest blue she'd ever seen. The Mediterranean stretched out before her, its surface never still. The sea was as filled with energy as she was, rolling over itself to get to shore.

It being the slow season, they practically had the hotel to themselves, which was a good thing, since they both came from big families who didn't quite grasp the concept of elopement. Three of Nick's brothers had come, along with wives and fiancées and parents. Only Ronan had stayed back in Happily Inc. Her mom and brother Cade had made the trip, as well as her cousin Drew. In truth, Pallas was glad to have them here, especially Grandpa Frank, who would give her away.

As if her thoughts had called him, Grandpa Frank knocked lightly, then entered her sitting room. "You ready to do this?" he said.

"Ready." So ready to see Nick. To marry him! "Grandpa Frank, are you crying?"

"Proud to see you wearing your grandmother's wedding dress. Adeline would've been mighty proud, too. You're a good girl, Pallas."

"That's so sweet." She tucked her arm through his. "Shall we?"

Her friend Violet had modified the bodice of the 1950s-style dress, then embellished it with antique buttons, transforming the knee-length gown from old-fashioned to vintage chic. Pallas felt like a princess as she walked down the marble steps on her grandfather's arm, the full skirt swooshing from side to side with every step. She wore her brown hair in a simple updo and carried a bouquet of pale blue hydrangeas and delicate white baby's breath.

Her maid of honor—and future sister-in-law—Carol was waiting for them in the lobby. She hadn't gone so far as to wear a dress for the occasion, but she did consent to a periwinkle silk blouse over flowy white pants.

"How are you feeling?" Carol asked.

"Nervous. Excited."

Carol hugged her, then preceded her out to the white stone courtyard. Pallas and Grandpa Frank paused in the doorway. A string quartet was playing softly off to the side. When she'd asked Nick if they could afford all of this, he'd just said, "I want you to have everything you want, Pallas. This is your day."

As the musicians segued into the wedding march, everyone stood and turned toward her. And there, just ten steps away, was the man she loved. Nick looked so handsome in his charcoal-colored Italian suit and blue silk tie. His chiseled jaw was clean shaven, his short hair neatly combed. He looked at her and visibly let out a breath he'd been holding.

She didn't even try to restrain her smile as she moved toward him as if in a dream. The happiness and love in his eyes filled her spirit to bursting. How did she get so lucky?

The Italian priest officiating the ceremony said in heavily accented English, "Marriage is what brings us together today."

Pallas nearly burst out laughing at the familiar line from *The Princess Bride*, one of her favorite movies. How very perfect!

Nick held both her hands in his, gaze locked with hers, as he repeated the traditional Italian wedding vows in English. "I, Nick Mitchell, welcome you, Pallas Saunders, to be my wife. I promise to be faithful to you always, in joy and in sorrow, in sickness and in health, and to love and honor you all the days of my life."

Pallas's eyes filled with tears. Through a tight throat, she said, "I, Pallas Saunders, welcome you, Nick Mitchell, to be my husband. I promise to be faithful to you always, in joy and in sorrow, in sickness and in health, and to love and honor you all the days of my life."

"Per favore, Signor Nick, kiss-a your wife," the priest said.

Amid the cheers of the people who loved them the most, Nick swept Pallas into his arms and kissed her.

And they lived happily ever after!

Read the full story behind Pallas & Nick's romance in

YOU SAY IT FIRST

Carol Lund
&
Mathias Mitchell
3/3/2018

AS THE SUN rose over the savanna outside Happily Inc, Carol Lund took a moment to appreciate the view of her giraffes silhouetted against the colorful sky. One giraffe, Millie, walked toward her, somehow both graceful and ungainly. Millie leaned her head forward and Carol obliged with a leaf-eater treat and an affectionate pat along her long neck.

Today was Carol's wedding day, the third of March. 3/3. Chosen in part because Mathias said the number three was an artist's best friend, and in part because the weather in March was perfect for an outdoor wedding. Carol couldn't imagine getting married anywhere but here. A large luxury tent had been set up for the reception, and a cadre of electric golf carts decorated with streamers stood ready to take guests from town on tours of the game preserve.

Tomorrow, after she and Mathias left for their honeymoon in South Africa, her father would feed the animals while she was gone. But Carol wanted to do it today—one last time before her wedding. Her animals grounded her. She didn't feel nervous at all about marrying Mathias, but the thought of standing up in front of all those people had her nerves humming.

She looked over her shoulder and saw Mathias on his back porch, watching her, holding a mug of coffee and wearing only low-slung sweatpants. As he waved, the sun highlighted the muscles of his torso. Her heart leaped. He was so handsome. And he loved her. Her! Bad luck for the groom to see the bride before the wedding? She didn't believe in bad luck anymore. Not when she'd gotten so lucky in the husband-to-be department.

She waved back, then went to work.

The wedding...

At four that afternoon, Carol stood still in the office at the game preserve as her sister fussed with her dress one last time. Violet had flown in from England a week ago, with her fiancé, an honest-to-goodness duke, in tow.

"I'll say this for you," Violet said with a twinkle in her eye. "You clean up well."

She had been horrified when Carol had clomped in at nine that morning, sweaty and disheveled, with a streak of gazelle poop across her cheek.

Violet had ushered her into a hot shower, and had spent the rest of the day making Carol beautiful. Carol didn't argue. She wanted to knock Mathias's socks off, and knew it would take a village to transform her ordinary self.

Now, as she stood on the precipice of her new life,

Carol pulled her sister into a hug. "Thank you for talking me out of the pantsuit."

Her wedding dress was an elegant silk column, with a deep scoop neckline that showcased her collarbones and cap sleeves. Violet had added tiny, sparkling button embellishments at the waist. Carol had insisted that the skirt end at her knees. A long skirt would be impractical for an outdoor wedding on the savanna, and Carol was nothing if not practical. Even so, it was the most feminine thing she had ever worn. Around her neck, she wore a simple white gold chain, from which hung a glass heart pendant in swirls of red and orange, a gift from her husband-to-be.

The door opened, and their father stood framed in the sunlight, which made his red hair look as though it were on fire. "Are you ready?"

Carol nodded. Violet went first, then Carol, with her hand looped through her father's arm. As she stepped outside, it took a moment for her eyes to adjust. When they did, a feeling of peace and happiness settled through her. Mathias waited for her at the base of the gazebo they'd built for the occasion. His dark hair was freshly cut, brushed back from his face. His dark suit made his shoulders look immense. But what really captured her attention was the smile on his face, filled with joy and love. She saw forever in that smile.

Her friends and family came to their feet as she walked past the rows of white folding chairs. On the other side of the fence, the giraffes approached with curiosity.

When Carol was within a few steps of her groom, he

stepped forward, too impatient to wait any longer. He surprised her by cupping her face between his large, warm hands and bending down for a deep kiss.

"You're amazing," he said when he pulled away. "I love you. I'm going to keep saying that for the rest of our lives." He leaned his forehead against hers and ignored the catcalls from his older brothers. After a lingering moment, he drew back and together they stepped up into the gazebo. Violet and Nick, maid of honor and best man, followed.

Carol knew that the one shadow on the day was that Mathias's erstwhile twin had refused to be his best man. Ronan still hadn't reconciled himself to the fact that they were half brothers, not full, much less the twins they had been raised to believe they were. So although Ronan had agreed to attend as a guest, he had refused to stand alongside Mathias at the altar. Time would heal, she told herself and hoped she was right.

The reverend greeted them with a smile, then invited Mathias to recite the vows he'd written.

Mathias cleared his throat, and Carol's heart melted. Mathias, who never seemed rattled by anything, was nervous. She handed her bouquet to Violet before putting her hands into his.

"Carol, you've changed my life. You've made my life. I'm yours, and I promise to do everything in my power to make you as happy as you've made me. I will be true to you and honest with you. When problems come, we'll face them together because we're stronger together than either of us could ever be on our own. You're my best friend. I love you. For always. I want to be the father to your children and the grandpa to your grandkids, side by side the rest of our lives."

Carol felt her eyes well up with tears, but she choked them back as she said, "Mathias, I love you more than I knew it was possible to love another human being… or even an animal."

A smattering of laughter came from the crowd, since Carol's love for animals was well known. Mathias squeezed her hands, encouraging her to continue.

"I'm a mate-for-life kind of girl, and you're it. My one and only. I I'm so grateful that you moved into the house next door. Your heart is as beautiful as the art you create. You fill my life with color and meaning. I look forward to our future together. From this day forward, you are my family."

They exchanged matching gold bands, then the reverend pronounced them husband and wife.

With a tremble so slight it was almost unnoticeable, Mathias kissed his bride. And they lived…wait for it… happily ever after!

Read the full story behind Carol & Mathias's romance in

SECOND CHANCE GIRL

Violet Lund
&
Ulrich Sherwood, Duke of Somerbrooke
6/9/2018

"YOU'RE NOT GOING to throw that, are you?"

Violet looked up to see her sister Carol skeptically eyeing the bouquet she held—a bouquet with not a single flower in it. It was made entirely of antique lace and buttons, the most treasured buttons in Violet's collection. The buttons were shades of pearl and pink and 18-karat gold, scattered with jewels to catch and reflect the light. She'd made it herself for her wedding day, the one nontraditional touch in her exceedingly traditional wedding to Ulrich Sherwood, Duke of Somerbrooke, and a whole bunch of other titles she hadn't yet learned to string together.

"Heavens, no!" Violet said. "Not only would I risk damaging my precious buttons, but I might knock some poor girl unconscious."

"'Heavens, no'? Are you getting a British accent already?"

"Mayhap," Violet said with a wink, then gave Carol an impulsive hug. "Oh, I'm so happy!"

"I know you are," Carol said, hugging her back. "And I couldn't be happier for you, even though this means we're going to live halfway around the world from each other."

"London to LAX takes less than twelve hours."

"I wouldn't do it for anyone but you," Carol said.

"Don't make her cry," their friend Silver warned. "I just finished her makeup."

She pulled out her cell phone and made the sisters pose for a few quick shots, which she immediately emailed to the friends who had remained back in Happily Inc.

The women were in Violet's parlor—the duchess's suite—at Battenberg Park, an estate that had been in Ulrich's family for more than five hundred years. Carol, her maid of honor, wore a champagne-colored dress with wide straps and a vee neckline. Her short red hair had been slicked back. Violet's bridesmaids—Silver, Pallas, Natalie and Wynn—wore dresses in the palest rose, each in a style that flattered her particular figure. Violet had strategically placed a mother-of-pearl button edged in gold on each woman's dress, a memento of the occasion. The same button was prominent in her button bouquet. She wondered what Britain's upper crust would make of the tattoo on the back of Silver's neck, exposed by her upswept hairstyle.

From paintings on the wall, generations of prior duchesses gazed down their noses with haughty but benign expressions, reserving judgment on the American upstart who had captured the heart of the duke. One of his ancestors, still very much alive, swept into the room as majestically as an eighty-two-year-old could.

"It's time, dear girl," Ulrich's beloved grandmother said. "Let me have a look at you."

Violet stood still while Carol and her bridesmaids fussed with her train and her veil. She felt like Cinderella when the birds and the mice readied her for the ball. She was a bit nervous about the pomp and circumstance of the upcoming ceremony, but not about Ulrich. Never about him. They were meant to be together, and somehow, despite living on different continents, they had found each other.

The women backed away and collectively gasped.

"You'll do nicely," Nana Winifred said. Violet could tell she was trying for a stiff upper lip, but the tears in her eyes betrayed her emotion. "Come now, your father is waiting. And more importantly, so is your groom."

Violet's heart skipped as she linked arms with the dowager duchess. Together, they walked to the grand hallway where her father and uncle Ted waited. The two men looked like bookends—standing ramrod straight in matching gray suits that only made their shock of red hair look brighter. And when they saw her, matching smiles appeared.

The next thirty minutes passed in a blur. Violet and her entourage—maid of honor, bridesmaids, father and uncle of the bride, groom's grandmother, and two distant young cousins of Ulrich, who would serve as flower girls—made their way to the carriages waiting along the drive. When Violet had tried to object to the open carriages, the dowager duchess had reminded her that the nearby villagers were curious and had the right to get a look at the new duchess. And Violet did feel very much on display as the carriage wound its way through the village to the charming abbey where she would marry the man she loved.

She was guided into the church. One by one, her bridesmaids and Carol left, then it was her turn to step into the doorway at the back of the church. Hundreds of people stood at her entrance, but she only had eyes for the man who waited at the other end of the aisle.

Ulrich.

Impeccably dressed as always, he looked more handsome than ever with his dark blond hair neatly trimmed and combed away from his face. Their gazes caught and held as she floated down the aisle toward him on her father's arm. As soon as he touched her hand, time righted itself.

He fingered her bouquet. "Buttons?" he asked with amusement in his piercing blue eyes.

"It seemed appropriate."

"Indeed."

And then her fiancé leaned over and whispered something very *inappropriate* in her ear about what he planned to do with the buttons on her dress as soon as they were alone. A fiery blush blazed through her, and it was all she could do to repeat her vows without stumbling over the words.

When the vows had been said and rings exchanged,

the officiant proclaimed to the congregation, "I present to you the Duke and Duchess of Somerbrooke!"

And they lived…wait for it…happily ever after!

Read the full story behind Violet & Ulrich's romance in

SECOND CHANCE GIRL